To

Caribbean High

GARY E. BROWN

With best wishes

Sint maarten July 21

2010

A NOTE FROM THE AUTHOR

For lovers of the sea and its lore, the Caribbean offers everything a thriller writer could want. That said, it should be noted that this is a work of fiction. Names, characters, places, and incidents are a product of the author's imagination or are used fictitiously, and any resemblance to actual persons, living or dead, events, or locales is coincidental. If some of the characters and places sound familiar, then you are using your imagination, too.

ACKNOWLEDGEMENTS

I am grateful to Peter and Lisa Robertson, Rita Clark and Julia Lillingston. When I was adrift, their enthusiasm came to the rescue. I owe a special thanks to Kathy Gifford for toiling over the manuscript, we shared a secret and any and all mistakes are mine. With the clock ticking, Dimitri Likissas answered all my emails and worked diligently on the layout and cover. Not a word would have been written or an ocean crossed without the encouragement of my wife and best friend. Jan, this is for you.

No man is an island

—John Donne 1572-1631

1

I woke up bleary eyed, hung over, and wondered just who the hell I was in bed with. Then I moved and my reflection, made doubly heinous by the crack in the bunk-side mirror, moved in sympathy. I moaned and focused one eye on the battered alarm clock, which was shattering the silence with the enthusiasm of a kid let loose on a tin drum.

It was eight-thirty on a steamy Caribbean morning. I was fifty years and fourteen hours old. Was the cup of life now half full or half empty and could I bring the sorry thing between my legs back to life by the workings of my dirty mind or would it need a touch of glue. The thought made me giggle, then cough. I fell back onto the pillow with a cry of, "Oh shit!" as the bongos in my head pounded out a tattoo that started an inch above my nose, peaked to a crescendo somewhere below my bald patch, then eased off halfway down my back.

Looking around was torture so I covered my eyes to protect them from the sun, which was bouncing malignant rays off the surface of the water and hurling them like harpoons through the portholes and into my sozzled brain.

It must have been a hundred degrees in the tiny cabin of my yacht *Strange Light*. The boat, thirty-six feet of rusting steel, had been my home and retreat for the last five years. It was bought and paid for by a pension from Her Majesty's Government, in whose navy I had served with dubious distinction, until a near miss with an underwater mine destroyed my left eardrum. Still, I'd fared better than the rest of my team whose remains made scant pickings for the fish.

By screwing my eyes shut I was able to keep the pounding in my head to a tolerable level and, by swallowing hard every few seconds, keep the nausea at bay. Something told me this wasn't going to be one of my better days.

I rolled over and the image of the cabin seared on the inside of my eyelids did a couple of three-sixties and stopped on tic-tac-toe. What I needed was a beer, but for now would make do with the bottle of water that was somewhere in the bed.

My fingers crawled across the soggy sheet like a crippled tarantula. Foray number one produced a slimy Kleenex. The next, a half-eaten sandwich that, by its sticky feel, contained jelly and peanut butter. Nice. I took a bite and slid the rest under my pillow for later.

Thoroughly enjoying my private game of blind man's bluff, my fingers set out again. I was playing the game to some crazy tune dredged up from childhood. "Du dum du dum a spiders bum. Du dum du dum what has he done. Du dum du dum a spid …" The spider stopped when it touched hot flesh and skittered back towards me as a clenched fist.

I cracked an eye and through the gummy slit saw a familiar hand. Susie! What if she was awake and staring at me? I shuffled sideways like a crab until I was as far away from her as I could get.

This was her thing. No matter where we slept she had to have the right-hand side of the bed. She once told me it was a territorial thing—that it gave her a sense of belonging. Okay by me as long as she didn't take to sniffing the air and turning around three times before she lay down.

I knew without looking that if she was asleep then she was on her back. Something I envied, but a position that eluded me unless knocked senseless, drunk, or both, as the multiple angles in my rearranged nose made me snore or cough up the residue of a once fifty-a-day habit.

I desperately needed a piss but the thought of climbing out of the bunk brought on fresh waves of nausea so, instead, I summoned up the courage to look at Susie.

I was right, she was on her back. Her head, sunk deep into the pillow, was framed by her hair, which cascaded over her shoulders like waves of dark silk. As I watched, her eyelids, pale against her nut-brown face, fluttered with the intensity of sleep and I wondered where her dreams were taking her. Wherever it was, gut instinct told me it was a million miles from me.

I lowered my eyes and followed a bead of sweat as it gathered speed, ran along her throat, and slipped away between her breasts.

Her breasts were small and tanned and one of them had squeezed its way out of her flimsy nightdress where, with each breath, it rose and fell as if to mock me. Tiny creases, not there a month go, rippled the skin at the top of her cleavage, telling tales of years in the sun. Then it hit me, selfish bastard that I am, that Susie was fighting God's little joke too.

What men insist are character lines, women call wrinkles, and once or twice of late I'd caught her looking at old photographs while pulling and stretching her face with her fingers to smooth out the crevasses. This bit of sadomasochism is less painful—and cheaper—than the surgeon's knife, but how long can you walk around pulling at your eyes like you're applying for a job in a Chinese restaurant?

I'd convinced myself long ago that I didn't give a damn how I looked. That was until Susie caught me in front of the mirror doing the finger thing. "I was picking my nose," I said, which got me nowhere and for days I had to put up with her tugging at the corner of her eyes and shouting, 'Flied lice, flied lice,' at the most inopportune moments. Women can be so childish. Anyway, it was far too late for me and the lines and scars I'd always wanted as a kid were now etched so deep into the leathery skin of my face that they resembled roads on a tea-stained map.

Shit, my head hurt.

Focus on something positive, I told myself, and my mind went straight to thoughts of doom, gloom and impending loss, which did me no good at all. So I concentrated on Susie's plump nipple and even thought about tweaking it.

Then I remembered what I'd done the night before and decided it would be a big mistake.

2

Susie had taken me out for breakfast and we were driving back to the marina where we had moored the dinghy. On the way, the road went past the old floating bar that lay tied to the dock at the end of the mangrove swamp. This was our usual hangout and where we hoped to spend the evening unobtrusively celebrating the fact that my brain, and most of my body parts, had made it to the half century.

That was the plan, but I should have known better. After all we were in the Caribbean; a place of pirates and lost souls, where time has a permanent kink, and a smile and a fuck-you attitude are all you need for a happy life.

As we drove by the end of the track leading to the dock I could see the old diehards drinking the last of their breakfasts. And when the bar's owner, 'Black Pete' Macalister, spotted my battered Jeep, jumped onto the bulwarks of the *Lucky Lady* and began revolving his hips and waving two cold beers in our direction, I knew we should ignore him and drive on by. But that's the problem with my ancient Jeep. Over the years it's been owned by so many island characters that, like an old horse, it knows its way from one watering hole to the next. So it came as no surprise when, without warning, the wheel spun in my hands and we skidded onto the dock in a cloud of dust.

By the time I climbed down from the Jeep, Pete was dancing a jig on top of the ship's anchor windlass while expertly juggling four beers. "Yee haw, it's the birthday boy," he roared and without missing a beat sent two bottles spinning towards us.

Pete had pulled this stunt on me before and I plucked the beer out of the air as it whistled past at head height. Susie wasn't so lucky; she ducked and the bottle exploded against the Jeep, showering her in beer and green glass.

"You lose," roared Pete. "You lose!"

"Oh shit, here we go again and eight hours early," said Susie, as I dug out my wallet and strode towards the grinning coconutters at the bar.

Some said the *Lucky Lady*'s luck ran out the day she sailed into St Peters and dropped anchor in the lagoon. Others said it was the best day of their lives. As a lover of sailing ships and strong drink, I tried to remain neutral. But sometimes, when my eye wandered to the faded sepia photographs screwed to the shelf above the bar showing the old ship running hard before the trades, I would feel sad and even a little guilty to be carousing amidst such history. Then someone would slam another round of drinks onto the ravaged bar and my melancholy would retreat back into the photo where, no doubt, it rightly belonged.

The boat was built at the end of the 19th century for a Scottish nobleman who saw it as the ideal means of getting his crazy son as far away from himself, and the rest of the family, as possible. Not wanting his son dead, only banished—although it was rumored the former had crossed his mind as a cheaper alternative—the dour Scot had built the yacht to the highest standards. Put together by the last of a dying breed of master shipwrights, using traditional skills learned and passed down over hundreds of years, the superb vessel was constructed from the finest materials that money could buy.

On the day of the launch, which just happened to coincide with his wayward son's twenty-first birthday, the nobleman handed the lad a *fait accompli* in the shape of a finely crafted one hundred and ten foot schooner. Along with the ship went a generous allowance to be paid annually providing, insisted the scheming father, his son stayed at least a thousand miles from the coast of Albion.

The ruse worked and the joyful miscreant was last seen heading west down the English Channel, dressed as Admiral Lord Nelson and accompanied by a motley crew of drunks, vagabonds, and the entire workforce of Portsmouth's largest and most notorious brothel. And the schooner *Lucky Lady*—or the *Lady*, as she is affectionately known throughout the Caribbean—has been getting people into trouble ever since.

3

Usually I never drink at a bar while sitting down. I had been cured of the habit years ago while on a three day binge in Papeete. Our submarine had dumped us ashore for some R&R after a tedious NATO exercise spent chasing, or being chased by, the bloody French.

It started well enough, with the usual inter-ship soccer matches organized by the chaplains and the like, but of course it couldn't last, and by the third day the French wanted to bring back Madam Guillotine and the Brits were all for refighting the Battle of Trafalgar. Instead they settled for a brawl that took out half the brothels and rum shops in town and raged up and down Boulevard Pomare for three hours.

The riot was nothing to do with me; I wasn't even on the waterfront. I was at the other end of town sipping tequila and entertaining the lovely wife of a French captain. I was just demonstrating, with a cigar and an upturned shot-glass, how we had sent a torpedo right up the chuff of her husband's ship when he burst through the door with half the crew. The kicking rearranged my nose and for years destroyed my backside's love affair with the barstool.

So, what had changed? Well, I was older and slightly drunk, and although the *Lucky Lady* had its share of rogues and villains it was reasonably safe, so by late afternoon both cheeks were firmly ensconced on leather and I was draped across the bar. Two of the boys had brought along their guitars and were switching between soft rock, reggae, and a couple of Jimmy Buffett standards that they always sang by popular request.

Susie was circulating with the girls at the front of the boat, away from the salty language and the same old stories and bad jokes. Now and then I heard her laugh, and a couple of times I swear I heard 'Flied lice' followed by girlie shrieks, but I didn't care as long as she was having fun.

I was feeling so damn good, kind of hazy and lazy, with my mind going nowhere.

The light was draining from the sky, darkening the horizon and marbling the clouds crimson and gold. Beyond the coast road the dusty palms stirred in the last of the evening breeze, reminding me of another time, another place.

I took a long swig of beer and watched a young couple strolling hand in hand along the beach, lost in another world. Occasionally they looked down as the Caribbean Sea bathed their feet in a swirl of warm sand and crushed shells. When they stopped and the boy turned and gently kissed her, I swear I could taste the salt on her lips. In that moment I wanted their love to last, I wanted it for them as I wanted it desperately for myself. Before they could break their embrace and the magic slip away, I closed my eyes and turned my attention back to the beer and reality of the *Lucky Lady*.

Things were heating up, yet I found it hard to shake off the reverie of the last few minutes. Then, in that strange way that can happen in a crowd, the music faded, winding down like a clockwork toy, until it stopped. In the pause, before someone found the key and rewound the spring, I realized that everything I valued was here on this creaking hulk.

Some of the drinkers were old friends; others, new. Some, whose last name I didn't know, I would trust with my life. All had a story to tell or they wouldn't be in the Caribbean. Some were loud-mouthed thugs who bragged about being mercenaries in Africa, but were no more dangerous than their imaginations. More lethal were the quiet ones; the lads who wouldn't remove their shirts on the beach in case someone saw the scars that even their girlfriends were afraid to ask about. Then there were the nomads with dodgy passports, and the rummies, tax evaders and black sheep. And here and there a gay couple, and why the hell not, they had as much right as everyone else to live and love in the sun and be left the hell alone.

The booze had me in its grip and any second I'd be off to the guitar players with a teary request for Jimmy Buffett's anthem to burned-out sailors; *Mother Ocean*. That's when Crazy Willie Jones decided I'd done enough reflecting for one day and bought me another beer. As I took a sip he wished me happy birthday, in Welsh, and slapped me on the back with enough force to drive a steel piling six feet into the ground.

"Thanks, Willie," I croaked and prayed to God he wouldn't buy me another.

What is it about birthdays that brings out the generosity in people and makes them want to buy you as much drink as it takes to make you fall over? They were all on a mission to get me pissed. Everyone wanted to buy 'Dick' Turpin a drink on his fiftieth birthday, and I, the Dick they were referring to, felt obliged to let them. Even total strangers were getting in on the act.

Having been christened Richard Theophilus Turpin was something I had at last come to terms with. It had taken a few years. Fifty to be exact. If you want to toughen-up your kids, give them a good name. Try putting them through a north of England school with a name like mine and you'll see what I mean. School days were amongst the darkest of my life and I say that after what seems like a lifetime of dark days. Yet, like most of us who were sluiced down the education drain, I came out with more than I went in with. Like a lasting hatred of my math teacher who used my name like a weapon. If I met the bastard today I'd kick his teeth down his throat even if it meant dragging him out of his wheelchair to do it.

The party was now well under way and reaching a point where it wouldn't matter a sailor's cuss whether I was there or not. So many people were dancing around the deck that the boat was tugging at her moorings as if to say, "Let's get the hell off this dock and away to sea." And through the booze I imagined the *Lady* sailing by with hundreds of happy drunks on deck, and Pete on the windlass juggling bottles as half-naked girls danced atop the bar and the ghost of the laird's son cavorted about the rigging in his three-cornered hat.

The thought had me whooping with laughter. Then the coconutters began passing around the cheap mescal, and whatever control I had over my own party went down like the worm in the first shot.

4

Winter brings a mass of boats to the islands of the Northeast Caribbean. From November to May, thousands of yachts cruise the tropical waters; the balmy trade winds pushing them north or south along the island chain.

Superyachts, one hundred and fifty feet or more, cater to the rich, famous and infamous. And for seven hedonistic months the airport on St. Peters reverberates to the sound of private jets bringing the blessed, with their bags of cash, to play in the sun.

The island has everything they could want: restaurants, casinos, golden beaches, cheap booze and even cheaper sex. You name it, St. Peters has it. But no matter how rich and famous, before flying away, most people end up slumming it with the pirates on the *Lucky Lady*. Tonight was no exception.

Most of the guys who drink at the *Lady* have done their time at sea, many in the military or merchant marine, before moving on to the big yachts where, if you can handle the bullshit, you can make good money. Who knows, perhaps the camaraderie of the sea is what bound us all together. And it's funny, once you've been to sea, just how easy it is to tell if someone's a seaman or a bullshitter.

Seamen come in many guises: male and female, black, white, heathen or believer. The sea makes no distinction and drowns them equally without bias or prejudice. And when I talk about seamen, I make no distinction. I don't give a rat's arse if it's a lost soul on a shoestring budget trying to nurse a leaky eighteen-footer around the world, or someone on the bridge of the largest and most sophisticated tub afloat. If he or she has been there, you can tell. But, as in all walks of life, the world of professional sailing has its share of wannabes; in fact the industry is full of them. Men and women who have it all: the looks, money and attitude, but they don't have an ounce of seamanship from backbone to brain. The *Lady* attracts them like a magnet, and why not, they're good entertainment, and I'm all for the dreamers so, when a bunch of them crashed the party, they were made welcome.

Her name was Debbie—it said so on a gold pendant around her neck—and I haven't met a Debbie yet who isn't trouble. While the rest of her crew was whooping it up with Pete and his mates on the aft deck, she was sending me sidelong glances across the bar. When she realized the cool looks were getting her nowhere, she started with the shy smiles. They didn't work either. Now, with the sun below the horizon and the only light coming from the colored lanterns strung from the rigging, I guess she was feeling brave.

Her expensive perfume hit me long before she wiggled a slender arm between Willie and me and placed her empty glass on the bar.

When she spoke I heard but the faintest whisper above the din from the band and the drunken racket coming from the aft deck. Missing one eardrum didn't help either, so when she spoke again I was forced to turn to catch what she said in my good ear.

She was beautiful. Her hair, a deep natural red, was expensively styled to look wild and windblown, and it shone like burnished copper in the soft glow of the lanterns. Unusual for a woman with red hair, her face was perfectly tanned, as if her skin could treat the harsh tropical sun as a friend, instead of the enemy it had become to the rest of us.

She smiled and twisted a strand of hair around a manicured finger in a pose both shy yet challenging. Then the lovely green eyes came into play in a way she'd no doubt used before to great effect.

I hadn't spoken; in fact I was having trouble focusing. Debbie was going through a practiced routine and, after all the booze, I was quite happy to watch and let her get on with it. She was in the islands and feeling cool. Her boyfriend was carousing with the lads at the other end of the boat and she wanted a diversion. She'd probably heard some crazy stories and found me ugly enough to be interesting.

Her smile told me she was enjoying the game as much as I was. As she rattled on she kept touching my arm with her fingers, sending signals to all the right parts of my body. She had to shout to be heard above the din and her voice held a touch of Irish, which I thought could account for the copper in her hair.

"Where are you from?" she finally got around to asking.

"England," I slurred, with no intention of making it easy for her.

The sudden glint in her eye told me she was asking questions that she already knew the answers to.

"Oh, that's nice," she said. "My boyfriend, Gordon Glokani the Third, has an English mother." She rolled her eyes when she said 'the third,' her accent making it sound like something unpleasant you pick up on your shoe. "His daddy's given us the yacht to drive around the islands. It's like a last fling for him before he goes into the family business. Would you like to meet him?"

"Sure, bring him on. We can swap sea stories and he can buy me a drink on my birthday," I said waving my empty bottle at Pete who was now on duty behind the bar.

"He might buy you a drink," she said, "but I doubt he'll talk about the sea, he hates it; he gets sick."

That bit of nonsense earned her a sideways glance; then I went back to waving my empty bottle around.

"There's a real captain on board but Gordon holds the purse-strings so he gets to play God." She giggled and staggered a bit yet something told me she was completely sober, and that triggered the warning bells in my head. But the bells stopped clanging in the time it took for her fingers to brush the back of my hand in what was more a caress than a touch. Besides, it was my birthday and what with the booze and the music I thought I could get away with a little mischief.

Finally Pete circled around to our side of the bar and yanked the empty beer bottle from my hand. With a flourish he produced a bottle of Patrón Silver Tequila and two glasses from behind his back and slammed them down on the bar.

"Come on, Pete, there's no way you're getting me on that stuff," I said. "Just bring me another beer."

"No way, José. The lady's boyfriend sent it over for the birthday boy, he must have heard about your Mexican blood." With that he produced three limes and a knife designed for skinning buffalo and went into his juggling act.

"What's that about Mexican blood," purred Debbie.

Immediately, without missing a beat, Pete told her how he once convinced his Swedish girl-friend that my Yorkshire accent was really Mexican and how, whenever I went to their apartment for dinner, she would play Mariachi music and cook fajitas.

Debbie thought this was hilarious, as had everyone at the time. And I must admit that Pete's joke had helped me through the bad days when I first came to the islands, wondering whether my body and mind would ever mend.

It was no secret that I was sensitive about my accent. A scholarship to grammar school pleased everyone in the village, but growing up five hundred yards from the pithead hardly prepared me for a school full of twits with Hooray Henry accents.

At first they tried to beat the accent out of me in the headmaster's office and, when the teachers weren't around, in the common room. All they did was thicken my accent to the point of incomprehension, which infuriated them even more, because although I couldn't talk the talk, I found the learning easy.

Despite the accent, I made it into Dartmouth Royal Naval College where the prejudice was even worse. However, it took a year before the piss-taking and the constant jokes about the miners finally got to me.

I was on duty during the night of the Admiral's Ball when a stupid looking gutless bastard of an officer began entertaining the wives by mimicking my accent. I listened, with a smile painted on my face, thinking all the while about the lads who'd marched out of the pits to a bloody death on countless battlefields to protect England and silly twats like him. When he started again I dropped him with a perfectly executed Liverpool Kiss that broke his nose in two places and landed me in the guardhouse, still dressed in my number one whites. It took a commanding officer with an accent thicker than Lancashire Hotpot to bend her majesty's rules and save my career, that and a rapid transfer to the submarine service.

"Are you going to dream the night away or are you going to introduce this lovely lady to the delights of the silver nectar?" Pete's voice brought me back to earth and although I should have known better, I told him to pour.

I love the barmen of the Caribbean, and of all the barmen I had ever had the pleasure of watching, 'Black Pete' was the best. In a land where Coca-Cola costs more than rum, the tourists loved him, especially those from England, where a shot of booze is so miserly there's a danger it will evaporate before reaching your lips.

Pete juggled the knife and the limes, pulling in extra glasses and throwing them high in the air. His act had attracted a large audience and he worked his way up and down the bar, slamming down glasses, nodding to people, and shouting, "You in?" as he went along.

When he had enough glasses in line, and touching rim to rim, he upended the tequila and, still juggling the limes with one hand, quickly ran the bottle up and down the line, making sure each glass was full to the brim. Amidst drunken cheers and friendly abuse, he then tossed the empty bottle over his shoulder into the bin.

"Okay guys, if you're new to this, here's what happens next." He picked up the limes, sliced them, and gave everyone in the round a piece. "Now, all you poor people who are drinking alone, you lick the back of your hand and sprinkle salt on it. All you guys who are accompanied by a lady, you get to lick each other's hand and sprinkle salt on it. And I mean hand; *that* comes later."

Pete held center stage and everyone loved him. He waited for the laughter to die down then he continued. "Okay. When I give the word, you lick the salt from the back of your hand, pick up the glass, down it in one and then suck on the lime. That's what's known by the pros as lick it, slam it, suck it. Don't be the last to drain your glass or you buy the next round."

With that he hammered his fist on the bar, licked the back of his hand and tossed the tequila down his throat while the competition were still getting their tongues in all sorts of unlikely place.

The night was going to be a blast.

Debbie's juices were flowing and she was hell bent on not being the one to buy the next bottle. Giggling and blaming the crowd, we pressed into each other as the tequila stripped away our inhibitions and sharpened our senses. When we slammed down another glass of molten silver, and passed on the limes to suck each other's tongues, my heart beat so fast I thought this birthday would be my last.

5

With beer and tequila sloshing around in a stomach that had seen no food for more than eight hours, I was ready to party. Yet something was telling me to heed the alarm bells in my cranium that suddenly had gone from the gentle tinklings of a wind chime to that of London's Big Ben striking noon. I was breaking all the rules that had kept Susie and me together. It was time to back off, get the fuck out of Dodge, and get on with the sailor's art of simply getting drunk.

As if reading my mind, Debbie slipped her hand into my shirt and dragged her fingernails down my chest. "Dance with me," she whispered and set off towards the music.

Now was my chance to end it, but it was no longer my brain that was doing the thinking and, like an adolescent fool, instead of running the other way, I waited three seconds then followed her to the dance floor.

It was around ten o'clock. Frank and Jimmy had put away their guitars and slipped something with a heavy Latin beat into the tape-deck.

The island has a large population of Latinos from Puerto Rico and the Dominican Republic. They're great people but their music can be lethal.

I'd seen it all before, from the bars of southern Chile to the back street bodegas of Madrid. The throbbing beat subtly weaves its way into the heat of the night, like voodoo. The drinks flow and fire up the least imaginative of the guys until they begin to throb with a desperate need to move. Unable to remain still, girls, their bodies slick with musky sweat, writhe against their partners, leading them in a dance so erotic it charges the night with lust. It was no place for the local vicar or someone who mistakes the carryings-on of the dancers for an invitation to grab hold of something that belongs to someone else.

Debbie forced her way aft through the crowd and I panted along behind her.

I looked back at the bar and, like I was their wayward little brother, saw Willie say something to Pete and then nod in my direction. It was the same when we served together in Special Forces: Pete, Willie and Dick, forever covering each others back.

I was still grinning when we made it to the edge of the dance floor—twelve square feet of battered deck covered with plywood—and found four couples slithering around on each other in perfect time to the Salsa beat. Dancing like this you suck in with your mother's milk or work very hard to learn.

This is where it usually went to hell. The lads would get boozed-up and think they could dance. But this wasn't the under the disco lights with half an inch of dandruff glowing on your shoulders like snow, and eight pints of Guinness sloshing around in your belly, kind of dancing. Usually they lasted about three minutes before scuttling back to the bar amid gales of laughter and a barrage of tossed beer mats.

Debbie didn't hesitate. She pushed her way to the middle of the dance floor, tossed her hair in challenge, and beckoned me forward with both hands.

As I strode towards her the lads at the bar began to cheer.

We came together in the classic position, face to face, my right arm around her back, her right hand in my left between us at shoulder height.

She smiled and pulled me into her hot body. It was almost a

parody, until she began to move. The rhythm slid through her like hot liquid and although her feet remained still the rest of her began to undulate in the arousing way of the expert Salsa dancer.

She was provoking me with her body, her eyes locked on mine. So I teased her, playing dumb, until a flicker of doubt entered her eyes, and then followed her into the dance.

Debbie was a natural. By the third dance the rhythm owned our souls and our bodies fused together like molten glass.

Suddenly, the music stopped and she peeled herself off me and stepped back. My eyes took in the shadows of her hardened nipples through the sweat-soaked cotton of her dress. Sparking like some mutant teenage hormone bomb, I fancied the rest of the night would be one of unbridled lust. And I was all for getting started when someone punched me in the back and said, "Hey, you pissed in my fucking dinghy."

Gordon packed quite a punch and although it didn't drop me, it sent me crashing into Debbie, numbed my shoulder, and sent pins and needles right down my arm.

Experience told me that Gordon the Turd was winding up for another punch, expecting I would take it with surprise.

My next move had him beat.

I leaned into Debbie, turned her sideways and, before she could react, kissed her, making sure that Gordon had a good view of my tongue heading for her tonsils.

If he'd punched me again, Debbie would have bitten off my tongue. But he didn't, instead he began to pray, or at least he bellowed, *"Jeeesus!"* then his mouth dropped open and for an awful moment I thought he wanted a kiss, but the moment passed and I pushed Debbie away and took his next punch on the arm.

"You son of a bitch, you pissed in my dinghy," he bellowed again and I began to think the guy was deranged. He wasn't the least concerned that I was planning to slosh my fluids into his delectable fiancé, but was extremely upset about the fluids he claimed I'd deposited in his miserable dinghy.

Admittedly, I knew what he was talking about. The *Lady* has a shortage of heads and on busy nights guys wandered to the aft deck, used the toilet with the view, and pissed over the side. This I learned the hard way when I dropped into my inflatable one night and found myself ankle deep in recycled beer. I was disgusted but not as disgusted as the poor girl puffing on a joint while relieving herself over the side of a nearby dinghy. My sudden arrival bounced her three feet in the air and backwards into the drink.

The music stopped and the memory fled. In the silence, the crowd pulled back, forming a small circle around Debbie, Gordon, me, and three strapping young lads who appeared to be Gordon's crew.

Beyond the circle, I could see Pete and Willie trying to force their way through the crowd. But there was no way they were going to make it before Gordon unleashed another haymaker. I needed to talk to this guy and calm him down. After all, it was a beautiful night and a great party; he wasn't worried about his woman so why the hell screw it up.

Gordon was a clean-cut, stars-bars-and-apple-pie kind of a guy, with short blond hair atop a deeply tanned face. His eyes, almost as blue as mine, showed a tinge of alcohol-induced red, which contrasted rather nicely with the expensive gleam of his perfect teeth. He was wearing a designer polo shirt with the New York Yacht Club logo embroidered over the pocket, and from his build I knew he was a workout freak. His cream Bermuda shorts were tailored to go with the shirt, and on his spiffy canvas belt he carried a brand-new two hundred dollar multi-tool in a monogrammed sheath. The only thing about Gordon that wasn't bright and shiny was his salt-stained deck shoes, which he obviously worked on for effect, and his attitude, which stank.

"Look, Gordon, it wasn't me but let's not spoil the party," I said and raised my hands into the 'I surrender' position. "Let's ask Pete for a hosepipe to wash out your dinghy. Then we'll pull out the bungs and take it for a spin around the lagoon until it's clean. What do you say?"

Before he could say anything I pushed past him and the gawpers and went to the rail.

I saw immediately why Gordon was pissed at the piss, so to speak. His dinghy was no sagging zodiac held together by peeling patches and propelled by a questionable outboard motor of undetermined vintage … like mine. But twenty-six feet of gleaming white Hyperlon wrapped around an inboard diesel and a consul that held enough electronics to guide a space probe.

Behind me I could hear Gordon approaching with his merry men and as soon as he was within range he just couldn't resist giving me a hefty shove in the back. "Okay motherfucker, get in and clean it out."

Wow, this was wonderful stuff, straight out of the movies.

Gordon's next line wasn't long in coming and I mimed right along with him. "You heard me motherfucker, get in and clean it out."

Americans have a great way with a curse. They are far more inventive than the Brits, and I could have listened to Gordon all night. In fact I wish I could have taken notes, so I could remember his expletives and used them later to impress my friends, but we were fast running out of time.

I turned and looked at him. He was pumped up, ready for action, and I knew he was done with the wild swings when the idiot dropped his hands to his side and began taking deep controlled breaths.

Perhaps I should have ended it there: pointed out that he wasn't in the dojo and whatever color martial arts belt he had was fit for nothing but holding up his shorts. But I doubt he would have listened.

He flexed his muscles as his goons moved in behind him, smirking and exchanging glances. They were like wolves waiting for the alpha male to claim the best of the kill before getting their noses into the blood to devour what was left.

I tried one more time. I didn't want this shit on my birthday or any other day. I didn't want this shit in my life.

"Look, Gordon, it's simple. We grab a few beers and invite a few girls along. Then we go out and look at the stars. With the bungs out, the dinghy cleans itself while we yahoo; then we come back to the *Lady* and get on with the party. What do you say? Shit, I'll even buy."

What he said wasn't long in coming. His right arm shot back in a rapid twisting motion that spun his hand into a karate fist. If he'd learned from a master then the punch would finish three inches beyond the back of my head. Designed to kill, the punch drives the shattered nose-bone upwards, severing the optic nerves and sending it into the brain.

Something about Gordon's attack told me he was a seriously unhappy guy, and I began to regret my little bit of fun with Debbie. To put up with a vicious assault like this, instead of just kissing her, I wish I'd boffed her right there on the deck!

Karate is more than a fighting technique; it's a discipline that takes years to learn. In the dojo, I bet Gordon had all the other students wetting themselves. But he wasn't in the dojo and I was no student.

The punch was at shoulder height when I hawked and spit in his face. I guess old Gordy thought I might have that dreadful disease that some think you catch from swapping saliva. When horror forced a moment's hesitation, as I knew it would, I drove my knee into his balls and augured him, shrieking and gushing vomit, into the deck.

With Gordon taking a rest, I backed up to the rail and waited for the wolves to move in.

They approached to within six feet. Then two of them turned and pulled automatics from their belts and leveled them at Willie and Pete, stopping them in their tracks.

At a grunted command, another goon stepped out of the shadows into the light. The glint of a knife told me he was ready to finish what Gordon had started. By the way he moved, this guy was in a different league—lean, good-looking, and deadly.

He stepped over the whimpering Gordon without a downward glance.

As he advanced a smile spread from his lips all the way to the corners of his reptilian eyes. This was a professional killer who loved his job; a psycho who would laugh as the knife went in.

I shuffled further along the rail.

Sensing this was more than your average bar room brawl, the crowd on the boat had thinned. The hardcore crooks and criminals had hit the road and were still running. Others had climbed over the side into their dinghies from where they could safely enjoy the show before motoring off to the next waterfront bar.

Silence enveloped the boat as I edged away from Snake Eyes, trying my best to sober-up and work out just what the hell was going on. We were supposed to be having a party. And the delectable Debbie was supposed to be part of a yacht's crew; not an accomplice to a group of professional assassins.

A steel band started up with *Yellow Bird* from a dock nearby. The sound drifted across the water on the breeze bringing with it the fragrant aroma of marijuana smoke.

I couldn't help it and started to laugh. After all I had been through I was going to die beneath the tropical stars to the rhythm of a steel drum band. Worse, the last thing I would ever hear would be that bloody awful song *Yellow Bird.*

My guffaw brought a puzzled look from Snake Eyes who'd probably never killed someone who laughed at him before. It puzzled him but it wasn't going to stop him.

I was fast running out of options. Perhaps I could somersault over the rail into the water without breaking my back across someone's outboard motor. Or maybe chance a frontal assault on the murderous bastard and his two bonnie lads.

Suddenly the small deck hatch between Snake Eyes' feet began to rise and what appeared to be the front end of an old-fashioned blunderbuss loomed out of the hole.

Sensing movement, Snake Eyes stopped and stepped back. I heard Susie shout, "Flied lice!" then he was gone as the freezing blast from a forty-four pound carbon dioxide fire extinguisher vaporized his shorts.

The unexpected attack was enough. Leaving Gordon to his fate, the three assassins leapt over the rail into the trouble-making, piss-filled dinghy, and roared off into the night.

Along the beach *Yellow Bird* died beneath the wail of approaching sirens. In the ensuing stampede, I slipped over the stern and swam away in the moonlight.

6

The banging on the side of the boat refused to go away. It just grew louder and louder as the miscreants hammered their way towards the bow. Suddenly, the noise stopped and the shaft of sunlight spilling across my bunk began to shrink, as a peeked cap, followed by a black face, appeared at the open porthole.

"Susie, there's someone to see you," I said.

This earned me a muffled, "Fuck off," from beneath the pillow.

"Well, at least we're still talking," I said as a nightstick began rattling backwards and forwards in the porthole like a demented bell clapper.

"Get up, Turpin, up, up, you're in big trouble, mon." The policeman rattled his nightstick again for effect and then nodded towards the back of the boat.

I slid off the bunk and wrapped a towel around my waist, then made my way shakily through the main cabin to the companionway steps and climbed into the cockpit.

Normally I would have laughed at the sight of the three of them standing in the tiny plastic dinghy that was ready to capsize at any time. But I could tell, before they spoke, that for whatever reason they were seeking my council it wasn't for a round of belly laughs.

Sergeant Ascari was an old friend, but the other two I didn't know. I could see that they weren't happy and I knew why. Most of the cops on the island can't swim and these guys were carrying enough hardware on their belts to take them straight to the bottom if they fell in.

I invited them aboard and Ascari hauled himself up and over the side. Before the other two could follow, he made a 'stay there' signal with his hand, and left them clinging to the gunnels of the rocking dinghy like frightened children.

"I'm not supposed to talk to you, just bring you in, but—"

"But," I finished for him, "there's no room in your police boat for four people, besides you're a friend. So, what's going on?"

He looked at me and shook his head, then took my arm and led me to the far side of the cockpit, out of earshot of the other two. "Dick, you were on the *Lucky Lady* last night, you got into a fight, and there are plenty of witnesses. Something bad has happened and it's more than my job's worth to tell you more. One of the men in the dinghy is the police chief's nephew, so for once behave yourself and follow us ashore."

Ascari was a good man, a good cop and, a rarity on St Peters, honest. He had studied law in England and America then returned to the island he loved to raise his kids and look after his aging parents. A while back his two sons had got into a bit of trouble with one of the island's drug lords and Pete, Willie and I had got them out of it. Nothing had ever been said but his kids were his life. He was a cop, so we never socialized, but our bond of friendship was strong.

I went below and dragged on some clothes, swallowed six aspirins with a swig of tepid water, and made my way back to the cockpit.

Ascari was already in the dinghy, which now was bobbing about thirty feet astern of *Strange Light*.

The sergeant looked towards me and rolled his eyes as one of his men pulled on the string of an ancient two horsepower outboard motor in an effort to make it start.

While they performed, I hopped into my inflatable and cranked the engine that for once in its miserable life started at the first pull. Minutes later, and with the plastic dinghy and its crew of terrified policemen hanging precariously from a towrope astern, we set off for the shore.

It was obvious where they wanted me to go, as what seemed like half the population of St. Peters was on the rickety dock where, a few hours earlier, the band had tormented us with *Yellow Bird.*

I brought the two boats alongside, threw a clove hitch around a rotten piling, and climbed up onto the dock.

The crowd was in carnival mood. Everyone was shouting and laughing, which was a bad sign. They knew they were in for some entertainment and I had a sneaky suspicion that I was the star of the show.

I forced my way towards the center of the mob and Ascari and his men followed.

As we reached the makeshift stage the crowd fell silent. A circle of uniforms surrounded something on the ground, something I didn't want to see. But I had no choice. Ascari gently pushed me through the cordon until I had the bad news of the day laying at my feet.

"Ha! Mister Turpin. Good of you to join us. Nice day for it wouldn't you say?" Colonel James Chalmond, better known by everyone as Chopstick, except to his face, was the island's Chief of Police. Grossly overweight, it was hard to tell where his shoulders ended and his neck began. His uniform was an immaculate mix of jungle camouflage and parade ground finery bedecked with badges that, if they were to be believed, made him a wing commander, an admiral of the fleet, and a five-star general all at the same time.

On any other island, Chalmond would be a laughing stock, but not on St. Peters. Here, backed by 'retired' drug lords and corrupt politicians, Chopstick was a man to fear.

I stepped around him and the first thing I saw was a scruffy deck shoe. It was lying in a pool of blood about six inches from the tanned and very dead foot of Gordon the Turd.

"Do you think he was murdered, Mister Chalmond," I said, which brought a bellow of laughter from somewhere.

Chalmond didn't reply but turned and, tipping his head so he could see from beneath the peak of his cap, stared into the crowd, which choked off the next guffaw as effectively as a knife in the ribs.

Having dealt with the mob, he turned his attention back to me.

"I'm glad to see you haven't lost your sense of humor, Turpin, as I fear you are soon going to need it. What!" he said in his affected public school accent.

"Fuck you," I thought and, doing my best to ignore him, took a closer look at my friend from the previous night.

Whatever the guy was into, it was now more serious than a dinghy full of piss.

Gordon lay with his back against an old rum barrel that doubled as a table. His chin was resting on his chest and, judging by the gash in his neck, it was the only thing holding his head on.

He was naked but for his cream Bermuda shorts which, his tailor would be delighted to know, still held a perfect razor-sharp crease. They also held a good part of his guts, which were hanging from two neat slashes carved across his belly in the shape of a cross.

Had it been a Samurai warrior committing seppuku, he would be proud of himself. But this was no warrior, just a dead, punk kid lying in a pool of congealed blood and rat shit. Yet it could have been worse; it could have been me.

Chalmond tapped me with his swagger-stick. "Well, Turpin,

what have you got to say for yourself. I would have thought that you of all people would have enough sense to take the body outside of the lagoon and sink it. What!"

"That's more your style, Chopstick," I said, putting plenty of emphasis on his nickname, knowing everyone was listening and it would really piss him off.

I was on dangerous ground but the fat bastard was beginning to annoy me. The six aspirins hadn't even put a dent in my headache and the stink of blood, mixed with that of our jolly police chief's hellish cologne, was about to make me throw up. I wanted to get this farce over with, catch up on some sleep, and if that meant a night in a jail cell then so be it.

"I should have had you and your band of renegades thrown off our beautiful island years ago, Turpin, but now, well, murder is a serious thing and I rather think you might hang." Chalmond was drooling at the thought.

"You know damn well that I had nothing to do with this," I said.

"So, you say you didn't kill this unfortunate fellow even thought you threatened to do so last night. If you didn't do it, perhaps you know who did," he sneered. He was on a roll, playing to the crowd, pushing himself up on his toes and slapping a camouflaged thigh with his swagger-stick.

The audience was hanging on every word and within hours we'd be the talk of the rum shops. Behind Chalmond, I could see Sergeant Ascari shaking his head in warning. But I'd had enough.

I stepped forward until I was grinning into Chalmond's face. "I heard he went out to buy some of that perfume you wear but he couldn't find any so he committed suicide."

Whatever he did signaled the end of the game and while one of his men tried to remove my kidneys with his truncheon, two more dragged me backwards through the cheering mob and into a waiting Jeep.

Before they jammed my face into the congealed blood and vomit that littered the floor, I caught sight of someone familiar at the back of the crowd. Although I couldn't identify the face, there was no mistaking the color of her hair.

7

Like many third world countries struggling to survive and prosper in the cutthroat world of tourism, St. Peters has two faces. One it presents to the world on its colourful tourism brochures, the other it keeps hidden behind a mountain of drug money, graft and corruption.

It also has two jails.

Built at the back of the new police station, jail number one is clean and brightly lit, and keeps Amnesty International happy by maintaining the minimum standards laid down in their bill of rights. This is where they take the drunken tourists, wife beaters, and Saturday night brawlers, and I could handle a few days there in an air-conditioned cell.

The other jail is something else. Supposedly unused in these enlightened times, it is hidden away deep in the mountains, where it began life as a colonial military barracks. This is where they re-educated the 'politicos' during the various uprisings that were common during the island's turbulent past. Locals refuse to go near the place claiming it is haunted by jumbies; ghosts of the tortured dead who walk the stone passageways looking for revenge.

The old jail had been closed for years. But rumor had it that Chopstick and the drug lords had been using it recently to enforce their own rules, inviting the competition to midnight orgies, never to be seen again.

Whatever the truth, the story wasn't lost on me.

I began keeping track of the time. I knew roughly how long

it would take to reach the new police station—and already it was taking too long.

Suddenly, we turned sharp left, and the Jeep was no longer thrumming over tarmac but bouncing along a dirt road and swerving around potholes. Two hundred yards further on the engine note changed, the driver shifted into four-wheel-drive, and we began the long climb into the mountains.

With each hairpin bend, my hopes of air-conditioning were strangled by thoughts of pain. And when next I inhaled the stench of my own sweat, I was shocked to catch the aroma of fear amongst the still pungent odor of last night's beer.

Those who claim there is nothing to fear but fear itself have never watched a friend have their fingernails torn out, or an electric cattle prod shoved up their arse, knowing it's their turn next.

In Special Forces we were given lectures on how to face up to torture and control our fear. A room full of psychobabalists told us how to survive interrogation by the enemy, and how to get our minds around the degradation and pain. They even brought in some guys who had been through such an ordeal and made us listen while they told their awful tales.

As the lectures went on, we were in awe of these brave men. Then they introduced us to a woman who had been captured in some dirty African war. By the time she had told us what they had done to her, and what she'd had to do to survive, we were ready to resign our commissions and drive a bus.

There are incredibly brave people who can suffer torture and remain unbroken, but they usually end up dead. In reality, most people collapse, quivering and begging, into heaps of their own piss and shit long before they feel the touch of a blade or inhale the sickening stench of their own seared flesh.

I know, because—God forgive me—I've experienced it from both sides. And if I was right about where they were taking me, I was about to experience it again.

"How's life on the floor, Turpin?" The voice from above caught me off guard and I raised my head only to have it slammed back down by a beautifully polished size fourteen boot.

This brought a bellow of laughter from the two cops in front, who were gripping the dashboard with both hands as the Jeep bounced and swerved along what now was little more than an overgrown track.

"Don't go worrying yourself, mon," said the driver over his shoulder. "We'll soon be there and then you can stretch your legs, or perhaps one of us will get to stretch them for you."

This brought more hoots of laughter and kept them amused until the Jeep hit a graveled surface, traveled a few yards, and came to a sudden, jarring halt.

A car door slammed, followed by another. The door of the Jeep was flung open and I was grabbed by the ankles and dragged out.

With my hands cuffed behind my back, my ribs took the full impact, but at least I managed to twist my head so that it was my deaf ear that hit the ground. As I struggled to force air into my lungs, two of them kicked me onto my back and I found myself looking up into Chopstick's smiling face.

"Ha, Turpin. There you are. It's barely noon and already I've had the pleasure of your company twice today. What!"

He turned to his two grinning constables and told them to stand me up. "That's better, now we can talk like gentlemen," he said and with surprising speed for such a ponderous man, struck the side of my head with his swagger-stick, which dropped me back into the dirt at his feet. "I do hope that wasn't your good ear, Turpin," he sneered, knowing full well that it was.

His men sprang forward and dragged me to my feet, only this time, instead of the swagger stick, he wound himself up and buried his fist into my stomach all the way to the wrist.

The pretense was over. Chopstick Chalmond had lost all trace of his Eton accent and his speech was now pure Kingstown waterfront. His piggy eyes were bright with excitement and I began to suspect that what I'd heard about our Police Chief's sexual proclivities was true. Flecks of saliva bubbled from the corners of his mouth and beneath his arms growing circles of sweat marred the trim of his immaculate uniform.

From my vantage point in the dirt, I could see that he was actually getting a hard-on, and it filled me with disgust to think that I was the focus of his lust.

My loathing lasted all of two seconds before the sight of the ridiculous bulge in his camouflaged trousers cracked me up and I grabbed my knees and began to howl.

At first they thought the tears and snot from my bloody nose were some kind of plea for mercy and seconds went by before they realized I was doubled up with laughter.

This was too much for Chopstick and he began bellowing like a bull. However, what he wanted to say and what he actually said were two different things, and all that came out of his mouth was a shower of spit.

He couldn't speak but his intentions were clear.

He fumbled with the flap of a shiny leather holster and yanked out an ancient Webley Mark 6 revolver that at short range would do as much damage as a cannon.

At the sight of the gun the two cops stepped back and my stupid sense of humor stepped back with them.

Chopstick had calmed down; it was not a good sign. He towered over me, legs apart and slightly bowed, as if his balls were too big for their allotted space.

The cop on my right raised his hands, "Colonel, this isn't a good idea," he said and took a hesitant step forward.

Chalmond ignored him and continued to stare and point the

gun. Then he slowly pulled back the hammer with his thumb. I watched the chamber turn. For a moment the sun caught the hollow tip of the .455 bullet before it disappeared behind the barrel with a well-oiled clunk.

It was too much for one of the cops who dropped his hands and sprinted towards the trees.

Laughing like a hyena, Chopstick tracked him with the revolver, then swung it back around and pointed it at my head.

His vocal cords were back in action and when the Eaton accent suddenly replaced his hideous laugh, I knew the man was totally insane. "I would say you are fucked, Turpin, fucked and at my mercy. Wouldn't you?" The word 'Fucked' came out as 'Farcked' and I thought God help me I'm going to laugh again and die.

Behind Chopstick the front of the old prison was turning pink in the afternoon sun. To the south, I heard the faint roar of a jet as it lifted off from the airport and climbed towards the mountains. The noise built then quickly faded away, returning the clearing to silence.

I glanced to my left, gauging the distance to the edge of the courtyard where the tangled forest stood deep in shadow.

A tic developed on Chopstick's right cheek, his eyes narrowed and he slowly squeezed the trigger.

I came up out of the dirt like a snake, one hand twisting towards the gun, the other, fingers extended, aiming for the hollow below his ribs.

The movement was little more than a thought before a blinding flash blew my head apart.

8

Dead is as dead does ... Dead is as dead does … The silly mantra was pounding through my brain, repeating itself over and over. Two distant red dots kept pace with the tune, swinging back and forth like laser gun sights.

I tried to turn my head but it wouldn't move. It was cold and dark, but then, being dead, that was no surprise.

Terrified, I watched the glowing red dots draw near; the fires of hell growing in size as they came to claim me. The flames moved up my body, consumed my legs, until they were on my chest and licking at my face.

"Nooooshit!"

I shot up, leaving a clump of blood-matted hair fused to the stone mattress. Dead men don't scream and if this were hell I'd just squeezed the life out of the devil's furry body with my bare hands.

I hurled the rat away and after a few sobbing breaths my heart settled down.

The last thing I remember was Chopstick's gun. The back of my head was on fire and when I touched it my fingers came away wet. Further exploration turned up a patch of raw flesh surrounded by a soggy lump the size of an egg. Satisfied, I lay back and carefully checked the rest of my body. My ribs were sore; two fingernails were hanging on by a thread, and I was naked. Other than some bruising, the rest seemed okay. No gunshot wounds and, as far as I could tell, nothing was broken.

All in all, I'd been carried off the rugby field in worse shape.

My head was throbbing like hell but my mind began to clear. Having decided I really was alive and likely to remain that way for the next few minutes, I sat up, swung my legs off the bunk, and cautiously lowered my feet to the floor.

I was in the old prison, in one of the stone cells.

Water was dripping somewhere and once, as I eased my way around the rough walls, I thought I heard voices.

A glimmer of light, low down to the left, led me to the door. It was steel, with no handle on the inside. When I lay on my stomach and pressed my eye against the narrow crack, I could see a few flagstones. The light was too soft to be artificial, so it must be daylight. But what time could it be?

I eased my way back to the bunk and sat down. After a while the light beneath the door began to fade and finally went out.

Some people go to pieces after no more than a few hours of incarceration. Hardened killers have been known to turn into screaming wrecks, breaking their knuckles against the door for fear of a future unknown. Others, imprisoned for months in stinking solitary confinement, stumble into the daylight tougher and prouder than when they went in.

The secret is to use the cell as a temporary refuge; a place to rest and plan. By quickly focusing the mind, before the cell becomes a cruel and terrible weapon that the enemy can use against you, you keep the upper hand.

My feet are exactly ten-and-a-half inches long, the span of my hand, nine. Placing one foot in front of the other, I measured the size of my cell.

Walking from the back wall to the door required nine steps, or ninety-four-and-a-half inches. The bunk was three hand spans—or twenty-seven inches.

The door was narrow, low, and opened outwards to the right.

By standing on the bunk I could touch the crumbling plaster on the ceiling. I measured the distance down the wall to the top of the bunk, then from the top of the bunk to the floor. The floor was made of flagstones with dirt packed between them.

There were no windows.

My nose led me to a drain in the left-hand corner; it was probably where the rats were getting in.

Once I had the dimensions, I sat down on the bunk and lay with my back against the wall. With the angles worked out, I knew the exact distance to the door and just how much room there was for various attacking and defensive moves.

There was one more thing to do. I found the dead rat and lay it by the door. As a weapon it was pretty useless, but I was counting on human nature. Few people fail to react when suddenly confronted by a rat and my dead friend could buy me a few precious seconds.

Of course nothing would help if someone simply threw opened the door and hosed the cell with automatic fire. But I had a feeling that wouldn't happen. Whoever had bludgeoned me to the ground had saved my life by getting me away from Chopstick. But why?

My internal clock told me I'd spent an hour working on the dimensions of the cell. At this time of year the sun set at around six-thirty, so by my reckoning it was now about eight o'clock.

All I could do was rest and wait. I lay on the bunk with my hands linked behind my head to protect the drying scabs from the rough stone.

An occasional mosquito buzzed around my face and an itch flared on my leg where one of them had feasted.

Sleep came quickly. Not the shock induced sleep of oblivion, but the alert sleep of combat. This is a technique taught in the military and one that served me well when I sailed *Strange Light* across the Atlantic Ocean alone.

Arriving in Martinique, twenty-one days after leaving the Canary Islands, I was ready to party and shocked by the condition of that year's crop of other solo Atlantic adventurers.

Tales of days without sleep and vivid descriptions of terrifying hallucinations brought on by solitude, constant motion, and sheer, mind numbing exhaustion, were traded to the curious for copious amounts of beer and cheap rum. Some of the sailors had been ashore for days and still had the look of zombies.

I approached single-handed sailing in a different way: following the same routine as living ashore, I went to bed at ten and got up at six, having slept a good eight hours.

The real sailors told me that this was illegal; that as the captain of a ship I was charged with keeping a good watch at all times. But I never did have much time for real sailors, with their flags and fancy clubs, and did my best to avoid them.

The sleep pattern worked for me. Once the boat settled into a rhythm, I slept soundly, but the slightest change and I was instantly awake.

While on active service I discovered others in my unit with the same ability. It was as if we had become sensitive to changes in air pressure and were able to sense unusual currents and vibrations. Then again, we might just have been scared shitless.

Whatever the reason, after my encounter with the mine, the gift seemed to leave me and I swear it was sailing that brought it back. Over time, the damage to my ear even seems to have sharpend my perception, so I was already standing when the cell door creaked and began to move.

9

Had they stormed into the cell, I wouldn't have stood a chance. However, this was no frontal assault; the door was being opened with care, silently, moving a fraction at a time.

Pressing my back against the wall to present a narrow target, I slid towards the door and took up position to the right of the frame.

Four deep, calming, breaths and I was ready.

The door moved another inch, revealing a sliver of light. Someone was using a low-powered flashlight or something to deflect the beam.

They had no idea. Surprise was on my side and if there were only two of them then I had a chance.

My eyes were accustomed to the dark, so I kept them away from the source of light.

A hinge creaked and the door opened another notch; it was followed by the unmistakable click of a gun's safety catch.

More light spilled into the room forming a dim path that eased its way towards the empty bunk.

I had to act or lose the advantage of surprise. I braced for a kick that would smash the door back into my assailants. If I could just make it into the passageway and in the sudden confusion extinguish the light, then the odds of my survival would go from zero to one.

My plan was sound but my timing lousy.

I wound up for the kick as the door flew open and the flashlight swept the cell. The beam shot across the back wall then fell, pinning the corpse of the rat to the floor. There was a sudden terrified shriek as my shadow, made gross by the angle of the light, leapt from the wall and followed me out through the door and into the passageway. I caught a glimpse of the rat as it danced away in a hail of gunfire. My shoulder made contact with something soft. The flashlight spun through the air then hit the ground and went out, plunging us into darkness.

The gunfire and yelling stopped. I threw myself to the floor. The stench of cordite bit into my lungs and I tried desperately not to cough.

"Stupid it is, you'll get us all killed." Willie's unmistakable singsong voice echoed off the walls then faded away, leaving a stream of pathetic little sobs in its wake.

Before I could speak heavy footsteps pounded down the passageway bringing with them another bouncing beam of light.

"Is everyone alright?" Pete steadied the flashlight and shone it at Willie. Susie was sobbing on his shoulder. Her arms were draped around his neck and in her right hand she gripped the short-barreled Walther P38K semi automatic that I kept hidden on the boat.

I coughed.

Pete spun around and bathed me in light.

"There he is, look you, and as naked as the day he was born," said Willie.

"Oh God, he's alive ..." Susie threw her arms round me and slammed my head against the wall.

"For God's sake get off," I roared. "You damn near killed me, and who the hell let you loose with a gun?"

"Sorry, Dick, we didn't know she had it, but she sure as hell killed that dead rat," said Willie, and the two guys started to laugh.

The flickering light made their shadows grotesque, stretching them upwards along the wall and across the ceiling.

"You arseholes," said Susie.

I grinned and looked at each of them in turn. "Okay guys you did great but could we save the celebrations until we get out of here?"

"It can't be too soon for me. This place gives me the creeps." Susie grabbed my hand and hauled me to my feet.

We made our way back to the open cell. Pete shone a light inside but he found nothing and we moved on. Ahead, the passageway turned to the left and disappeared into the darkness.

Susie slid her arm around my waist and clung on. She'd heard all the stories about the old prison and, though she said they were bullshit, she was spooked.

We'd taken a dozen steps when Pete raised his hand and signaled us to slow down.

"What is it—" I clamped my hand across Susie's mouth.

"Shush."

She shivered and dug her fingernails into my arm. The adrenalin, that for the last few minutes had kept her going, had drained away and she was starting to shake.

"Don't leave me, Dick. Please." The dim light cast a flickering shadow, highlighting the fear on her face.

"It's okay, we're all here," I said and after a reassuring hug she relaxed her grip on my arm.

Pete crept forward and we followed.

Ten yards on, we came to another bend. Pete pointed to his flashlight and made the cutoff signal with his hand. Willie nodded and instantly both flashlights went out.

The darkness was sudden and absolute.

I waited for Pete. After a couple of seconds he touched my arm and began whispering in my good ear.

"We had a good look around when we arrived. The place was deserted. All the cells were empty except yours. Yours was easy to find; it was the only one that was locked."

"But you opened the cell with a key. I heard it."

"I know; someone left it hanging from a hook by the door."

He stopped talking while we both listened, then, after a moment, he went on.

"Look, I don't know what's going on but I've got an uneasy feeling. The Jeep's outside the front door and that's the only way in or out."

Pete's uneasy feelings had been known to save lives, so I wasn't taking any chances.

"Willie, can you hear me?" I murmured.

"Right here, Dick."

"I'm the one who got us into this shit so give me the pistol. I'll go out first and make my way along the wall to the left. Pete, you count to ten then go out to the right. Make your way along the wall but stay within twenty feet of the door, and keep low. Don't approach the Jeep until you're sure the three of us are there. Willie, when you see me alongside the Jeep; give it a few seconds and then bring Susie out."

We slipped into our old combat routine. I kept telling myself that I hated it. But I knew the other two were enjoying the rush as much as I was.

I took a deep breath and stepped through the door.

The Jeep was parked exactly where Pete said it would be with its front end pointing away from the building, towards the road.

Across the courtyard the wind, eerie in the fermenting night, stirred the branches of the trees. Constantly changing, the shadows solidified in the moonlight and then melted away.

I gripped the automatic with both hands and waited. Then, as Pete moved along the wall behind me, I edged towards the Jeep and squatted down by the rear wheel.

After a few seconds Willie and Susie joined me.

We waited for Pete, counting the time.

"Where the hell is he?" said Susie.

"Behind you," said Pete.

Susie let out a scream, my heart slammed into my ribs, and we tumbled into the Jeep like circus clowns.

"Go!" I shouted.

Pete jammed the key into the ignition and spun it to the right.

Nothing.

In the silence the courtyard lit up like the Fourth of July.

10

Pete slid his hand under the dashboard and came up with a fistful of ignition wires. In the glare we could see the clour-coded spaghetti had been neatly snipped.

Susie shrieked and leapt out of the Jeep. The moment her feet hit the ground the offside wing mirror exploded, showering her in bits of metal and glass.

“Don’t move!” I screamed and spun around, lunging for the back of her shirt before she could run for it.

Willie beat me to it, grabbed each shoulder and threw her backwards onto the seat.

Whatever weapon they were using was high-powered and silent.

Pete glanced across and I responded with a nod. He slowly raised his hand and after a moment’s hesitation wrapped his fingers around the top of the windshield. Without warning the driver’s side mirror slammed into the doorframe and the spent bullet whined off into the night.

Whoever had the rifle was good. One mirror could have been luck; two was a deadly warning to stay in the Jeep. Ignore it and the next shot would kill.

“There are three vehicles and they’re about fifty yards apart. The middle one has a small searchlight high up, probably on its roof. I think that’s where the shooting’s coming from. It’s your call, Dick.” Willie’s voice was calm and matter of fact.

I slid the .38 into the torn fabric covering the back of the passenger seat and pushed it down into the foam. “We do nothing,” I said, trying to keep my voice as calm as Willie’s. “They’ve proved they can take us out whenever they want, so we wait. Just don’t move. Willie, keep hold of Susie, something tells me she’s expendable.”

That brought a stifled ‘Fuck you’ from the back seat and a chuckle from Pete.

I was straining to make out shapes in the harsh glare when suddenly all six headlights went out leaving us pinned in the single narrow beam of the searchlight.

To the left of the searchlight an engine coughed to life. It was followed seconds later by one on the right. Two vehicles slowly moved towards us across the courtyard, their tires crunching gravel as they came.

They stopped at the edge of our circle of light, which illuminated their front ends leaving the rest of the vehicle in shadow. Both were hefty four-by-fours, a sticker across the windshield identified them as belonging to the Jolly Mon Hire Company.

We waited, listening to their powerful engines ticking over, sacrificing the Earth’s dwindling resources on the altar of air-conditioning.

“Don’t turn around or make any sudden moves.” The voice behind us was little more than a hiss. “You are quite right, Turpin. I will kill the girl first if you fail to cooperate.”

As if on cue, the doors of the two four-by-fours opened and three people stepped out. One of them slipped into the shadows but not before the light reflected off an AK-47 held with both hands.

We were no threat to whoever was running this operation. They knew it and, perhaps with the exception of Susie, who I could hear muttering, we knew it, too.

"Susie, take it easy and please keep quiet," I said, knowing Willie would have a firm grip on her arm.

There was a short bark of laughter and a figure stepped forward and peered down into the Jeep. "You wear your nakedness well, Turpin, most men would put embarrassment before danger."

"Feel free to join me," I said. "This is St. Peters; we won't be the only ones running around naked tonight."

That brought another bark of laughter, followed by a sharp command, and my missing clothes were tossed into the Jeep.

"Please join me in a walk once you are dressed. Perhaps we can work out a way of keeping you and your friends alive." The accent was American, but there was a trace of something else in the voice.

For a moment I thought about following him in the nude, just to see if he could maintain his cool. A fully dressed man can usually bully a naked woman. However, confront him with a naked man, who stands up straight and thrusts his head and his dick forward in a show of animal aggression, and he's likely to back off. The ancient Scots knew this when they painted their balls with woad, whipped off their kilts, and hurled themselves naked at the invading English.

Having no woad, I tucked myself into my shorts, slipped on my shirt, and went after the man who seemed to have our lives in his hands.

The sky was brightening in the east as I followed him towards the forest where he stopped before entering the line of trees.

He must have heard my approach but never once looked back. As a show of bravado it was impressive, but it was more than that, the guy was letting me know that he was in complete control.

I stopped within touching distance and waited as he turned.

Tall and well built, he wore a cream tropical suit that had never seen the inside of a chain store. His brown hair had receded and formed a straight line across the top of his head, connecting one neatly trimmed sideburn to the other. He had a deep-water tan and flashed a gold tooth that complemented the heavy medallion hanging from a chain around his neck.

Everything about the man was chic. From the Rolex chronometer on his wrist, to the way he shrugged off his jacket and swung it over his shoulder; his moves were done with the practiced skill of a film star at the Oscars.

"You killed my son and I think you may know the whereabouts of something that belongs to me. Now I have something that belongs to you. Three things, actually," he said nodding towards the Jeep.

The sound of a shot echoed off the walls of the old prison sending a flock of roosting birds screaming in terror from the trees.

"Make it two things that belong to you." He thrust out his hands. "Stop! If you move towards me, the executions will continue. Of course, my men may choose to kill them anyway."

His laughter turned my bowels to water. My life had gone to hell. Someone had killed Gordon the Turd and because of it my friends were dying.

"Listen, you miserable sack of shit. I have nothing of yours and I don't kill people for crashing my birthday party. I kill people for killing my friends."

"You make that sound like a threat, Mister Turpin. Perhaps another execution is called for."

"Perhaps it is," I said and slid out the Walther that Susie had taken from the stuffing in the back of the seat and buried in my clothes.

"I was warned not to underestimate you, Turpin. Now I find your attitude highly intimidating, and I really don't like being intimidated."

"You're lucky I didn't find the woad," I said and thumbed back the hammer.

A puzzled look crossed his face then he tried another barking laugh but it died on his lips when his eyes met mine.

"What would you say if I told you that all your friends are okay and will remain that way unless you do something stupid, like pulling the trigger?"

"I'd say you'd just bought yourself three chances of staying alive."

The sun had tipped the horizon. Outside the prison, crimson light reflected off the windshield of my old Jeep and the polished chrome of the two land-cruisers. Beyond them, the truck with the spotlight blended in with the jungle, military camouflage softened the outline but failed to disguise the blue police light on its roof.

I casually nudged my prisoner around until he stood between me and whoever was targeting me through the riflescope.

"Now's your chance to explain," I said and jabbed him hard in the gut with the barrel of the gun.

He grunted and took a step back.

There was rustling in the undergrowth around us as the first predators of the day drove the killers of the night back to their lair. A large gecko, its tail scarred and peeling, strutted by with the bloody remains of one of its brethren dangling from its mouth. Maybe it would spit it out and make with the barking laugh.

"Who are you and what do you want from us?" I said.

He let the question hang.

The strengthening sun played on the angles of his face and I could see the resemblance between him and the boy who had been gutted and left on the dock. I thought that would be a good place to start, but he beat me to it.

"My name is Glokani. Gordon—Alexander—Glokani," he said. Then, as if I was holding nothing more dangerous than a bar of chocolate, he stepped around me and walked back towards the courtyard.

11

He played the game well, confirming something although I wasn't sure what. Shooting him now would sign our death warrants but I was keeping the option open and if he had hurt any of my friends then he would die.

As we approached the vehicles Snake Eyes stepped out from behind the nearest land-cruiser and hissed at me. He carried a .22 Ruger MK II automatic with a silencer, which he shook in my face like a charity box before stepping into line behind me.

Our procession carried on and came to a halt next to the second land-cruiser. On Glokani's command, Pete, Willie and Susie stumbled into view ahead of a cop with a riot gun.

It was Chopstick's nephew, the cop who was in the dinghy with Sergeant Ascari, and the one who minutes earlier had tossed me my clothes.

With all the firepower on display it was only a matter of time before someone got hurt, so I engaged the safety catch and slid the Walther into my belt. No one tried to stop me. It was a good sign.

Glokani turned and spoke to the cop. "Turpin had a gun; you could have got me killed."

The cop tried to smile but could only manage a twitch. His eyes circled the courtyard, focused briefly on the police vehicle over by the trees, and then flicked back towards Glokani, and something behind my back that I couldn't see.

"I'm sorry, Mister Glokani," he stammered. Sweat ran down

his face and his hands began to shake. Suddenly, he remembered the riot gun, but it was already too late.

There was a muffled cough and his right eye turned crimson. He fell to his knees. For a moment his body remained upright in disbelief then slowly toppled forward into the dirt at my feet.

Across the clearing the police truck crashed into gear and sped towards us spraying gravel from beneath the wheels.

If Snake Eyes was worried he didn't show it. He grinned down at the dead cop and kept the Ruger pointing at his head as if thinking shooting him again might be fun.

Glokani simply waited for the truck to arrive as if it was picking him up for an island tour.

Pete, Susie and Willie eased their way over and we stood in a group waiting for the next act.

When it came they sent in the clowns.

The truck was still moving when the front passenger door flew open and a uniformed cop jumped out. He trotted alongside the truck until it stopped, then, with parade ground precision, pulled open the rear passenger door and saluted as Chopstick stepped out.

"Well, well, well. Mister Turpin, not only have you escaped from prison, you've managed to kill one of my policemen while doing so." He lifted the dead man's head with a polished boot, totally ignoring Snake Eyes and the gun. "Mmm, my sister's boy, such a shame," he said and let the head drop with a sickening thud back into the blood congealing on the ground.

When she heard the Police Chief's voice, Susie whimpered. It was the keening of an injured animal and it brought a grin to Chopstick's face.

12

Only four people on St. Peters knew about Susie's past. Unfortunately Colonel Chalmond was one of them.

Before she washed up in the islands, Susie had been one of the few women on the South African police force during the dark days of apartheid.

Her wealthy parents were horrified by her choice of career, but supported their stubborn daughter as best they could.

Three months into her new job, her patrol was ordered into Soweto during a riot. On a previous sortie a police officer had been abducted and hacked to death. And although she didn't know it, her guys were looking for revenge.

Towards dawn, a scream led her patrol to a dilapidated shack. The leader told her to wait outside while the rest of them cocked their weapons and went in. Minutes later they came out laughing and said they should move on.

As they walked away another scream tore through the building. Before they could stop her, Susie threw herself through the door.

In a back room she found a naked, thirteen year old girl surrounded by four white cops. They had beaten the child senseless and were taking it in turns to rape her.

Horrified and ashamed, Susie pushed the barrel of her gun into the neck of a thrusting cop, forcing him away from the bleeding girl. Then she marched the four of them outside. When they hesitated she fired into the ground at their feet. When the rapist tried to tuck himself into his pants, she fired again and told him to leave his dick where it was.

Out on the street, Susie demanded her patrol leader arrest the four cops. Then she went back into the shack, but the girl was gone. When she came out, so were the rapists.

Her fellow officers told her to let it drop. They said it was just a minor incident in a night of madness. When she refused, they claimed to have seen nothing.

Susie made a full report to Internal Affairs. They told her that in the interest of police morale no action would be taken.

Weeks later Susie was snatched from outside a restaurant by four hooded men. They dragged her into an alley and almost beat her to death. Then they took it in turns to do to her what she had stopped them from doing to the child.

After the attack, an anonymous phone call led an ambulance to the alley. For months Susie lay in hospital while the doctors worked on her broken body. Finally, able to walk, she was released and went to live with her parents in their Cape Town home.

Suffering from depression, she hid away, rarely leaving the house and hardly eating. Weeks turned into months until one day her father asked her if she would like to go sailing. At first she refused, but her father wouldn't let it go and, after weeks of trying, she finally agreed.

It was the start of her recovery.

Every weekend she joined her parents as they sailed their Mura 29 around Mossel Bay. Slowly her depression eased and the bad days grew further apart. One Sunday, while rounding off the day with drinks at the Royal Cape Yacht Club, they met Captain Frank Toller, a seventy-four year old sea gypsy heading for New York at the end of his third circumnavigation.

Toller entertained them with his sea stories and ended up joining the family for dinner. At the end of the night he told them he was looking for crew and offered Susie a ride to the Caribbean. With the blessings of her mother and father, she took it.

For the next four months Susie fought off the advances of her randy septuagenarian captain as they laughed and joked their way across the Atlantic Ocean.

After stops in St. Helena and Brazil, they arrived in St. Peters, where the old roué finally accepted that, after eight thousand miles of trying, he wasn't going to get into Susie's pants. So he sent for his wife, dumped Susie on the dock with a hug, a duffle bag, and four months pay at fifty bucks a day.

Within hours of arriving in St. Peters, the old goat's story was the talk of the waterfront. And by the end of the week the gang of renegades and misfits at the *Lady* had Susie safely under their wing.

And that is where we met. We became a double act of damaged goods. The intensity of our on-off relationship baffled our friends. We would laugh and party and then split up. Susie would go back to her tiny beach apartment and I would take *Strange Light* to sea or drink myself into oblivion at some bar. But no matter what happened in our crazy lives, we always came back to each other.

Somehow Chopstick had got hold of Susie's story, probably from a bent politician with contacts in the South African underworld. In his twisted mind, Susie was a murdering oppressor of his people. Worse, she was an educated woman and she was mine.

13

Using their machine pistols, the cops pushed Willie and Pete to one side then prodded Susie forward.

Those who didn't know her thought she was tough. But she had endured too many horrors and her toughness was a brittle façade. Life in the islands had helped make her whole, but there was no way she could survive the abuse that was coming her way.

Before I could react, Snake Eyes drilled his silencer into my kidneys and snatched the automatic from my belt.

Susie was trying to be brave. She knew what was about to happen and the look in her eyes broke my heart.

"Keep your filthy hands of her you fat bastard," said Willie, which earned him a gun barrel across the side of the head and he went down.

Chopstick flexed his swagger-stick between his meaty fists, then raised it and touched Susie on the nose. When that got no response, he tapped her lightly on the forehead.

He snorted with laughter.

Susie continued to stare at the ground. The sadistic bastard was tormenting her soul, and her vacant look told me her mind was shutting down.

He stroked her cheek with the silver tip of the swagger-stick then dragged it down across her lips to her chin. "Look at your bitch, Turpin," he said and forced her head backwards.

Tears streamed down Susie's face. "Please," she sobbed.

"Please what, bitch. Your three fucks can do nothing; I'm your lover now." He angled his wrist in an effeminate way and, in a parody of affection, stroked her cheek with the side of the cane. Then he moaned and drew back his arm for a slashing blow that would peel the flesh from her face down to the bone.

"That's enough!" The shout came from Glokani.

Chopstick hesitated and then froze as Snake Eyes pulled the gun out of my kidneys and pointed it at his head.

Glokani strode forward and forced Chopstick's arm down to his side. "Enough of this nonsense, you'll get your chance soon enough if our friends here don't co-operate. Now, clean up your shit and get out of my sight." He nodded towards the cop on the ground.

I was hoping Chopstick would rant and rave and get himself killed. He glared at Glokani, his piggy eyes weighing the odds. Then his nerve gave out and, with a last sneering look at Susie, he pointed his swagger-stick towards the ground. "Pick that up," he growled, and two of his goons lifted the dead cop and threw him into the back of the truck.

Tonight another floater would drift out of the lagoon and head for Panama. In the morning Chopstick's worried sister would call the cops and file a missing persons report. Chalmond would get a twisted kick out of that.

As the cops drove away, Pete helped Willie to his feet.

I nodded towards Susie. "Get her out of here," I said. And between them they led her across the courtyard towards the far corner of the old prison. She went with them like a child.

Glokani spoke to Snake Eyes who came forward and handed me my gun. His reptilian eyes never left mine as I dropped the magazine and checked the load. When I was sure there was ammo in the clip, I slid it back into the handle and chambered a round. Then I asked him how long it had taken for his balls to thaw out.

"By the time I'm through with your Susie, you'll beg me to kill her," he spat. The use of her first name sent shivers down my spine.

"You won't do anything without the permission of golden boy here, so fuck you," I said, nodding towards Glokani.

"You are quite right, Turpin, he won't. But make no mistake; I hold the power of life and death. Right now I need you alive but that could change if we can't do business."

"And what kind of business would I have with a man like you?"

"This kind of business."

He tossed me a small drawstring bag. The bag hit me in the chest and in a reflex action I pinned it there with my arm. He glared at me and then, for the second time that day, turned and walked away.

I watched him head towards the nearest four-by-four. Once he was safely inside, Snake Eyes shouldered me out of the way and followed him. At the door he took a final look around, slid the Ruger into his shoulder holster, and climbed in.

The vehicles reversed through a hundred and eighty degrees, drove across the courtyard and stopped.

After a while there was movement in the shadows at the edge of the trees and a figure clutching an assault rifle stepped into the sun. Moving like she wanted another dance, Debbie wound her way to the side of Glokani's truck. As she approached, the passenger door swung open. She slid the gun onto the seat then turned and threw me a mock salute.

Such a friendly gesture deserved a reply, so I swung up my left fist and slapped my right hand into the crook of my arm.

Debbie threw back her head and laughed then disappeared inside the truck. The door slammed and they roared out of the courtyard in a cloud of dust.

14

It was obvious that Glokani had orchestrated the entire violent charade right from the time of his son's death, and for all I knew he had organized that, too. He traded in death and I wondered what else.

I looked at the bag in my hand. Drugs were a good bet. St. Peters is on a direct route from South America to Europe and the USA. The cops, when not taking money to look the other way, caught drug mules by the hundreds as they flew in and out of the country.

The mules, hired in Columbia and Venezuela, were taught to swallow condoms full of opiates one at a time until their bellies were full. The ones who were paid received a pittance compared to the street value of what they carried. The ones who were not paid did it because their families had been threatened, or to help free their sons and daughters from the clutches of the pimps and pornographers.

Every week some poor sod died shitting and retching during an international flight. The filth from a burst condom surging through their body while the flight attendants struggled to hide the uproar in case it disturb other passengers as they settled down to watch Hollywood's latest romantic comedy.

I hated the drug lords and the island had them by the hundreds, like rats, only according to the politicians they were retired businessmen. They lived in splendor on the hill overlooking the harbour and owned the casinos where they laundered their filthy money.

When one of their sons was found dead in a sleazy back alley from an overdose of heroin and cocaine, the family paid for a full-page obituary in the local paper, calling their sweet son's loss a tragedy. I called it poetic justice.

A shout brought me out of my reverie. I looked up to see Pete pounding towards me throwing up as much gravel as the recently departed trucks.

"You okay?" he shouted. The words were barely out before he slid to a stop.

"I'm fine. What about Susie and Willie?"

"Willie's not good … Glokani's men took Susie with them."

"Jesus! Why, Pete?" Snake Eyes' last words ripped into my brain. "Come on," I said and we sprinted for the Jeep.

Willie was sitting in the front passenger seat. "I'm sorry, Dick. Two goons were waiting for us; there was nothing we could do. If we'd even tried, Glokani's men would have killed her."

"How the hell did they get her out past me? I was watching them the whole time"

Willie was gutted. "They had another car stashed behind the building. We didn't even know you could get out that way."

I climbed in behind the wheel and rested my head on the back of the seat.

The sun was climbing and across the courtyard the forest shimmered in the heat.

Willie slammed his fist into the dashboard. "What's it all about Dick, what the fuck is going on?"

"Same old and lots of it," I said and tossed him Glokani's gift.

We watched him undo the knot and upend the bag; waiting for the white powder to fall into his hand.

“Bloody hell!” he cried as his palm disappeared in a shower of diamonds.

15

It took us ten minutes to recover the gems from the floor of the Jeep. And another five to dig them out from where they had fallen between Willie's legs and disappeared through the tears in the fabric of the seat.

When they were all in the bag, Willie lay on his back across the front seat and with the help of his penknife spliced the ignition wires back together. He turned the key and the Jeep started up.

Perhaps we should have gone after them straight away. Things might have been different if we had. Instead, we left the Jeep ticking over and walked back to where Snake Eyes had killed the cop. There wasn't much to see, just a dark patch on the ground and a few flies buzzing around trying to decide if it was worth the effort or not.

As we brooded over the killing, I told Pete and Willie about my conversation with Glokani, and how he'd studied my reaction after telling me his assassin was killing them one by one.

Pete thought it over. "He wanted the answer to a question, he needed the truth, and the ruthless bastard knew exactly how to get it." He bent down, picked up three small stones and tossed one towards the trees. "He got his answer but there's something else. That's why he took Susie and gave you the diamonds. Whatever his game is; we're still in play."

He shook the stones in his hand, as if he were rolling dice, and then tossed another into the trees.

"Do you know what I think, boyo?" said Willie. He fished

something out of his pocket and looked at it. "I think we're in deep shit and it's going to get a whole lot deeper. Before they took Susie away, one of the goons gave me this."

He hesitated, then handed me an expensive looking business card. On the front was a picture of a motor yacht and below it, embossed in gold, the name *Temptress*. I flipped it over. Scrawled on the back it said: Dinner. Marina. 8:00pm. Sharp.

I handed it to Pete. He studied it, wrapped it around his last stone, then dropped it into the dirt and ground it in with his foot.

As we drove across the island, we tried to come up with a plan. Going to the cops was hardly an option. And all we could hope for was that Susie was being held on the yacht and not in one of Chopstick's torture chambers.

Pete was all for swimming out to the motor yacht and starting a one-man war with his old Special Forces K-Bar.

Willie's plan was more flamboyant. He wanted to round up a few of the boys and mount a frontal assault on the yacht. He was trying to be serious, but by the time he'd finished describing how he would storm the busy marina with the gang from the *Lady* in tow, we were roaring with laughter. The more excited he got the thicker his Welsh accent became until he was almost singing.

Feigning shock at our reaction, he paused in mid flow and threw us a hurt look. "Just think how it will look on the front cover of *Yachting World*, boyo," he said setting Pete and me off again.

He carried on ranting about his crazy plan, but fell silent when I pulled up on the dock next to his dive shop.

They climbed out of the Jeep, turned, and looked at me.

Willie put his hand on my shoulder. "What are we going to do, Dick?" All traces of mirth were gone and his eyes were as cold as ice.

I looked across to the marina where the big motor yachts were laying against the dock. "No need to steal from the kitchen when the owner's invited us to dinner. See you at eight," I said.

As I drove off, I could see them watching me in the rear-view mirror.

16

St. Peters sits like a knuckle at the northern end of the Windward Islands, at a point where the archipelago turns west towards Hispaniola. The island was christened by Christopher Columbus who sailed by in 1492, tossing out names while on his way to somewhere else.

From the sea, the central mountains are visible for forty miles. On its leeward side, the land is lush and green and rises gently as it leaves the wide coastal plane. Further inland, fertile valleys cut through the mountains and crystal clear springs tumble into rocky pools beneath a canopy of almost impenetrable rain forest.

On the windward side, the land is brown and arid. Here the mountains crumble like decaying battlements into the sea, to be battered by waves that have traveled, unopposed, all the way from Africa.

Looking down from an aircraft, the island resembles a giant bear wading chest deep through the ocean. The mountains form the head, while two volcanic ridges, one running to the north, the other a similar distance to the south, make up the shoulders. From the shoulders, two arms sweep down towards the west. These gradually become narrower as they level out around the Caribbean's largest lagoon.

The whole island is a tourist's dream, but at certain times of the year heavy traffic and bad roads make it a resident's nightmare.

On my way into town, I got stuck behind an ancient tour bus belching out smoke as it struggled to climb the mountain road.

Through its back window I could see the tour guide walking the aisle. He was spouting bullshit into a microphone while no doubt praying the tourists wouldn't compare notes with their friends on the other buses; at least until whatever cruise ship they left on was well below the horizon.

When the bus rounded a sharp bend, revealing a stunning view of the Caribbean that even the guides couldn't lie about, it came to a halt and blocked the road.

I had driven this way a thousand times and the beauty of the scene never failed to move me. We were at the road's narrowest point. To the left, a few bushes clung to the mountainside. To the right, the edge of the crumbling blacktop fell away a thousand feet to the ocean below. If the tourists had seen the cracks in the middle of the road, where the whole hillside was slowly moving, they would have thrown their cameras in the air and run. But they were happily snapping away at the water beyond the cliff where three yachts, their sails held taut by the stiff trade winds, were plowing creamy furrows through the azure sea.

In the distance four small uninhabited islands hovered like a mirage in the heat. It was a day of rare beauty, even by Caribbean standards. The only hint of danger came from a smudge on the far horizon where occasionally Montserrat's living volcano spewed a plume of grey ash into the clear air.

I was brought back to reality by the impatient blasting of car-horns. A few more honks and the bus driver took the hint. Amidst a choking cloud of oily smoke, the bus jerked forward—the driver manically doubling the clutch and crashing the gears until he got it right. As it rattled passed a faded sign that read *Tourism is Everybody's Business,* a taxi sped around the corner on the wrong side of the road, forcing the bus up the bank and into the bushes. As it roared by, the taxi driver blew a stream of marijuana smoke out of the window and gave the tourists the finger.

It took a few minutes for the bus to reverse out of the trees. Unable to pass, I followed it down the mountain until it stopped to let the bemused tourists out at a rum shop. Half a mile further on, the road leveled out at a crossroads where the traffic lights had been stuck on red for three months. I carefully turned left and drove down a shady avenue of royal palms into Cannon Town, the island's capital.

Cannon Town lies between two headlands at the head of a deep, half-moon bay. During the Napoleonic wars, two forts protected the town, one on each headland. Thanks to restoration by the historical society, each fort boasts a massive cannon that two hundred years ago was capable of firing a hundred pound ball nearly two miles. The heavy guns were put there to keep out the marauding English, who had a reputation as hooligans long before soccer was invented. The English, the Spanish, the Dutch, and the rest of the piratical bands that roamed the Caribbean, simply ignored the guns and landed elsewhere before marching into town to entertain the locals with pillage and rape. If they fired the guns today they would blast a collection of empty rum bottles, cigarette packets and used condoms right across the bay.

Cannon Town is the island's only deep water harbor and a favorite port of call for the growing number of cruise ships that unleash tens of thousands of passengers on the island every year. You can spend a pleasant morning watching the cruise ship passengers hurrying ashore through the army of shouting taxi drivers, time-share sellers, t-shirt venders, dope-heads and peddlers of sundries and other dubious wares. However, today I had more on my mind. I headed for the town's other big attraction, Bridge Street. Here, hidden amongst the duty-free shops selling electronics and fake Rolex watches, were some of the finest diamond merchants in the world.

Ignoring the more serious stores that offered quality gems at seventy per cent off, I turned right down a litter-strewn cobbled passageway known as Treacle Cock Alley. Halfway along I came to a small sign in the shape of a diamond that hung from a rusty frame above a nondescript door. A grimy window, set to one side, held a collection of cheap jewelry that was more tarnish than shine.

I opened the door and a tiny temple bell rang in welcome. As I stepped inside, the door closed behind me and, with a faint electrical hum, a hidden bolt locked it in place. There was another door ahead, this one made of steel. The whole thing resembled an airlock in a submarine.

A small video camera looked down from a bracket high on the wall. I gave it the finger and the metal door slid open. A bearded two hundred and twenty pound Indian, wearing a Heckler and Koch MP5 machine pistol and a large smiley pin, is far more effective than a dead rat. I was expecting it, so didn't scream, but it was a close call.

The Wooly Mammoth held the gun to one side and gave me a lopsided hug that made my good ear pop. Then he pushed me away, bellowed for tea, and said, "Welcome, friend, to our humble emporium."

17

Mohamed Singh's business was clean. By clean, I mean Mohamed and his family ran a legitimate diamond business with interests on three continents and a history that could be traced back nearly three hundred years.

No drug dealing or money laundering. I know, because Pete and I once delivered a ninety-foot motor-sailor from Gibraltar to the Caribbean for Mohamed and his family. And before we accepted the commission, Pete had his contacts at the Drug Enforcement Agency check them out.

When we arrived in St. Peters with the boat, Mohamed threw a party that would have got anyone else thrown off the dock—had their family not owned the marina. On the third day, with no sign of the party winding down, I staggered out of the head and bumped into a tiny old lady in a purple sari who introduced herself as Mohamed's mother.

"Ah, you must be Mister Turpin," she said in beautifully enunciated English. "Please, come and sit with me for a while." Taking my arm in a strong grip, she led me to the foredeck where we could be alone. She sat down on the cabin top and patted the space beside her. It was a simple request from a gentle old lady but it carried all the authority of a military command.

There are times in life when you find yourself in a rare presence. I would have laughed at the thought of this tiny woman giving birth to the Woolly Mammoth. But even though I was drunk, I knew I would demean myself by doing so.

We sat for a while without speaking, content to listen to the revelers aft. And once I caught sight of someone heading our way along the side-deck, only to be firmly turned back by the Woolly Mammoth himself.

I was about to speak when she touched my arm. "Mister Turpin, before you and your friend agreed to bring our yacht from Gibraltar to the Caribbean, you had an American law enforcement agency run a check on my family."

My gasp of astonishment brought a smile to her face and before I could form a reply she silenced me by laying her tiny brown hand on top of mine.

"Please, answer a question for me," she said. "Had we not checked out okay, would you still have delivered the yacht for us?"

I turned and met her steady gaze. "No, ma'am, you'd have had to find someone else," I said.

"And had we tripled your fee, Mister Turpin. What then?"

"Then you'd have been triply disappointed."

"Mmm …" She held my eyes for a few seconds then looked away. "I suppose you're wondering how we found out about you snooping into our business?" she said.

"The thought did cross my mind."

"We had *you* thoroughly checked out before we offered you the job. You're an interesting man, Mister Turpin, and today I wanted to meet you for myself to see if what I heard was true."

"And ...?" I spluttered.

She chuckled and patted my knee. "Oh yes, Mister Turpin, I do believe it is."

"You shouldn't believe everything you hear…" I began, but she cut me off with a wave of her hand.

"You have no need to explain, but, if you wish, you may escort me to my car."

I stood and led the way aft. As we walked along the deck, Mohamed smiled and nodded respectfully to his mother.

We stopped at the end of the gangway. "The yacht is such an extravagance, Mister Turpin, but my son works hard, so perhaps he deserves it."

She accepted my hand and stepped down onto the dock.

Mohamed followed our progress and, before we turned the corner and disappeared from view, raised his glass in salute. I read it as a toast to friendship. Looking back, I should have seen it as a warning.

In the parking lot she led me to the latest custom BMW sports convertible. I opened the door and she slid behind the wheel. She fussed over a couple of cushions until she could comfortably see over the wheel and then closed the door. The engine gave a throaty roar and she revved it twice for good measure.

"Don't look so surprised," she laughed, "being old doesn't exclude you from having fun. Oh, and by the way, Mister Turpin, my name is Elisa, never, ever, ma'am. Remember that next time we do business. And we will, I promise. After all, we both check out." With that she let out a whoop and floored the accelerator. The Beemer's tires howled in protest as the car shot across the parking lot and out into the road.

My association with the Singh family proved to be very lucrative indeed. Over the next few months Pete and I moved Mohamed's boat around the Caribbean for him. We cruised through the islands, taking members of his family and various business associates to all the popular vacation spots.

Contacts made on these jaunts brought us more and more work and we found that we filled a particular niche. Most of the jobs involved security. Wealthy clients, many of them linked in some way to the diamond trade or commodities market, hired us when they chartered a boat of their own. Although these were usually superyachts with their own skipper and crew, they liked the idea of having locally based security advisers along, people who were familiar with the islands and had the qualifications to run a ship.

To keep a low profile we went along as guests and left the everyday running of the yacht to the skipper and crew. Occasionally some perceptive captain or mate would pick up on something we did or said, grow suspicious, and start asking questions. However, most of them knew better than to hassle the guests. Those who didn't—and pushed too hard—we usually won over with a firm but friendly discussion at the bar.

In September of 1995, Pete and I were chaperoning an Arab prince and his entourage from Fort Lauderdale to Europe, when their one hundred and thirty foot motor yacht was caught by the tail-end of hurricane Marie, two hundred miles southwest of the Azores. The hurricane was an act of God. But the disabling of the yacht's 1000 HP Cummings diesels two days before it struck was not.

The approaching storm effectively ended a plot to kidnap the prince, but the loss of the engines also deprived us of a chance to outrun the storm or put our bows into the worst of the seas.

Caught at dusk in the mounting fury of the storm, we lay beam-on to the breaking seas. During the night, the motion of the boat grew more and more violent until by midnight each roll was jamming the bridge clinometers against the stops.

At what passed for dawn, our view to the horizon was one of endless marching waves. I ventured on deck and almost died. It was impossible to see or breathe as the crest of each towering wave was ripped apart and driven towards us by the howling wind. After fourteen hours the storm began to move. This created rogue waves that ran so high they collapsed under their own massive weight. Occasionally we'd hear one coming and brace ourselves before it broke over the boat and tried to force us under. By midday the windward side of the yacht was a shambles. Stanchions, davits, two life-rafts and the large inflatable tender had been swept away beneath an avalanche of water.

The Arabs, huddled in terror on the galley floor convinced they were going to die, spent their final hours praying to God to save them. In the darkened engine room, Pete and I and the rest of the loyal crew were also praying. We prayed to the gods of internal combustion and, after hours of spewing and swinging wrenches, had the port engine going.

With power restored, we were able to bring the boat around to face the storm, which was beginning to die down as the center of low pressure moved away. Five hours later, we had the starboard engine running. It ran hot and we were constantly shutting it down to prevent it seizing, but while it was running we were able to limp northeast towards the Azores.

For two days we nursed the damaged yacht towards Horta on the island of Faial. We hardly saw our employers. They lay low, spending the remainder of the voyage either in their cabins or on the bridge, where they spoke into the satellite phone for hours on end.

We arrived at Horta's massive breakwater an hour before dawn and were met by a pilot boat that took us to a quiet area of the commercial dock. No sooner had we secured the mooring lines and rigged the gangway than four hard-looking men in dark suits ushered a high ranking police officer onboard. Following a brief inspection of the yacht, the officer was taken to the state room for an audience with the prince.

Pete and I remained on deck, helping the crew to clear away the mess caused by the storm. That's where they found us. The crew saw them coming and moved away from us in fear. Then one of the suits spoke, and I understood why. I'd been expecting Portuguese, but received an order barked in Arabic instead.

The Arabs led us to the prince and, in the presence of the police officer, asked us to sign a document stating that the problem with the engines was caused by bad fuel and clogged filters. I had no wish to be involved in the politics of the Middle East, so took the offered pen and signed.

Pete did the same.

The suits looked at the document, nodded to the prince, and pushed us out of the room. Fifteen minutes later two official looking cars arrived at the bottom of the gangway. The back doors were flung open and two of the suits dragged a very frightened steward and engineer off the yacht and drove them away. The prince and his entourage were then helped into the other car and they sped off towards the airport without thank you or farewell.

We spent the next few days in Horta trying to drink the bar at *Pete's Café Sport* dry. Something every transatlantic sailor worth his salt has tried to do. But they were re-stocking the bar from somewhere and after a few days we ran short of cash. We gave it one more try then pooled what was left of our money and bought tickets home.

Back in St. Peters, we checked our bank accounts.

I found enough money in mine to support life as a beach bum for years to come.

Pete found enough in his to buy the *Lucky Lady.*

18

Mohamed and I reminisced until his niece arrived with the tea. She placed the tray on a small lacquered oriental table that barely cleared the floor. I squatted to pick up my cup and my knee cracked like an ice cube dropped into a glass of warm rum. Mohamed grinned and shook his head. The grin disappeared when I took Glokani's bag from my pocket and poured the diamonds onto the tray between the sugar bowl and the chocolate wafers.

"Oh, Dick," he sighed, "what have you and the boys got into now?"

He didn't touch the diamonds but simply stared at them and sipped his tea.

Behind me a door slid open and the faint scent of vanilla drifted into the room. I stood as Elisa walked towards me. "Dick, it's so nice to see you," she said. "You hardly ever come by anymore." She offered me her hand, which I took. Then she waited to receive a kiss on both cheeks. "Those knees of yours need seeing to. I could hear them crack from my office." She chuckled and pointed to a surveillance camera set high on the wall in the corner of the room.

"Dick has something to show us, mother." Mohamed moved the tea things to one side.

Elisa knelt at the table, lowering herself down with the ease of a twenty year old.

"Come," she said and pointed to the carpet beside her. When I was settled, she unzipped a small leather case and removed a black velvet mat, which she unfolded and placed on the table in front of her. Next she dug out a loupe and a pair of felt-tipped tweezers.

With everything in place, she reverently brushed the diamonds off the tea tray and onto the mat. Using the tweezers she picked up the nearest gem and, turning it slowly, held it to the light. She fitted the loupe to her eye and brought the diamond in close. She studied it for a moment then carefully placed it on the velvet, keeping it apart from the rest of the diamonds.

The minutes ticked by while the pile of diamonds slowly moved from one side of the velvet to the other.

Elisa was meticulous, picking up each diamond in turn and offering it to the light.

She stopped once to look at me, and what I saw in her eyes I didn't like.

Fifteen minutes of this was all I could stand. But when I tried to interrupt, Mohamed brought his finger to his lips and demanded silence.

I ignored him and tried again.

Elisa nodded and continued to stare through the loupe.

Mohamed stood and angrily beckoned me to follow him. He propelled me to a door at the far side of the room that slid open as we approached. When I hesitated, he placed his hand in the middle of my back and firmly guided me through.

The room we entered was brightly lit and arctic cold. It was scrupulously clean. A man and a woman were seated at a table full of electronic equipment in the center of the room. Outside it was ninety-five degrees in the shade but in here they were wearing sweaters and jackets.

As we walked by, the two of them looked up and smiled.

The girl I recognized from the *Lucky Lady*. We'd chatted a few times when she'd stopped by for a drink or two after a day at the beach. For a small island, where we all know each others business, she was a bit of a mystery. I knew she was Dutch, but had no idea what she did or where she worked. And when I asked, she changed the subject. Now I knew why.

I stopped to speak and again Mohamed silenced me with his finger. Ignoring the couple altogether, he drove me across the room towards another door. As the door slid open, he removed his shoes and placed them carefully in a basket by the wall. I followed and he muttered something about beach bums as I chucked my flip-flops towards his shoes.

Mohamed's private apartment was straight out of the pages of *Good Living* magazine. And, even though it lacked windows, a clever combination of air-conditioning and concealed lighting gave it the feel of a drawing room whose patio doors had been thrown open on a glorious summer's day.

Mohamed walked to a wet bar and returned carrying two cold Carib beers, which he set down on mats on top of a teak and ivory coffee table. Then he lowered his bulk onto an ancient floral patterned settee—the only shabby thing in the room.

I ignored the offered beer and continued my inspection. In all the years I had known him, this was the first time I'd been invited into his private domain, and I was impressed.

The floor was made of polished hardwood covered by a tasteful scattering of Persian rugs. Besides Mohamed's incongruous settee, several matching armchairs of rich Moroccan leather were dotted about the room. A state-of-the-art entertainment center dominated one wall. In counterpoint, an impressive collection of first editions stood in neat rows along another. The Renoir I recognized from a book, but the Chagall and Monet had me beat. Every shelf, nook and cranny, held a piece of art.

In the center of the room, a sculpted spiral staircase of polished wood led to the upper floor, and I wondered what treasures he had hidden away up there.

"Dick, perhaps I can show you around later, right now we need to talk." Mohamed's words took away the magic, filling the void with a feeling of unease.

Curious, I walked to the sliding door and gave it a push. It was locked, and I could see no way of opening it. There had to be another door, but a circuit of the walls turned up nothing.

I headed for the stairs.

"Yes. There are other ways out but you'll find them locked too, so come and sit down, your beer's getting warm." Mohamed's voice was threateningly sincere.

"Listen, I came to you as a friend," I said, "but that's okay, coming here was just another fuck-up in a week full of them." I took a step towards him. "Friend or not, Mohamed, now would be a good time for you to open the door."

He bellowed a laugh. "Don't be so hard on yourself, and for goodness sake calm down. You came here because you are in trouble. What you see here are simple precautions in case you brought that trouble with you." He patted the cushion next to him and slid the beer across the table.

I ignored the gesture, grabbed a straight-backed chair from against the wall, and slammed it down opposite him. The slam lost its effect in the thick weave of the Persian carpet and we both smiled.

"For one awful moment I thought you were going to use the chair on me. Thank God you didn't, its seventeenth century Chippendale, Elisa would never forgive you." Mohamed picked up his beer and took a sip. "We had you under surveillance the minute you entered Treacle Cock Alley. With your reputation, you can hardly blame us. The moment you dropped your little package on the table we sent people into the streets to see if you were followed. You were not."

He paused, waiting for a reaction. When I said nothing he carried on, only this time there was steel in his voice.

"Yesterday you were arrested for killing a man in a bar room brawl and today you walk into my family business with a bag of diamonds which, by the way, Elisa has already ascertained are of the finest quality and totally fucking illegal. Now, I suggest we drink a couple of beers and when Elisa joins us you can explain why you brought such danger here."

We didn't have long to wait before Elisa's arrival broke the oppressive silence that had descended over the room. I stood and she waved me down with a flick of her hand. She beckoned Mohamed to join her at the bar where she poured herself a scotch—no ice, no water, no nonsense. They spoke in Urdu. Elisa remained calm but occasionally Mohamed raised his voice to make a point. After a few minutes they turned and walked towards me.

"Mister Turpin, tell me, what do you know about the diamonds that you brought here today?" Elisa asked the question then swirled the scotch around her glass and took a long drink. Not once did her eyes leave mine as if, by looking directly at me, she could detect truth from a lie.

"Very little," I replied, keeping my eyes steady. "Mohamed says they're illegal, so I imagine they're conflict diamonds. I know that for years some African countries have been trading illegal gems in order to finance their endless civil wars."

When I offered nothing more, she finished her scotch and passed the glass to Mohamed, who took it without a word and headed for the bar.

There was a moment of silence then she fished in her pocket and brought out Glokani's troublesome bag. "Those were my first thoughts, too. I felt sure that what you brought here were indeed conflict diamonds, diamonds that you might want us to evaluate and then sell on your behalf. Had that proved to be the case, I would have been honor bound, by our long friendship, to return them to you, after which all ties with our family would be severed."

She left that floating in the air while she accepted another glass of scotch from Mohamed. Then, in a movement similar to Glockani's just hours before, she tossed me the bag. "Don't look so worried," she said. "They're not conflict diamonds. In fact they have never seen a mine or river bed."

"You mean to tell me they're not real!" I leapt to my feet. All the shit of the last two days for a bag of worthless paste, it didn't make sense.

"Steady, Dick, she didn't say they weren't real." Mohamed stepped forward and placed a restraining hand on my arm. "They're real enough. In fact they're twenty-two carat and flawless, they just didn't come out of the ground; they're manufactured."

"They're what! But how ...?"

"How, indeed?" Elisa blinked and took another sip of her scotch. "I think now would be a good time to tell us exactly where you got them."

For the next hour I walked them through the last two days of my life. I began with my birthday party and left nothing out. They asked a few questions, and we stopped once while Mohamed refreshed our drinks, but mainly they just sat and listened.

I finished, and Elisa broke the silence with a sigh. Then she stood, touched Mohamed's shoulder, and together they walked to the door where they spoke in whispers.

After a few minutes Elisa looked my way. "Dick, there is someone I want you to meet," she said, and turned and left the room.

She was back to using my first name. It had to mean something but I had no time to work out what before she returned with the guy from the computer room in tow.

"Dick, I'd like you to meet Edwin. Edwin's on loan to us from our Amsterdam subsidiary." She ordered Edwin to sit next to me while she went off to fix him a drink.

While Elisa twirled bottles, I took a careful look at the man from Amsterdam. Edwin was no beauty but he had the kind of face that some women would find attractive. He had disguised his baldness by shaving his head, but he didn't shave it every day and it was partly covered with blonde stubble. What he lacked on his head he more than made up for on his face. And with his thick, closely cropped beard and mustache, he reminded me of those weird guys you see advertising designer underwear in overpriced magazines. He removed his jacket and hung it over the back of the chair, then rolled up his shirt sleeves. His arms were tanned and corded with muscle. In contrast, the knuckles of each hand were etched with fine white scars, similar to those on my own. The man had the physique of a solo long distance sailor and, although almost skinny, what there was of him was as hard as nails.

I decided that whatever Edwin did with computers was good for him; perhaps he juggled them.

When Elisa was sure we were comfortable and provided with drinks, she nodded at Edwin, and for the next half hour he told me more than I ever wanted to know about my diamonds.

19

Why we value diamonds so much is one of life's great mysteries," Edwin began. "Formed millions of years ago as the earth began to cool they are, after all, only crystals. And although De Beers, the company that controls ninety per cent of the market, would like us to think otherwise, there is virtually an unlimited supply and, for De Beers, that is a big problem.

"If all the diamonds in the world hit the market at once, you would buy them for ten cents a pound. The diamond cartel makes sure that that can't happen although some conflict diamonds, mined illegally and sold to finance civil war in some African states, along with a small percentage of diamonds smuggled out of De Beers' own mines, do find their way onto the market."

Eddie the Expert stopped his discourse to pick up the troublesome bag. He undid the lace and worked the neck open with his thumb and index finger. As he worked, Mohamed reached over and laid the velvet mat on the table in front of him.

Eddie nodded his thanks and then continued.

"De Beers control the diamond trade with military precision. Their operatives span the globe keeping track of every diamond, legal and illegal, that reaches the market. They run their business like a secret society, and they are virtually untouchable. Their influence reaches to the very top of most governments. Simply look at what the 'first ladies' are wearing at their charity concerts and you'll understand how it's done."

He upended the bag and dragged it across the mat, leaving behind a glistening path like slime from an enchanted snail.

"What you have in your possession is the power to bring down a financial empire and topple governments. You are an alchemist, Mr. Turpin. You are probably also a dead man." He chuckled and carefully picked up one of the diamonds between the points of the velvet tipped tweezers. "It's like turning base metal into gold, only what you have here is obviously more than a dream."

I gazed at the diamonds while trying to make sense of what he was telling me. "You say that these are real diamonds but they didn't come out of the ground, they were manufactured in a laboratory," I said.

"Yes. Scientists have been manufacturing industrial diamonds for over half a century and you can find them on everything from saw blades to the space shuttle. But manufactured industrial diamonds never came anywhere near gemstone quality. That is, until now. Recently, a company in the United States discovered a way to produce high quality synthetic gemstones. By passing atomized graphite through metal solvents, they found it would bond to a tiny diamond seed and begin to crystallize layer by layer. After a few days they had created a near perfect gemstone diamond. The process requires extreme heat and pressure. In effect, they recreate the geological conditions under which natural diamonds are formed; only they do it over a couple of days, not millions of years."

"Do De Beers know about this?" I asked.

"Yes. They don't like it but there's nothing they can do about it." He picked up another diamond and held it to a loupe that he had fitted over his left eye. After a few seconds he removed the loupe and offered it to me. "Obviously, De Beers are concerned. The diamonds you have here are real in every way but an expert, if he's good, can identify them as having been produced by a machine. Also, during the manufacturing process, they take on a yellow tint. The jewelers don't have a problem with that because yellow diamonds fetch a premium price." He paused and took a sip of his drink while I attached the loupe to my eye. "Now, Mr. Turpin, tell me what you see."

I squinted through the loupe at the diamond between my fingers. "You say this is manufactured."

"Yes."

"You say that manufactured diamonds are yellow."

"Yes."

"This one's pink."

"Exactly, and that is why you have a problem. What you are holding is impossible to create, yet someone has." He tipped the diamonds back into the bag and pushed himself to his feet. "Come. There is something else you should see."

We followed him through the sliding door and into the computer room. He walked to a table and took the diamond I was holding and placed it into an optical processor. He pressed his eye to the scope, made a few adjustments, and flicked a switch. After a few seconds he straightened and stood to one side.

"Take a look. This machine sends ultraviolet light into the diamond. By analyzing the return path of the light, we can usually pick out diamonds that are manufactured. Earlier, I ran the test on your gems. Almost all were perfect, but two had a slight flaw; something so infinitesimal that even the most knowledgeable experts would probably fail to spot it.

I looked through the eye-piece but all I could see was a diamond. Eddie spent a few more minutes explaining the intricacy of diamond manufacturing and then switched off the machine.

"Pink diamonds are the most precious gems on earth. If the flawless ones are machine made, and I suspect they are, then someone has mastered the manufacturing process. That knowledge is lethal." He handed me the bag of diamonds. "The wise thing to do is watch your back, Mr. Turpin, watch your back."

His voice was low, little more than a whisper. Before I could reply, he turned and walked away.

20

The sun was setting over the distant islands as I made my way home along the mountain road. At any other time I would have pulled over at the lookout just to watch the crimson ball fall off the edge of the world. But Eddie the Expert had unnerved me and the ruddy hues of sunset triggered thoughts of blood and gore.

I drove straight to the *Lucky Lady*. The evening sky had faded with its customary speed and it was almost dark by the time I stepped aboard. I made my way aft along the starboard side. At the bar amidships, the happy hour crowd was pounding down two-for-one drinks, filling the evening with noise and bonhomie before heading off for dinner. Most of the drinkers were tourists, and paid me little attention, but a few of the regular diehards—at least those still able to focus—nodded as I pushed by. A group of them were onboard on the night of the brawl and had been amongst the first to leg it when the cops showed up. Now they were back, propping up the bar, and doing their best to look mean.

I made my way into the deckhouse and the door leading to the living quarters below. The door was always open, but finding too many of his valuable customers in a drunken heap at the bottom of the steps, Pete had installed a rope across it at waist height. I took a quick look around and then ducked under the rope.

At the bottom of the companionway the faint hum of a generator, along with the smell of bilge and ancient wood, stirred pleasant memories of long days at sea. Entering the passageway that ran the length of the ship, I turned right. A polished brass handrail ran unbroken along the port side. To starboard the rail gave way to three cabin doors. The doors were open to allow air to circulate through the old boat.

Voices drifted out of the main saloon, leading me towards my favorite place on the old schooner. Pete had ripped out all signs of tacky modernization, installed by the previous owner, and lovingly restored the saloon to the designer's original plans, dug out of the maritime museum in Glasgow, Scotland.

Thousands of hours had gone into stripping paint and removing Formica from the mahogany panels, locker doors, and bulkheads. Refinished, they now shone with varnish as thick as shot glass. The original oil lamps were still in place and their flickering light bathed the cabin with a soft glow. Two teak settees, upholstered in bottle-green leather, formed the letter L where the aft bulkhead met the hull. Their armrests, carved into an erotic display of twisting mermaids, had the power to make you blush. A small burgundy and gold Abyssinian rug covered a section of the floor, leaving enough space around the edges for guests to admire the oak boards, which ran the full length of the cabin. The boards were close-grained and knot free. And given the age of the ship, more than four hundred years had passed since they began life as an acorn.

A carved teak table inlaid with ivory and strands of silver wire—some as thin as human hair—dominated the center of the cabin; it was Pete's pride and joy. I was with him in Hong Kong when he bought it from the owner of an ancient trading junk that was about to be broken-up. The tabletop depicted a busy harbor scene of the late 1800s. The work was exquisite, finely detailed, with sampans and junks gliding through the busy waters of Kowloon Bay. In the background, the peaks of three hills disappeared into a mantle of cloud. Up close you could make out flocks of tiny seabirds wheeling through the sky or swooping low over the stern of the fishing boats as the crew cleaned their catch. Nine writhing dragons were hidden like a code within the inlay. It was a work of art, and probably priceless. The owner refused to talk about the table's history, saying only that it must be removed from Hong Kong, quickly and without fuss. That was enough to make Pete offer all the money he had, and most of mine to boot.

I stepped into the saloon. Someone had covered the table with a padded cloth, beautifully inlaid with an Uzi machine pistol and other weapons of evil intent. Pete looked up and slammed an automatic into a shoulder holster. "Hi, Dick," he said and grinned at Willie. "You've caught the girls dressing for dinner."

21

I sat down at the table and over the next half hour told them all about our little bag of goodies. They listened without comment until I had nothing more to say. Then we sat dumbly looking at each other until the silence was broken by the chiming of the bulkhead clock.

Willie was the first to speak, but not before picking up the Uzi and jacking back the charging handle, which made a satisfying snick. “Let me get this straight, boyo. First, Glokani junior gets himself filleted and you’re the prime suspect. Next, his old man grabs Susie and in exchange gives us a bag of priceless home-made diamonds that are more than likely going to get us all killed. Then, being a good sort, he invites us to dinner on his yacht along with a group of hired killers who just happen to have the full support of our crazy police chief, a man who has sworn to rip out your heart and eat it! I say we round up the boys and end this nonsense now, before it gets totally out of control, because you don’t need to be a genius to know where this is going.”

Pete waited until Willie had finished his tirade. Then he pushed himself away from the table and laced his fingers behind the back of his head. “You have a point, Willie. But what guarantee do we have that it will end if we storm the damn yacht? If Susie’s not on board, then she’ll be killed for sure. We have no idea what this is about or why Glokani wants us involved. The slick bastard comes across as the head honcho but he may just be a cog in a much bigger wheel.”

While Willie and Pete knocked it about, I strolled over to an open porthole and looked out across the lagoon. A warm breeze was ruffling the water, making the reflection of the lights in the marina dance.

What Willie said made sense: end it now before it dragged us all down. But where would that leave us? For years we had survived on St. Peters by quietly going about our business and steering clear of local politics. The island was our home and refuge, and as long as we hovered on the right side of the law we were mostly left alone. If we must, then we would do it Willie's way, but not yet. Trying to sort this out with firepower would be a mistake. Chopstick had a heavily armed squad of goons at his disposal, paid for by the boys on the hill. If we took them on, not only would we risk losing Susie, we would probably start a war. The solution lay in finding out what Glokani wanted and, if possible, giving it to him.

There was a sudden beep. I turned my gaze from the porthole and focused on the desk where a bank of video monitors showed various areas of the *Lucky Lady*. The monitors, there to warn of trouble, were the only bits of high-tech gadgetry Pete had on the boat.

"It's Toby, one of Sergeant Ascari's sons. He tripped the alarm at the top of the companionway," said Willie. He quickly grabbed a cover and threw it over the table, hiding the guns.

Footsteps echoed along the passageway and young Ascari stepped through the door into the saloon. Toby was wearing a Bob Marley t-shirt that hung low over his cut-off jeans. His hair was a mass of dreadlocks and he sported a thick, black beard that, to his father's horror and many a girl's delight, he'd streaked with blond. He was clutching a beer in his left hand and I remembered seeing him earlier at the bar.

Toby grinned when he saw Pete. "How you doin', bro', staying out of trouble?" he said. Pete laughed and they did the handshake and gave each other a hug. Toby shrugged off the embrace and turned to Willie. After they had touched fists, he came to me and we did the same.

"How's the music business? I heard you've played a few gigs since you came back," I said.

"Business is cool, man, and it's great to be jammin' with the boys again. There's so much musical talent on this island, I guess I just got lucky."

The luck he was referring to was a scholarship to the Boston School of Music, and there was no luck involved, talent and hard work had taken him there.

"So, what's next?"

"One more year and I'll have my degree, then who knows. I've had some offers from the States and Europe, but I might come back to the island and see if I can help. There are changes coming and I—"

He bit off the words in mid sentence and began twirling a dreadlock around his finger. I followed his eyes to the table where Willie was trying to push the perforated mettle stock of the Uzi further under the cover.

When Toby spoke again his voice had lost its confidence. "Look guys, I really have to go, my friends think I went to take a leak." He turned and gave me an envelope. "My dad asked me to give you this."

He headed for the door.

"What changes are coming?" said Willie.

Toby stopped and pointed at the table. "With what you have there, I think you already know," he said, and then he was gone.

Willie made to go after him but Pete stopped him with a wave of the hand.

"Okay, boyo, have it your way, but will somebody explain to

me just what the hell that was all about?" When Pete didn't answer he looked at me, but I had no answer either. "Oh, I see. The lunatics are running the asylum," he said and pulled the Uzi from under the cover and gave it an angry polish with an oily rag.

We grinned at him.

"What?" he snapped and started to laugh.

I looked at Toby's envelope, it was sealed and I slit it open with my finger. Inside was a single sheet of paper from a spiral-bound notebook. On it was a list of names copied straight from the pages of the villains' *Who's Who*.

I scanned it and passed it to Pete.

Pete read it and passed it to Willie. "What do you make of that?" he said.

Willie studied the paper then turned it over and studied it again. "I'd say that's tonight's guest list." He shook the Uzi in our direction. "To hell with the popguns, boyo, what we need is a fucking tank."

22

We met at the entrance to the marina a few minutes before eight. The marina guard, whom I didn't recognize, looked us over with obvious distaste. "Name," he snarled and glanced at a clipboard.

"Turpin,' I replied.

"And these two?"

"Why don't you ask them?"

He grunted, enjoying the power-play, then unlocked the gate and waved us through, keeping a suspicious eye on the Welshman.

Willie had done us proud. He was wearing a *Lucky Lady* T-shirt with the buxom mermaid logo on the front, and the words *The liver is evil and deserves to be punished* written across the back. His lime-green shorts were emblazoned with pink parrots and ended six inches below his knees. He was barefoot and carried a pair of old flip-flops in his hand. It was a dramatic change for a guy who just hours before was ready to storm the yacht wearing battle fatigues and a flak jacket.

When Pete remarked on the way he'd dressed for dinner, Willie replied, "Fuck 'em."

Pete, on the other hand, was looking pretty suave. His blue batik shirt hung loose, but it couldn't hide the contours of his powerful shoulders. He wore the shirt island style, so that it hung down over his waist, covering the belt on his white cotton pants. A new pair of leather deck-shoes rounded things off; I was impressed, it was the first time I'd seen him wearing them.

I'd spent the last hour onboard *Strange Light*, checking she was okay. She was, but she was in a hell of a mess. The boat had been thoroughly searched. Clothes were strewn about. Books had been ripped open and discarded. Tools and safety equipment were in a heap on the cabin sole and every locker door was hanging off. Where the screws of the head-linings had proved too difficult to remove, they'd simply jammed the screwdriver under the edge and forced them down.

A quick inventory told me nothing was missing. Whoever had carried out the search was obviously looking for something in particular and, unable to find it, had left without taking anything else. I was pissed-off about the mess but grateful that they hadn't cut the hoses and sent her to the bottom.

What upset me most was the damage to Susie's belongings. Her dresses and underwear were flung about like rags. Both her photo albums had been torn apart and the pictures of her family, which she kept in frames on a shelf in the saloon, had been smashed and tossed to the floor where they formed a pathetic little heap. Trinkets from her box of treasures were amongst the debris: a tiny pink animal from the end of a cocktail stick, a shell, two old theater tickets; a brass horseshoe on a broken key chain. I picked up a torn piece of paper. Scribbled on it was a poem that I'd written to her shortly after we'd met. All her secrets now lay scattered and ground underfoot.

I slumped onto a bunk and thought about her. The bastards had destroyed her memories and now were threatening to kill her. I tried to work it out, but nothing made sense.

The door of the head had been ripped off its hinges, but thankfully the shower still worked. I lathered up and then sluiced off, letting the water ease the ache in my joints.

From the mess in the saloon, I picked up a tan cotton shirt and a pair of crumpled cargo pants, and that was my attire as we walked along the dock towards *Temptress*.

The motor yacht was lying stern-to at the far end of the dock, about as far away from the other boats as she could get. As we approached, I recognized her as one of the latest superyachts out of a famous shipyard in Germany. Over one hundred and sixty feet of gleaming steel and aluminum, stabilized, and driven by twin Caterpillar 3512, 1500 HP turbo diesels that would suck down twelve gallons of fuel per hour. On a full tank she would carry you in luxury for three thousand miles at a steady fifteen knots.

The yacht was lit from stem to stern, riding in a halo of her own lights that spread outwards about three hundred feet before ending abruptly in the inky waters of the marina. Floodlights along her upper deck pinpointed a forest of radio antennas, satellite communication domes and radars. A Bell 206 Jet Ranger, gaudily wrapped like a child's Christmas present, sat on a raised platform aft. The helicopter's rotors were hinged back and it was secured to the deck by heavy cargo straps. Two thick yellow cables snaked ashore from the yacht's transom and disappeared into a utility box on the dock. In one night the yacht would consume enough electricity to keep a coastal village going for a week.

Twenty feet from the gangway I heard the crackle of a two-way radio, and caught the tell-tale glow of a cigarette in the bushes to our left.

To keep the vermin off the boat, the bottom of the gangway was raised some eighteen inches from the ground. Obviously it hadn't worked because through the open doors of the aft stateroom I could see the guests walking around sipping drinks.

I was surprised to make it to the stern of the yacht without being challenged, and we were debating what to do next when a speaker, built into the handrail, crackled to life and Glokani's disembodied voice invited us to step aboard.

Pete led the way, Willie and I followed. We were halfway up the narrow gangway when two heavies appeared at the top. Pete hesitated, looked back, and nodded towards the dock. I turned as two men closed in behind us, cutting off our retreat.

"Step this way gentlemen. One at a time, please." The heavy at the top of the gangway waved Pete forward.

Pete shrugged and carried on climbing. At the top he passed through an archway and stepped down onto the deck.

An alarm chirped out a warning.

"If you are carrying weapons of any kind, now would be a good time to tell me," said the heavy. His voice left little doubt as to what would happen if we were lying and I prayed that Pete and Willie were sticking to the plan.

Pete shook his head and was led to one side where a second heavy patted him down.

The search was professional, and thorough, and the loose change that had tripped the metal detector was returned without fuss.

Willie and I went through the same procedure; the metal in our pockets tripping the detector, followed by the body search. Satisfied that we were unarmed, we were instructed to remove our shoes and leave them in the basket next to the gangway. Boarding rules and rituals over, the heavy led the way to the open doors of the stateroom and handed us over to a waiting steward.

The steward was immaculate in a white uniform complete with gold shoulder pips. He bowed and offered us a tray of champagne.

"You might as well fuck off with those, *boyo*, 'cause I don't think we'll be here long," said Willie. This didn't bother the steward one bit and he simply turned and offered the tray to Pete.

Glokani appeared at my elbow. "Oh come, come now, Turpin,

can't you control these men of yours, no need to be rude on a beautiful night like this." He took two glasses from the tray, offering one to me with a polite nod.

His tailor had again done him proud and he looked every bit the owner of a multi-million dollar yacht. The white Armani suit and contrasting pale blue shirt deepened his tan, and the shadows, cast by the recessed lighting in the deck overhead, turned his face to carved mahogany. He wore the same heavy gold chain around his neck, and he'd added another that held a Spanish doubloon. He'd crossed the line with the doubloon and now, instead of looking like a crook, he looked like a cheap crook. The thought cheered me up.

"What do you think of my yacht?" he asked.

"What do you think of your dead son," I replied. His eyes narrowed to slits. The question hung between us until he broke the silence with his barking laugh, something I was beginning to detest.

"What is it with you English? You think I should mourn? My son should have been flushed away before my seed had chance to take root. You did me a service by killing him."

"I didn't kill him, and you know it."

"What I know is hardly the problem. The way I see it, the authorities have enough evidence to hang you for murder and jail those friends of yours forever as accomplices."

"We want Susie back. Is she onboard?" said Pete reasonably.

"You are in no position to make demands. Why don't you accept a glass of champagne and we can discuss her future over dinner?" Just then a gong sounded. "Ah, perfect timing. Gentlemen, if you care to follow me." He turned and we followed him into the aft stateroom.

As staterooms go, this one wasn't bad. A fitted carpet covered the entire floor; as rich in colour as Devon cream, it butted against walls of embossed velvet delicately embroidered with threads of silver and gold.

As I trailed our host, I noticed several old masters in heavy gilt frames. Each masterpiece sat in its own alcove and was protected by motion sensors linked to roll-down metal shutters discreetly built into the deck overhead. The security left little doubt as to the value of the paintings or their authenticity. It was enough to make you weep.

Each piece of exotic wood, gilt, or polished brass, was bathed in its own soft pool of light cleverly designed to ease your eye from one treasure to the next.

A round mahogany table inlaid with a compass rose dominated the middle of the room. At its center was a silver tray bearing a crystal decanter and eight monogrammed glasses. Eight chairs, each bearing a coat of arms across the back, were drawn up to the table. The same heraldic crest adorned an antique roll-top desk that sat athwart-ships next to a glass and mahogany door, which our courteous host held open for us to pass through.

Everything was slightly understated and far too tasteful for a man who dangled gold chains and a Spanish doubloon around his neck. But then, if you have the cash, you can buy taste by the yard from an interior designer.

Glokani ushered us along a short passageway towards another door. As we approached, the door was opened from the other side by our friendly champagne steward who bade us enter. He still wore the uniform with gold pips, but had swapped the tray for a silenced Ingram MAC-10 machine pistol with a 90-round clip.

"You can fuck off with that, too, boyo. Now we're definitely not stopping," said Willie, and pushed past him into the dining room.

23

The steward closed and locked the door. Then he crossed his arms and leaned back against the wall, leaving the MAC-10 hanging at his side from a canvas strap looped over one shoulder.

An appraisal of the dining room revealed more elegance, but the art work on display was sullied by the trash around the table.

As we entered the room, conversation tapered off and finally stopped. I looked around and from what I remembered from Sergeant Ascari's list, all the scumbags were present and correct. With one addition—at the far end of the table, the Minister of Finance was chomping on a plate of canapés.

Our host beckoned us forward and with a sweeping gesture presented us to his guests. "I was hoping to surprise you, Mr. Turpin, but once again you have surprised me. Am I correct in assuming that you knew exactly who was on our guest list before you arrived here?"

If he was expecting a reply, he didn't get one.

"Perhaps in future I should pay more attention to the coconut telegraph," he said which earned him a ripple of laughter from the scumbags.

Another uniformed steward, complete with his own MAC-10, pulled out three chairs on Glokani's right. "Gentlemen, please be seated," he said and waved us forward.

Pete drew back and kicked the chair with such force that it

slammed into the table, splintering wood and scattering wine-glasses.

The crud rose in uproar, toppling more glasses and sending a flood of red wine across the damask tablecloth like blood from a severed limb.

Before I could make a move, we were clubbed to our knees and our heads forced onto the table by guns at our necks.

"Enough! Get 'em up, get the fuckers *up*." Glokani had finally lost his cool.

Pete shot me a glance. "Having fun yet?" I said as we were hauled to our feet and dragged backwards from the table.

"I brought you here for a civilized conversation and you dress like clowns and behave like animals." Glokani was struggling for control and losing the battle. He turned, took a few steps, then spun and slapped a glass of wine off the table and sent it flying across the room where it did a thousand dollars worth of damage to a square-foot of wallpaper.

"What's wrong with that, bad year?" I thought Willie had gone too far but Glokani ignored him and looked down the table at his guests. No one would meet his eye and after a few seconds they began to sit down.

"If you cause any more disruption I will give that psycho Chalmond your South African tart, with strict instructions *not* to kill her, until he's had his fun. And that also goes for your two friends here; they step out of line one more time and the girl dies. Do I make myself clear? Now, you will do as I say and listen, then you will get off my yacht." He sat down and signaled his men to move away from us.

We waited for him to speak, but he sat with his arms folded and looked towards the minister of finance at the far end of the table. The minister rose and made his way to our end of the room. He eyed the smashed chair as he went by and only seemed to relax once he was safely opposite Glokani, with the width of the table separating him from Pete.

St. Peters is a polychromatic society envied for its racial harmony by other islands in the region. And while some of the island's politicians are black, others, like our Finance Minister Joost van Norte, are white.

Van Norte looked the part. He was one of those lucky men who will never go bald. He wore his thick sandy hair very short in what used to be known as a bristle cut. His green eyes observed the world through tiny gold-rimmed glasses, which he slid to the end of his nose and looked over whenever he had to read something up close. This was his favorite pose and the one that always featured in the local newspaper when his office sent out their propaganda.

Tonight he was wearing a blue and white pinstripe shirt that was open at the neck to reveal more sandy hair on his chest. He had removed his jacket but, unlike many at the table, preferred to keep his shirtsleeves down. Maybe he wanted to draw attention to his chunky gold cufflinks, or perhaps he was hiding a tattoo of a naked lady that danced when he flexed his arm.

It was said that Van Norte could trace his ancestors back to the Dutch pirates who ruled the island towards the end of the seventeenth century. If his involvement with Glokani was anything to go by, he was a keeping up a tradition that would sit well on the old family tree.

He didn't wait for an introduction, which said something, though I wasn't sure what. And he didn't beat about the bush when it came to the three of us but waded straight in. According to the minister, we were a band of villains who had been tolerated on the island for far too long and instead of being grateful we had involved ourselves with forces unknown in a plot to overthrow the state. He said his friend, Mister Glokani, a man of vision, along with many of the island's leading citizens, whom, he insisted, we had the pleasure of meeting tonight, had created the means for his government to make the island the wealthiest and most powerful in the Caribbean.

He paused for effect then managed to get halfway through his next sentence before he was cut off, and I wondered what had taken Willie so long.

"Get to the point you bent bastard and save the campaigning for the poor sods out there who don't know any better."

Before anyone had time to react I hauled the bag of diamonds out of my pocket and slammed it down in front of Glokani.

"Save the side show for later and tell us about these instead," I demanded.

Glokani put an elbow on the table and rubbed his forehead with the palm of his hand. After a couple of seconds, he looked at Van Norte and dismissed him with a nod.

Van Norte hesitated, then thought better of it and, glaring at Willie, walked back to the far end of the room and sat down.

Glokani reached for a silver cigarette box and took out a black cheroot. He tapped the end of the cheroot on the lid of the box then threw it down and stood to address the room. "Along with my associates here, I have been conducting talks with certain members of the island government who have agreed to, shall we say, sponsor a business arrangement that will benefit all concerned. In the past, I have provided these gentlemen with certain goods, but changing habits and the increased vigilance of foreign law enforcement agencies are now playing havoc with our profits. As most of you know, *Temptress* recently arrived here from Europe. Unfortunately, because of business elsewhere, I left my son in charge of the boat. His job was simple: bring two people out of Europe unobserved and deliver them safely to this meeting tonight."

Before he could go on, Pete broke in. "You're referring to the guys who made the diamonds. Right?"

That certainly got the scumbags' attention and they leapt to their feet and began shouting. Above the uproar I heard the stewards cocking their MAC-10s and was praying that Pete and Willie would make it to the door before one of them lost it and opened fire.

Suddenly, the room went quiet. In the fracas Willie had wrestled one of the stewards to the floor and relieved him of his gun and was now using it to poke the wax out of Glokani's ear.

"Now here's a fine mess," said Willie. "Is there no honor among thieves? You didn't tell the scumbags that you were able to make diamonds, did you, and now look at 'em."

Glokani shook his head like a dog trying to dislodge a flea, but it did him no good; Willie kept the barrel right where it was.

"You're fucking with the wrong guy," Glokani hissed. "They were to be told when the system was in place and running smoothly. Turpin, tell this Welsh ape to get his hands off me or I swear to God, within the hour Chalmond will be slicing pieces off the girl."

The man was clever but he was capable of making mistakes. We had found out more about the diamonds than he wanted us to know and now, thanks to Willie, the crud knew it too. But we had pushed him to the limit and I had no doubt that the threat to Susie was real.

As if reading my mind, Willie yanked the barrel of the MAC-10 out of Glokani's ear. Then he released the magazine from the handle of the gun and threw them both on the table.

Following Willie's lead, Pete tried to help the disarmed steward to his feet but all he received for his good manners was a cuss followed by a vicious shove in the chest.

To my surprise, Glokani rapidly regained his poise. And in an effort to save face, stood as if nothing had happened, casually shot his cuffs, and began to speak. However, as soon as he opened his mouth, he was shot down in flames by another angry voice from the far end of the table.

"The black guy said the diamonds aren't real. Explain yourself, and it better be good. If you're trying to scam us, you'll end up butchered like your son." There was a chorus of muffled assent, which ended abruptly when the steward slammed the magazine back into the MAC with the heel of his palm.

Glokani looked around and with a sigh ordered his gunmen out of the room.

We were getting down to the nitty-gritty and it was on a strictly need to know basis.

24

Glokani waited until the last of his minders had left and closed the door then made his way across the room and stood by a curtained window. He drew the shade to one side and looked out gathering his thoughts. After a few seconds he turned to face his audience. All eyes were on him as the explanation began.

"Yes, you were told you would be involved in the distribution of illegal diamonds. But now, thanks to these … three ... you know it goes a little deeper than that. I asked you here tonight to meet two men, Uri Andropof and Michael Wies. Until a few months ago, Andropof worked at a laboratory on the outskirts of Lodz, in what used to be East Germany. Andropof is a talented chemist who likes to dabble in genetics and, according to my source, has made some remarkable discoveries. I won't go into the details of his work, only to say that during some of his experiments into human cloning, he went beyond the bounds of what is considered acceptable behavior. Andropof's laboratory shared the building with a small factory that manufactured industrial diamonds. The diamond plant was legitimate and had moved to Lodz from France to take advantage of local government tax incentives. The man in charge of the diamond plant was Michael Wies, a Swiss national and a friend of Andropof's from their days at the Sorbonne."

He pulled a handkerchief from his pocket and mopped his brow, then tucked the handkerchief away, walked back to the table and sat down.

"For some time, Andropof had been secretly helping Wies with the diamond manufacturing process. In return, Andropof allowed Wies to take part in his twisted experiments. Between them they worked out a way to steal a few diamonds, but they wanted more. A small plant can only produce a few diamonds at a time, so they began experimenting with ways to shorten the process. The owners of the plant were happy to let Wies get on with it and even gave him a grant towards the work. Wies and Andropof took apart the existing formula and rewrote it. For months, nothing they did seemed to work and the time it took to create a diamond remained the same. Then one morning, as Wies removed the latest batch of diamonds from the experimental incubator, he noticed the coloring had changed. Unable to believe what he saw, he carried out exhaustive tests. The results were incontrovertible. They had stumbled on a way to create one of the rarest and most valuable of all gemstones—a flawless pink diamond."

He stopped speaking and reached across the table for a glass and a carafe of water. There was a moment of silence broken by an angry shout. "Get on with it, Glokani. We don't need some Swiss fucking yodeler's life story. Just tell us where we fit in?"

Glokani glared at me as if to say: you're to blame for all this, then he took a quick sip of water and carried on.

"Wies' discovery put him in a difficult position. He'd stumbled on a way to produce untold wealth, but how could he get the diamonds onto the market? Slipping a few undocumented yellow stones into the system had never been a problem. But he knew the undocumented pinks would change the nature of the game. Looking for a solution, he added a single pink diamond, along with a cryptic note, to the packet of yellows he sent to his fence in Antwerp. He had been dealing with the same man for years without any trouble. The man brokered the diamonds, took his commission, and deposited the money from the sale into Wies' bank account.

"Sending the pink diamond was a big mistake, so was his choice of broker. The man was an undercover agent for De Beers. Apparently De Beers viewed Wies, and his few yellow diamonds, as insignificant. They were content just knowing the source, and would only act if the numbers became a threat. However, the pink was a different story. Within hours of it arriving in Antwerp, Interpol, acting on behalf of the diamond cartel, had come up with a detailed plan of the factory in Lodz. Two nights later an agent entered the building and conducted an illegal search. He made it past the security guards and as far as Andropof's lab, where he stumbled across some of the geneticist's more creative experiments. The story goes that he didn't stop running until he crossed the German border. The outcome of that break-in was an international warrant for the partners' arrest followed by a full-scale police raid to shut down the facility. Of course, they were too late; Andropof and Wies had disappeared taking the diamonds and formula with them."

Glokani risked breaking his narrative and took another cheroot from the silver box. He placed it between his lips and began patting his pockets in search of a light. One of the scumbags beat him to it and flicked open a gold Dunhill lighter. Glokani thanked him and leaning forward, touched the cheroot to the flame. He drew smoke deep into his lungs, then, sensing his audience's growing impatience, went back to his story.

"The laboratory where Andropof worked belongs to an organization with facilities throughout Eastern Europe. The organization is owned by a South American cartel, whose main business is importing raw materials from Afghanistan and Nepal and turning them into recreational drugs for consumption in the West. That was my connection. Refining the drugs was just a way for Andropof to finance his secret experiments, and I doubt the cartel even knew what he was doing. The guy cared nothing about the drugs, all he cared about was his experiments, but he knew they wouldn't buy him any help. He had to find a way of getting out of Europe undetected. Also, he needed a place to set up another lab, preferably where no one would ask too many awkward questions. I offered him a way out. In return for my services he agreed to bring Wies with him and together set up a similar operation to the one they ran in Lodz.

"In a nutshell, gentleman, certain members of this island's government were willing to allow Andropof to establish a research facility on St. Peters. In return they would receive enough income from the manufacture of diamonds to stabilize their regime and turn the country into a regional military power. You gentlemen were to provide the security for the operation and filter the gemstones into the system via your narcotics distribution networks, just as we agreed. You were not told the full details for security reasons. Yes, I admit you were led to believe that the diamonds coming your way were conflict diamonds. However, tonight you were to meet Andropof and Wies and receive the final details of the operation."

There was silence around the table as Glokani ground out his cheroot in a crystal ashtray and poured himself another glass of water. We were coming to the bottom line and I had the feeling he was steeling himself for what he was about to say. But before he could say anything, the silence was broken by the same angry voice.

"Supposing we go along with what you've told us and accept that you were going to let us in on your little secret tonight. What's the problem?"

Glokani stared at his antagonist, knowing everything hinged on what he was about to say. He drew a deep breath. "The problem, gentlemen, is that I trusted a boy with a man's job. I left my son in charge of security. Unfortunately he thought more about partying; a weakness that cost him his life. As I have already indicated, his loss means nothing to me, but the person he was supposed to guard, does. While my son was acting the playboy, Andropof disappeared."

Predictably, it was the scumbag's regional spokesman who again chimed in. "So what, your son lost the genetics freak, we still have Wies and that's all we are interested in. Right?"

"Wrong. Apparently, like you, Andropof realized our interest would go no further than Wies, so he wrote himself some insurance. About a week away from the islands, Wies failed to show up for dinner. The crew made a thorough search of the yacht, but he was not on board. The weather was calm so they turned around and spent twelve hours searching for him, zigzagging backwards and forwards over their previous track. They found nothing. I questioned Andropof when the yacht arrived, but of course he denied having anything to do with the disappearance of his good friend."

There was a round of muttering followed by another question.

"What about Turpin and these other arseholes, what have they to do with all this?"

"Good question," said Glokani. "Very few people knew about this operation. My son was one of them, his girlfriend another. Certain information led me to believe that Turpin and his buddies had something to do with my son's death and Andropof's disappearance. I'm no longer sure that that is the case. However, I think Turpin and his sidekicks can help us get him back."

"Why not bring in this girlfriend and let us hear what she has to say."

Glokani looked at the floor, he was about to lose a lot more face, so I decided to help him along.

"He can't, she's run off with the help," I said.

This earned Glokani more serious abuse and the uproar brought the stewards tumbling through the door, MAC-10s leading the way.

Glokani heard them coming and motioned them back into the passageway. Then he turned, slammed his fist onto the table, and demanded quiet. It had little effect.

"We put a lot of our money into this operation. We own this island and you don't fuck with us. You deliver or we'll turn you and your toy boat into a million dollar funeral pyre. You've got forty-eight hours. We've got nothing more to say." With that his guests pushed back their chairs and followed their spokesman towards the door.

The look on Glokani's face said he was about to call his men, but he thought better of it when the scumbags flung open the door and pushed past his private army with shouts of contempt.

"Do your friends always leave before they've eaten?" said Willie.

Glokani slumped in his chair and reached for a glass of wine. He had lost his poise and no longer acted the cool movie star. Like a vicious dog, he dominated by fear. Dogs detect changes in body odor. Humans pick up on body language. Both species are excited by their victim's terror and use it to their bloody advantage. Rapid eye movement may get your throat torn out. Running can prove fatal. Some dogs are driven insane by the urge to attack and will rip at their own flesh in the lust for blood. Yet there are some dogs that don't know what to do when their victim shows no fear and raps them across the snout with a rolled up newspaper. I was seeing one now: Glokani was sulking like a dog that had been struck on the nose with the Sunday edition, fifteen-pound supplements and all.

I'll give him his due, the cowed look didn't last long and he was his old vicious self by the time the gun-toting stewards streamed back into the room.

Glokani pointed at me. “Turpin, you and your heroes will find Andropof and the girl and bring them to me. You heard what they said; you have forty-eight hours.”

“What makes you think we can find them?” I said.

“You’ll find them or you’ll get your bitch back in pieces.”

“And if your men or the scumbags find them first, then what?”

“Then tough shit. I’m still not sure about you, but right now you seem like my best bet and like it or not you’re on the payroll.”

25

After the air-conditioned luxury of the motor yacht, the night was heavy and oppressive, and the heat made it uncomfortable to breath. To the northeast, lightning flickered along the edge of the clouds and only the brightest stars were visible through the haze.

We turned left outside the marina and walked along the local dock. A few old fishing boats were tugging at their moorings, their lines occasionally dipping below the water's oily surface, only to reappear with a sudden creak as they fought to hold their restless charges in place.

It was ten thirty by the time we made it back to the *Lucky Lady,* and for once the place was quiet. Tourists are thin on the ground in July and only a few people were hanging around the bar. The travel brochures claim we live in paradise, yet, like people everywhere, most of the local population had to get up early and head off to work in the morning.

Willie and I made our way below leaving Pete to talk to his bar-staff. He appeared a few minutes later carrying a loaded six-pack of Corona long necks. He popped the caps, gave us one each, and left the others within easy reach on the table.

Willie was the first to speak. "Want to know what I think? I think our friend on *Temptress* is finding out just how easy it is to end up with a million dollars in the Caribbean."

Pete fell for it. "And just how do you end up with a million dollar in the Caribbean?" he said.

"You start with two million, boyo."

Pete laughed then asked the question that had been bothering me all night. "Where do you think Snake Eyes was while we were being entertained?"

I took a long swig of Corona. The beer was almost frozen and slipped down my throat like a glazed rasp. "I reckon Snake Eyes has moved in on the boss and that somehow he and delectable Debbie have taken Andropof and stashed him away somewhere. No doubt Debbie drew suspicion away from herself by playing the part of Gordon's grieving girlfriend. That way she could hang around a bit longer to see what Glokani planned to do. It would also account for her appearance at the old prison."

"What about Snake Eyes? He was at the prison, too," said Willie.

"Snake Eyes proved his loyalty by blowing away the cop. I doubt Glokani even suspected them until they didn't show up tonight and by then it was too late to call the meeting off."

"How did you know Debbie wasn't there?

"I didn't, it was just a guess, but it certainly got a reaction."

Willie mulled this over. "So where do we go from here?" he said.

"Glokani must be asking himself the same thing, because right now he's up to his arse in alligators. He's lost his cash cow and seriously pissed off the scumbags. He thinks he's tough but even his kind operate within certain rules. Now he's dealing with something he's never seen before. An island fortress run by merciless crud that are more afraid of their wives and girlfriends seeing them sneaking out of the whorehouse than they arc of him, his guns and his money."

We all reached for another beer at the same time. I wasn't sure about the others but the action of the last couple of days was finally catching up with me. The beer wasn't helping either and I began to doze.

Pete and Willie continued their discussion. I followed it for a while until my mind became a jumble of distorted images of all that had happened since I stopped for a birthday drink just two days ago: Pete lining up the tequilas, Susie laughing from the aft deck, Chopstick looking down the barrel of his gun; the flies crawling through the dirt, rubbing their obscene little legs together in the dead cop's blood. Susie looking scared, Susie naked and broken, Susie, Susie … Susie.

26

I came out of my sleep like an uncoiling spring, one that's rusty and lacking a good part of its tensile strength. I was tucked up in a bunk in one of the cabins. Daylight streamed through a prism set in the deck overhead. The boat was slowly moving forward and then astern.

I swung my legs over the side of the bunk just as Pete came in with a steaming cup of coffee. "What happened to the glory days, Pete, fight all day, screw all night, and a two mile swim back to the ship in the morning?"

"You fell asleep at the table. It's called being fifty."

"Thanks. What time is it?"

He handed me the coffee and looked at the Citizen dive watch on his wrist. "Just after five," he said. "Grab a shower and come into the galley, Willie's on the loose with bacon and eggs."

I took a sip of coffee and headed for the shower. When I stood the motion of the boat was more noticeable. The *Lady* was moored to a dock at the farthest end of the lagoon and, with the exception of the Friday night party, when Pete made enough money to fill a wheelbarrow and so many people danced on deck that the old girl rolled like she was at sea, the heavy yacht rarely moved.

I dressed and followed my nose to the galley and a heaping plate of fry-up that sat on the table. The galley was deserted, but it was obvious that the other guys had eaten by the mess. Willie had done his usual job with breakfast and if I had to die, one of his cholesterol bombs wouldn't be a bad way to go.

Footsteps sounded in the passageway and a moment later Pete and Willie jostled their way into the galley. Pete went straight to the stove and grabbed the coffee pot. He poured Willie a cup then turned to refill mine. The boat gave a powerful surge and he slopped coffee onto the table.

"There's a tropical storm developing," he said as Willie handed him a paper towel. "According to the forecast it's still five hundred miles out, heading northeast, but if this surging gets any worse then we might have to move the *Lady* to the hurricane mooring."

Willie looked up and rolled his eyes, aware of the problems facing those who live on their boats through the Caribbean summer.

Pete tore more paper from the roll and dabbed thoughtfully at the spilt coffee.

Hurricane season runs from the beginning of June to the end of November. In the early summer, low-pressure systems develop over the Sahara Desert and then sweep west across the African coast. Even early in the season, depressions, or tropical waves as they are called, bear watching as they can develop into tropical storms, or worse, hurricanes.

The hurricane season peaks during August and September, when only fools sail the waters of the Caribbean. By then anyone in their right mind has either voyaged south to the so-called safe zones of Trinidad and Venezuela, or hauled their boats out of the water and moved ashore.

It was different for Pete. To stay in business the bar had to remain open all year round. When a storm threatened, he would take the boat off the dock and move it to a more sheltered area of the lagoon and run the bows deep into the mangroves. With the bow secured to the trees, he would then lead heavy lines from the stern to a series of concrete blocks air-jetted into the floor of the lagoon about a hundred yards out.

Every summer Susie and I fought over what we should do with *Strange Light*. I refused to pay the scalpers to haul it out, and I wouldn't run away south. Instead I preferred to lie to my own anchors and ride it out. I've seen off several hurricanes in this way and, thanks to the strength of the steel hull, the one time I did end up in the trees only my ego was damaged. Hunkered down while hundred and thirty mile an hour winds try to blow you out of the water, and coconuts smash into the hull like cannon balls, might not be everyone's idea of fun. But aging adrenalin junkies can always find an excuse and I'm never the only idiot out there.

Pete opened a locker and pulled out a dog-eared chart of the Southern North Atlantic. He unrolled it on the table and placed his coffee cup over Cuba. "This storm isn't going to help us find Susie. Even if it misses us by a hundred miles the rain on the outer bands will close the roads and make searching the island impossible. Last night the center of the storm was here, at seventeen degrees north, fifty-nine degrees west." He tapped the chart with a knuckle. "According to a report on the news station coming out of St. Thomas, the storm's building in intensity and slowing down. The experts are saying it's going to pass to the north but by the way the *Lady* is surging, they could be wrong. I reckon the seas beyond the outer reef must be ten feet high already."

To add weight to Pete's argument the heavens opened and rain snare-drummed across the deck. Willie reached up and closed the skylight. By the time he sat down the shower had already moved on.

I looked down at the chart. "Glokani said forty-cight hours. He's wrong. He can't leave *Temptress* tied up in the marina; he has to go to sea. If Pete's right then the channel through the reef will soon be impassable. That floating art gallery won't stand a chance unless he gets it out of the lagoon and heads southwest away from the eye of the storm. By my reckoning we've got less than twelve hours to find Susie."

27

It was time to go over everything in detail: to look back at what had happened and try and fit the pieces together. I was missing something. Last night, dozing at the table, I almost had it. Now the thought was back, hovering just out of reach.

We'd done this before after being in action, usually while relaxing at the end of the debriefing. There was always something else, something we'd missed. Sometimes it was nothing important and might, had we thought of it at the time, have saved us a few meaningless seconds or increased our comfort by a notch. Then there were times when we realized that what we had missed could have saved lives. Those sessions were tough.

Willie went first; sifting through his memory, placing in chronological order everything that had happened over the last few days. We listened carefully. If we thought he was off the mark, or spoke about something that Pete or I hadn't seen or heard, we interrupted and talked it out.

Pete went next and by the time he'd finished we had recent events mapped out in detail. Even so we still had no clue as to Susie's whereabouts or that of Andropof, Snake Eyes, and the girl.

When it was my turn, I went through the night of the party and my run-in with Gordon the Turd.

Our description of the happenings at the old prison matched, throwing up nothing new. So we went over my discussion with Mohamed and his mother and moved on to Edwin's lecture on the dangers of possessing the pink diamonds.

When our session was over we sat and stared into our empty cups like fortune tellers seeking answers in the tea leaves.

"A wise man would watch his back," I said.

Pete looked up. "What?"

"A wise man would watch his back. That was Eddie's parting shot—a wise man. Wiseman ... Wies. Shit! He knew about Wies. He was telling me he knew about Wies and the diamonds!"

I leapt to my feet.

Willie looked at Pete. "Steady on, Dick,' he said. "That's a pretty big assumption to make."

"No, it's not. I know I'm right. It's been bugging me. I almost made the connection last night. Eddie knows, but why not just come out and say-so. Come on, we have to talk to him."

Pete left the cabin and returned a few minutes later carrying a large plastic container. He flicked back the catches and lifted the watertight lid. From inside he removed a Glock 9mm automatic and the parts of the Uzi machine pistol that Willie had lovingly assembled the night before. He passed the pieces of the Uzi across the table; Willie had it back together and loaded in ten seconds flat.

"Scumbags, bent cops and a slime ball with a million dollar yacht. Toss in a hurricane and it's enough to get you high." With that Willie hefted the gun and followed Pete out the door.

I fished another Glock out of the box, slammed in a full clip, and chambered the first round. My thumb found the safety catch and slid it into place over the red dot. I had no intention of blowing my nuts off, so checked the safety again before pushing the gun down my waistband and covering it with my shirt. With a spare ammo clip in each pocket, I headed for the door.

It was still early but thanks to the distant storm the humidity was already high. The first rays of the sun were chasing the shadows from the mountain, but instead of the pale blue of morning, the sky was opaque, like the eyes of a dead fish left too long on the slab. Along the beach the palms were holding a whispered conversation, bending towards each other and then recoiling as if what they heard wasn't to their liking.

I reached the Jeep and found Pete looking through a pair of binoculars towards the seething white line that marked the outer reef. "It's already rough in the channel and it looks like a couple of the markers are gone," he said, and handed me the glasses.

I brought the glasses to my eyes and adjusted the focus. As I studied the horizon the sound of a powerful wave, destroying itself on the distant coral, rumbled towards us on the salt-laden air.

Willie climbed into the driving seat and spun the engine. After exchanging looks, Pete jumped in beside him and I took up my usual position in the back.

Willie looked over his shoulder. "Where to?" he asked.

"Take a right and head for the Meadowlands," I said. "We need to talk to Mohamed. He'll be at home at this time of day and he'll know where we can find Eddie."

The road to the Meadowlands runs west along a thin strip of land. A quarter of a mile from where the *Lady* is moored, the road crosses an ancient drawbridge which opens to let boats pass into the sheltered waters of the inner lagoon. On busy high season days, crowds gather to watch the big yachts come in. The channel can be tricky, especially around the time of the new or full moon when the current can cause serious problems for any uninformed yacht captain making his first trip through the bridge. The captains who get it right receive a loud cheer, but the loudest cheer goes to those who get it wrong, especially if they put a scratch in their gleaming topsides or, even better, a large dent. It sounds mean, but according to one rich and philosophical boat owner, who had clipped the bridge twice, the crowd was welcome to the entertainment. "It's the same as watching a boxer, who makes a million bucks per fight, get knocked out," he told me one night while buying a round for the bar. "The crowds cheer because he's on his arse but the boxer knows—when he gets back up—he's the one with the million bucks. So fuck 'em."

The Jeep rattled over the bridge and I looked out across the beach to the outer lagoon. From November to May, this area is usually full of boats. It's a nice place to anchor as the reef keeps out the swell and the trade winds blow away the mosquitoes. Today the anchorage was deserted but for the wreck of an abandoned freighter that lay with its rusting decks awash; victim of an earlier hurricane and uncaring owners who were content to pollute the beautiful bay with their discarded junk.

The drive to Mohamed's house usually takes about forty-five minutes and passes through the most delightful scenery in St. Peters. For the first two miles, the road runs along the edge of the beach, passing the occasional store or gaudily painted rum shop. After a couple of miles the road turns inland, hairpins through a banana plantation, then winds its way back towards the coast where it skirts a series of rocky inlets, the blacktop often giving way to sand as it crumbles near the water's edge.

Most of the inlets are deserted but, in some, tiny fishing villages nestle amongst the trees. This is all that is left of the St. Peters of long ago, where tiny wooden homes with roofs of red zinc cluster around churches of such fanciful denominations they can be found nowhere else on earth.

This is the part of the island that the greedy developers want the most, and the part the last of the true islanders refuse to give up. Any movement to oust the present corrupt government would come from the people of the Meadowlands. The authorities knew it and left them alone in the hope that the rampant development all around them would eventually force them out.

Willie tortured the old Jeep and got us to Mohamed's in record time. The house stands on a low headland overlooking a sandy bay. Once the home of a British admiral, it was built of yellow brick brought to the island centuries ago as ballast in ships trading rum and slaves.

As the house flashed by behind stands of trees the sun touched its façade, but today, instead of mellowing the old bricks, it soured them with dark foreboding.

Willie stood on the brakes and we spun off the main road onto a cobbled driveway. For a moment the house was hidden from view by the drooping branches of an ancient banyan tree.

We drove on until we came to a sliding electric gate set into a wrought-iron security fence, and coasted to a stop in front of a metal box housing a red button and a microphone. I reached over and pressed the button. A servo whirred on a small camera attached to the gatepost overhead. The camera scanned the area behind us, then, as if satisfied, focused on the Jeep.

We waited in silence. After a while I hit the button again.

"Dick. What brings you out here at this time in a morning?" Mohamed's words came pouring out of the wall with the tinny resonance of someone speaking into a coffee can half-a-mile away. There was no friendly greeting, but it was early, and perhaps he was hung-over, so I let it go.

"Mohamed, we need to talk. It's about the—"

My conversation was cut off by a buzz and a click, and moments later the metal gate began to roll back. Willie put the Jeep into gear and drove through. As we cleared the gate, it slid back into place behind us.

The driveway wound its way up a gentle slope set between rows of neatly tended royal palms. The lower portion of each tree was painted white to protect it from the sun. About ten feet from the ground each trunk was encircled by a wide stainless-steel band designed to keep climbing rats at bay.

As the driveway approached the house, it circled a roundabout covered with tropical flowers and shrubs. Beyond the roundabout, the road forked left down to the small cove where Mohamed kept a twenty-four-foot Boston Whaler that he used for commuting to town. Its twin 115 HP outboards solved the traffic problems of the tourist season when thousands of hire cars and buses seemed to be on the road at once. With the approaching storm, I thought Mohamed would have moved the boat to the inner lagoon for safety and was surprised, on glancing down into the cove, to see it tugging at its moorings just beyond the end of the little dock.

We followed the road to the right and drove along the front of the old stables. The stables had been converted into a garage, the doors were open and Mohamed's Range Rover was parked inside. To the left of the Rover was a white vintage MGB TC. Next to the sports car stood two Harley Davidson motorbikes—a 1250cc standard Softail and a lavishly customized Fat Boy with a 1340cc engine. Another SUV was half-hidden behind the garage, this one a battered Ford that I didn't recognize.

We parked opposite the flagged steps leading up to the front door of the house. Pete and I hopped out leaving Willie behind the wheel, looking as casual as he could for a man with a loaded Uzi beneath the seat.

At the top of the steps a brick porch, supported by granite columns, gave shade to the high double doors. The doors were pillar-box red and furnished with gleaming brass handles that must be hell to keep bright in the steaming humidity.

To the right, set between heavy clay pots of jungle ferns, a worn iron boot scraper bearing the date 1794 added to the sturdy elegance of the old Georgian house. If not for the camera mounted above the doors, you would think nothing had changed since the Admiral was last here over two hundred years ago.

Pete moved into position beside the plant pots, making sure he was not in direct line with the door.

I raised my hand to ring the bell. Before my finger reached the button, the door opened and Mohamed stepped out. "Dick, Pete," he said. "To what do I owe the honor of a visit this early in the morning?" He threw a quick glance over my shoulder and nodded at Willie.

Mohamed wore a khaki safari shirt buttoned almost to the neck. One of the buttons was in the wrong hole, dragging the collar to one side. Where the shirt was tucked into the top of his cargo pants it was askew and hanging out, as if the whole lot had been thrown on in a hurry.

His eyes followed mine and he refastened the offending button and tucked the shirt into his pants.

"Well, what can I do for you, not more bags of mischief, I hope?" His voice was full of forced joviality but he made no move to ask us in or even offer the customary handshake due to old friends. When I shuffled to one side, he matched my step and, using his bulk to block my view of the hall, made it clear that today we weren't welcome.

I took a deep breath and asked my question.

"We want to talk with Edwin, your diamond expert. Can you tell us where he is?"

Mohamed then did something I never thought he would do: he mimicked my accent. "We want to talk to Eddie," he sneered, "tell us where he is." As far as it went the accent wasn't bad. Then he dropped the pretense. "Same old double act, Popeye and Olive Oyle, Mutt and Jeff, Batman and Robin, Dick and Pete. Why do you want to see Eddie?" He ran the sentences together, the words dripping with scorn.

"You missed Willie out. He could be Bluto," I said. He looked at me as if I was nuts, so I dropped the sarcasm and tried again.

"Look, why not just ask us in so we can talk?"

After a few muttered words that I didn't understand, he sighed, then stepped to one side and invited us in.

We had been to Mohamed's home many times and usually looked forward to the visits. The lofty rooms were always cool and the genuine period furniture, although valuable, was well used and turned what could have been a drab museum into a comfortable home. Today we had no time to enjoy the ambiance and were hustled down the hallway to the conservatory at the back of the house. Made of glass and aluminum, the conservatory opened onto a wide patio overlooking a swimming pool, and an improbable-looking lawn that seemed wildly out of place amongst the riot of tropical flowers in the surrounding gardens.

Mohamed led us across the lawn to a small gazebo with a well stocked bar. He lifted a flask from a coffee percolator and poured himself a cup of steaming brew, then placed the cup on a matching saucer, ladled in cream and sugar, and gave it a brisk stir. After taking a sip, he turned and looked at us.

"No thanks, we've already had coffee," said Pete.

Mohamed ignored Pete's wit and addressed himself to me. "Okay, Dick, what do you want? I have much to do today, so get to the point."

He waited, then brought the cup slowly to his lips and took another tiny sip.

I managed to keep the friendliness in my voice. It was difficult but I gave it a go. "Yesterday I came to you for advice and your friend Eddie told me about my little bag of diamonds. He also held something back and now I need to talk to him. Do you know where he is?"

"Yes, he's in Miami, he flew out last night."

"What do you know about a man named Wies?"

"Nothing. Never heard of him."

"Does the name Andropof mean anything to you?"

"No."

"Who's here with you?"

"None of your business, now why don't you leave."

He took another sip of coffee but this time most of it slopped down the front of his shirt.

"Don't you want to know how Susie is?" I said.

"Yes … of course. Susie, how is she?"

"We don't know and that's another reason why we're here. We thought Eddie might be able to help us."

"Why would Eddie be able to help you?"

"Because Eddie knows a lot more about those diamonds than he told me yesterday."

"That's nonsense. He told you the truth. You've got yourself into trouble again; you've been doing it all your life. You brought your troubles to me, and I did what I could. I wish you luck finding Susie, but there is nothing else I can do. Now really, I must be getting along."

He chunked his coffee cup on to the bar and strode off across the lawn with us in tow.

When he came to the door of the conservatory, instead of leading us back the way we came, he turned right and beckoned us to follow him along a path leading around the side of the house.

"I'd like to use the bathroom," I called to his retreating back.

"What?'

"I need to take a leak. Do you mind if I use the bathroom?"

I waited for his reply.

He hesitated, stopped and turned.

Our eyes met. "Yes, yes of course," he said.

He shouldered his way between us and, with a grunt, walked through the conservatory and into the house.

The bathroom was halfway down the hall and to the left. I

pushed open the door and stepped inside. To make sure my timing was right; I used the toilet, flushed it, and then noisily washed my hands.

Back in the hall Mohamed was waiting to escort us to the Jeep. I opened my mouth to speak but he hustled us out and down the steps, and when I looked back our friend had closed the door.

"What was all that about?" said Willie as we climbed into the Jeep.

"Just drive," I replied.

He started the engine, gave me a hard stare, then slipped the Jeep into gear and moved off.

As we approached, the automatic gate began to roll back. We hardly made it through before it slid shut behind us.

Willie turned right at the old banyan tree and drove out onto the road leading back to the *Lady*.

I leaned forward and touched him on the shoulder. "Drive for a quarter of a mile and then stop. Chopstick's in the house."

28

Willie turned right onto a dirt road that led through the trees. We bounced along over ruts and exposed roots until we were almost at the beach, then he pulled over and killed the engine.

Pete was the first to speak. "What makes you so sure that Chopstick's in the house?"

"Perfume, that damn aftershave he wears. When Mohamed led us through to the conservatory, I thought I caught a whiff of it then, but I couldn't be sure. I think Mohamed caught it too, that's why he didn't want us back in the house. When I asked him if I could use the bathroom, he was screwed, he had to take a chance, but if he's checked, he'll know we're on to him, the bathroom reeks of it."

"Dick, Susie could be there." Willie reached for the dashboard but Pete stopped him before he could turn the key.

Willie pushed him off. "What the hell," he said. "Glokani's unleashed his dogs and they're out of control. Chopstick doesn't give a shit about money or diamonds; he'll take his payment out of anyone he can strap to a table, and right now that's Susie. We've got to go back."

"Steady, Willie," I said. "We are going back, but not the front way. There are more people in the house than Mohamed and Chopstick. I counted four used coffee cups on the breakfast bar, and my guess is someone was monitoring those security cameras. That means at least five people, maybe more. We've no chance of getting back inside unless we go in fast, and from a direction they don't expect. That means the water."

Willie hopped out of the Jeep and hauled the Uzi from under the seat. He ejected the extended thirty-two round clip, checked it, and slid it back into place. He fished around beneath the seat and pulled out two extra clips. One of them had a dab of red paint across the end—meaning every second round was a tracer. Satisfied, he put the tracer rounds in his right-hand jacket pocket and stowed the other clip in his left.

Uziel Gal never wanted his lethal invention to carry his name. One look at Willie's face and I understood why. Poor Uziel, they ignored him and named the murderous little gun after him anyway.

Pete checked his automatic then adjusted the strap that held a seven inch U.S. Marine Corps K-bar to his right ankle.

They looked at me expectantly, so I tugged the pistol from my waistband, ejected the clip, gave it the once over and slammed it back into the grip.

"Plan, Dick," said Pete.

"We follow the shoreline back to the house," I said. "We can make it nearly all the way on the beach. We may have to scramble over some rocks, and in a couple of places we might have to swim, but not too far. It'll bring us out behind the house, about a hundred and fifty yards from the gazebo. If we think the security cameras have picked us up, then we go in fast. Surprise is the only thing we've got. We need to get into the house before they work out what's happening. The room containing the surveillance monitors is on the second floor. We'll try for that first. Take out the monitors and they're blind."

"Shit. What about Mohamed," said Pete, "we've known him for years? And what if you're wrong and Chopstick isn't in the house?"

As always, Willie came straight to the point. "If Dick says Chopstick's in the house, then he's there. I don't know what the hell's going on with the Woolly Mammoth, but I tell you what, he's in deep shit, boyo, and we're not going to sort it out standing here. If he's involved with kidnapping Susie, then he'll be on the receiving end of this." He shook the Uzi and headed for the rocks at the water's edge.

Pete shook his head and grinned. "You do … ah … know about Willie and Susie?"

"I do now!

I tried not to laugh as we followed Willie into the rocks. Why I found it so bloody funny, I couldn't say. Our on-again-off-again relationship had been in crisis for months. However, like any betrayed lover suddenly faced with the truth, the idea of putting a warning shot through Willie's head did cross my mind. But I quickly consigned it to the bin of bad thoughts where such things belong.

Without putting up much of a fight, Susie and I had slipped into the old married couple routine; over time passion had become duty, and love—whatever that is—had become little more than a clinging, dependent friendship. If Susie and Willie wanted to be together then I would fight for their right ... The ever gallant Dick playing King Arthur to Willie's Lancelot. Stupid sod!

We moved off along the beach. The tide was low, and on this side of the island the seas were only just beginning to feel the effects of the approaching storm.

After a quarter of a mile the beach tapered off and we rock-hopped, following Willie as he picked out the easiest route. Twice we had to enter the water where the rocks became too steep to climb or the shale cliffs too crumbly to secure a handhold.

We were approaching a tiny cove when Willie stopped and flattened himself against a large rock. He looked back, made a slowing motion with his hand, then touched a finger to his lips.

We edged alongside, pressing ourselves into the rock.

Willie waved the Uzi towards a narrow strip of sand beyond our hiding place. The evil grin was back on his face.

I slipped the automatic from my belt and released the safety catch. Taking hold of my right wrist with my left hand, I raised the automatic, bringing it alongside my face, ready to fire.

From behind, a faint click told me that Pete had done the same.

Without giving us a chance to look, Willie leapt out from behind the rock. He was carrying the Uzi across his chest, index finger of his right hand on the trigger, left hand cradling the barrel halfway along its stubby length.

"Oh shit, here we go," said Pete and together we sprang from behind the rock and took off after Willie.

A naked couple on a large beach towel were going at it for all they were worth. The girl—her long dark hair swinging forward over her eyes—was riding the guy, gripping his shoulders and banging his head on the sand with each thrust. Pieces of clothing were strewn along the beach. Two empty champagne bottles lay on their side next to an old-fashioned wicker picnic basket.

Willie pounded by waving the Uzi, his hair flowing, clothes black-wet and covered in seaweed. The guy saw him coming and tried to throw the girl off. Mistaking his moves for heightened passion, she went right on thrusting and banging his head on the sand.

When the stud saw Pete and me galloping towards him with pistols drawn, he let out a terrified shriek. This excited the girl even more and by the time we disappeared into the rocks at the far side of the beach, she was screaming, "Yes. Yes. Ohoooo ... *Yes!*"

We were still laughing when we reached the next headland. "I wonder if they'll name the baby Sandy or Son of a Beach?"

gasped Willie as we fought for breath.

"You're fucking crazy," said Pete setting off another round of gasping laughter that was instantly cut off by a burst of gunfire.

We dived for cover then realized that whoever was pulling the trigger wasn't shooting at us, at least not yet. The shots were distant, but had to be coming from somewhere in the grounds of Mohamed's house.

We got to our feet, rechecked our weapons, and took off towards the last headland.

Getting ourselves around this one would be tough. A high concrete wall topped with razor wire isolated Mohamed's estate from the outside world. The wall ran along the top of the headland and followed the cliff down to where it entered the sea. At its base, the water was deep, and there was no way around it without a swim

From what I remembered of the house and grounds, the headland gave way to a thin strip of beach. Beyond the beach a rocky spur curved seaward protecting the cove and the small wooden dock where earlier we'd seen the Boston Whaler.

If there were any security cameras, we couldn't see them.

We discussed it and agreed we could make the swim.

It was impossible to keep the weapons dry, however, water wasn't the problem; the problem was the sand. Willie's Uzi had been designed to take the abuse, but we would have to be careful with the pistols.

I went first. A slight current tugged at my legs but then eased off in the deeper water away from the rocks. The sea reached my chest and I lay forward and started an easy breaststroke. I swam straight out until clear of the turbulent backwash then turned and swam parallel with the cliff.

Willie took up position on my right and I could hear Pete stroking along behind us.

My clothes were getting heavier and I was questioning the wisdom of keeping them on when the beach came into view on our right.

We made our way to the water's edge and, keeping low, waded ashore.

Thirty yards of sand separated us from a line of trees and scrub. It was the perfect killing ground. If anyone had seen us, this is where the bloodletting would begin.

We zigzagged, staying far apart, making it difficult for anyone to take us out with a single burst of automatic fire. Legs pumping, we reached the tangle of scrub and threw ourselves down in the sand. From here, and slightly to our right, we could see the gazebo beyond a stand of palms.

"We'll cross the path that leads to the cove and come at the house from the back," I whispered. "Go easy. If we make it to the conservatory door then there's a chance we can get inside without raising the alarm. If they spot us then all bets are off and it's code red. I'll head for the stairs and the surveillance room while Pete checks the ground floor. Willie, you take the door to the cellars and look for Susie. If she's in the house, I reckon that's where she'll be."

They nodded and we moved off, using our elbows and knees to scurry over the ground and into the trees.

After a few minutes, we came to the path. Pete squatted, looked left and right, and then made his move.

He was nearly halfway across when he stopped, spun on the balls of his feet, and dived back into the trees. "There's someone on the path about twenty five yards away. He's just sitting there looking towards the house," he gasped.

I pulled him close. "He'll have the information we need. Can you take him without killing him?"

In reply, Pete slid the Glock into his shoulder holster then reached down and slipped the Special Forces K-Bar from its sheath. Razor sharp, the blade was forged of black carbon steel with four serrations down its trailing edge. A weight in the carbonate bolster gave the knife balance. On active service, I'd watched Pete hone the blade for hours, only calling quits when he could shave with it. In his hands it made the perfect sap, or silent killer.

Pete moved off, gliding like a wraith through the trees.

When he was about five yards from his target, Willie and I followed. We could make out the figure of a man sitting on the path. Pete moved into position behind him, keeping the knife at belly height, blade up, at a forty-five degree angle. Held like that he could use the handle of the knife as a sap or drive the blade up under the ribcage into the heart.

We waited for Pete to strike, not daring to move for fear of giving him away.

Pete raised the knife and edged forward, hesitated, then hooked his arms around the sitting figure and dragged him backwards into the trees.

29

Mohamed was barely alive. Blood was running from his ears and his forehead had grown a tiny third eye. The front of his shirt was in bloom, the crimson stain spreading with every heartbeat.

We carried him to a clear patch of sandy ground and lay him down. I unbuttoned his shirt and using a dry piece of his shirttail to wipe away the blood, found another tiny hole. Both wounds were made by a small caliber hand gun, probably a .22.

He coughed and pink froth flew from his mouth. His breathing was ragged and, as he fought for air, a gurgling wheeze came from deep within his chest.

Pete gently rolled him onto his side. Mohamed gagged and threw up a stream of bloody mucus that ran into his beard and hung in ropes down to the ground. He opened his eyes and made a small mewing sound. Then he raised his head and tried to speak.

I leaned forward and brought my face to his so that he could see me.

"Dick, you came back, you son of a bitch, I knew you would." His voice was barely a whisper and his breath held the stench of the grave. "It was such a sweet deal, Dick. Pink diamonds served up like fast food and our own little island to play God on."

I looked at Pete, then back at Mohamed. "You were Glokani's contact, you and Eddie," I said.

"No. Not Eddie. Eddie came at mother's request. Eddie is a De

Beers agent. He and mother were doing legitimate business."

"But Eddie knew," I said. "He tried to warn me."

"That means that momma knew too. Momma and her damn code of ethics, she betrayed her own son." His sobbing laugh was cut short and he hawked up a mouthful of blood. This time it was thick and arterial red.

"Easy, Mohamed, easy," I said.

He no longer had the strength to hold his head clear of the ground and lay with one eye in the dirt, his nose and lips pushed to one side.

"I set it up with Glokani and those clowns in government," he wheezed. "No one was supposed to get hurt, just incredibly rich. Then you walk into the office like a fucking pirate and dump a bag of Glokani's pink diamonds in Eddie's lap."

"Why, Mohamed. Why get involved in a scam when you already have everything?"

He spread his fingers and dragged his hand through the dirt until it found mine.

"No, Dick, you have everything, you and your crazy friends. You do what you want and don't give a shit. I wanted freedom. No more momma and family running my life. You still don't get it do you, you stupid fuck. You don't even know what you've got."

He coughed again, drowning in his own blood.

I touched his face. "Mohamed, listen to me. Who's in the house? Where's Susie?"

"I came after you to tell you. Can you believe that, Dick? I couldn't let it happen. They cut Glokani out of the deal … they're heading for an island in the Bahamas."

His voice grew fainter.

"In the house ... Chopstick and the one who shot me, two more are with the girl. The girl is … the girl is … Susie is … Dick, I'm sorry, I—" His words ended in a heaving shower of blood.

His body shook and then lay still.

I looked up at Willie and Pete then pried Mohamed's fingers from my hand and let them join the rest of him in the dirt.

"I'm sorry, Dick; I know he was a friend," said Pete.

Willie's show of sympathy was a tad more forceful.

"I heard what the bastard said about Susie and this is what I think about your fucking friendship." He kicked Mohamed in the head then leapt over the body and took off at a crouching run towards the house.

Pete quickly covered Mohamed's face with the bloody shirt and we sprinted after Willie.

We found him behind a stand of trees, staring at the conservatory. He didn't speak, just nodded in the direction of the house.

To get to the conservatory meant crossing a flowerbed and a thirty yard stretch of manicured lawn. We scanned the building and the trees, looking for cameras. Pete pointed towards a fall-pipe that ran down from the guttering at the right-hand corner of the roof. It was difficult to see from this angle, but what looked like a small gray box was attached to the wall below the eves.

Willie nudged me out of the way and made a move towards the lawn. Before he could take another step, I grabbed him by the collar and yanked him back into the cover of the trees.

"Not so fast," I hissed.

Willie threw down the Uzi and took a wild swing. I leapt back and his fist whistled past my jaw. If he'd lost it completely then another punch would follow. He had, but he pulled the punch when I pointed my gun at his head.

We stared at each other until Pete began to chuckle. Then a grin split Willie's face and the crazy bastard began to laugh.

"Okay, boyo, I hear you. Let's do it right." He mouthed the words as if nothing of significance had happened. I was used to fighting alongside Willie, but fighting alongside Willie in love was a different thing.

I shook my head and slowly lowered the gun. Then I pointed to the Uzi at his feet. “We stick to the plan, Willie. You stay here and cover us. I go first and Pete follows. Once we reach the wall next to the conservatory, give it thirty seconds and then run across. If we’re still alive when you get there, we’ll work on the next move.”

Willie nodded and took up position behind a tree.

Pete and I shuffled forward and squatted down at the edge of the flowerbed. I paused and when Pete tapped me on the shoulder, made my run.

I held the pistol out in front, my eyes bouncing from window to window, corner to corner. After what seemed like an eternity, I slammed into the wall of the house and turned to cover Pete.

Seconds later he zigzagged towards me, making it across the lawn without breaking a sweat.

We counted to thirty, but Willie didn’t move.

A minute went by, then two.

Suddenly, he broke from the trees. Half way across the lawn he swerved and headed straight for the front of the house.

“Oh shit, not again,” I hissed then sprinted after him.

We rounded the corner in time to see Willie storm up the steps and reach for the door. A double blast from a shotgun blew the doors off their hinges and hurled him backwards down the steps.

I crept forward, keeping the brickwork between myself and the remains of the door.

Willie was on his back amongst the shattered wood and masonry. I reached for his wrist, hoping to find a pulse.

“Bastards,” he roared and fired half a clip into the hall. Then he sprang to his feet and disappeared into the smoke, cutting off a tormented scream with another burst from the Uzi.

“Clear!” he shouted as we raced after him, leaping over what remained of the guy with the shotgun and into the house.

We had no time to check all the rooms, but sticking to the original plan, Pete began a sweep of the ground floor as I headed for the stairs. I kept the Glock ahead of me in a two-handed grip. My shoes made no noise on the thick carpet but after Willie's arrival I doubt it mattered, whoever was in the house had fled.

The door to the surveillance room was open. I gave the room a quick once-over and stepped inside, heading for a bank of monitors set up on a large table. It was a sophisticated system, perhaps not as sophisticated as the one in Mohamed's shop, but extensive none the less. If each monitor had its own surveillance camera then there must be fifteen of them scattered around the house and grounds. The cameras covered all of the property, including the beach where we came ashore, and the lawn opposite the conservatory. That they hadn't seen us meant they were probably busy legging it, leaving only the hapless sod downstairs to fight a rear-guard action.

Two of the monitors showed parts of the house that I had never seen before.

I spun and found Pete standing in the doorway. He nodded towards the surveillance equipment and strode into the room. After a quick appraisal, he pointed to a monitor marked number five that showed a view of the cove. The Boston Whaler was gone from its mooring and Chopstick Chalmond was standing, naked, on the dock.

As I headed for the door, Pete stopped me and pointed towards another screen.

I looked but the screen was grey and appeared to be turned off. Then I saw movement, little more than a shadow.

Pete adjusted the contrast and Willie came into focus.

He turned towards the camera. Susie's broken body lay cradled in his arms.

30

We found them in the wine cellar in a miasma of blood and Bordeaux.

Willie had laid Susie down on the table where she had died and covered her naked body with his shirt. He was sobbing.

Pete lay his hand on Willie's shoulder and said something to him that I couldn't quite hear.

Willie stroked Susie's matted hair, kissed her on the lips, then reached for the Uzi. "There's another body at the back of the cellar," he said and sprinted across the room, his boots echoing like doom as he bounded up the stairs.

I gently pulled the shirt from Susie's body and looked at what Chopstick had done.

Two canvas straps hung from her wrists. They were still wet with her blood. There was blood on the table, and in pools on the floor. Her lips were torn and her eyes swollen shut. Huge welts covered every part of her body. She'd been savagely bitten, and all that remained of her nipples were two ragged circles of raw flesh.

I staggered back from the table. The dim light reflected off something on the floor: Chopstick's swagger-stick. It was matted with gore for a quarter of its length.

Guilt swept through me and I sank to my knees.

Bile rose in my throat.

Susie was still alive when Mohamed led us though the house,

and I'd done nothing to help her.

Pete covered Susie's body then knelt and took me in his arms. I lay my head against him and wept. I wept for Susie and Willie, and I wept for myself. Rage swept over me and for a moment I wept for the bastards who had done this for they would need all the pity they could get.

Pete held me until I was calm. Then he helped me to my feet.

"Is this your diamond expert?" he said leading me to a dark corner of the cellar.

By the look of the blood, Eddie hadn't been dead for long, which meant they probably tortured him while Susie was in the room. I tried not to dwell on the horror of that as Pete crouched down and turned Eddie's remains towards the dim light. There was a small caliber bullet hole above Eddie's right ear and four thin cuts across his chest.

Pete found Eddie's clothes in a pile in the corner and carefully checked the pockets. "Whoever did this was after information," he said. "They probably wanted to know who he told about the pink diamonds. Snake Eyes would want the information so he could make his own plans. I don't know how this guy was involved, but my guess is he couldn't tell them much. Perhaps he was simply in the wrong place at the wrong time."

"Like in the same room with me," I said.

Pete gave me a hard look. "That's a dark road to go down, Dick. You want to take it? Fine, we'll all go down it together when this is over. Right now we need to find Willie before he starts World War Three." He went to Susie and touched her cold cheek then ran for the stairs taking them three at a time.

Pete was right. There would be time for sorrow later. I took a final look at Susie's tortured body and bolted for the stairs. As we left the house, I grabbed the shotgun from the dead man in the hall. It was a Mossberg 590 combat pump-action with an eighteen inch barrel and modified handgrip. I jacked a round out of the chamber and showed it to Pete. "Tungsten slug," he said, "no wonder it took out the door."

We emerged into watery sunshine. The wind had risen and even with my bad ear I could hear the building fury of the sea.

We turned right at the bottom of the steps and sprinted past the garage towards the road leading down to the cove. Short bursts of gunfire told us exactly where to go.

Chopstick must have missed the boat and walked straight into Willie as he made his way back towards the house. They were facing each other on the path, standing about thirty yards apart.

Willie had the strap of the Uzi wound tightly around his wrist, his finger inside the trigger guard.

Chopstick had his hands above his head. He saw us and began franticly waving his arms and shouting in our direction. Whatever he said was lost as another burst from the Uzi ripped into the dirt at his feet.

Willie was executing the evil bastard one bit at a time.

We jogged forward until we stood at Willie's back then took a good look at our police chief.

His obscene belly hung down over his prick. He was slick with sweat. Darker patches around the top of his legs and on his face could only be blood—Susie's blood. He was a living nightmare; the bogie man, a twisted mind and warped soul just waiting to go to hell.

"You there, Turpin, call this maniac off. We can do a deal …" he bellowed.

He was holding on to the Eton accent, I'll give him that, but his voice was an octave too high and his words ended in a stuttering whine.

Willie put more rounds into the ground at his feet.

Chopstick tried Pete next. "You there, you're a brother. Don't you see what they're doing to you? Free yourself man. Help me. What do you want? Girls? Money? Name your price, but for God's sake help me."

Willie had finally got what he wanted, Chopstick was sobbing. Great tears rolled down his fat cheeks and, as we watched, his bladder let go sending a stream of steaming piss into the dirt.

Willie said nothing, just stared. He ejected the clip from the Uzi and dropped it on the ground. Without taking his eyes off Chopstick, he fished a full clip from his right-hand pocket, slammed it into place, and chambered a round. He set the leaver to single shot and began walking the bullets across the ground.

Chopstick watched in horror as the rounds advanced. He watched like a man watches the head of deadly cobra, hypnotized, unable to move.

Willie gradually raised the gun, taking each bullet closer. The range was short, but the eye picked up the line of each tracer. I was counting the rounds and knew the last one in the clip, the thirty-second, would have an exploding head.

Chopstick was blubbering. He took one step back, then another; keeping pace with each round in a macabre dance of death: Bang! Step. Bang! Step. Bang!

I heard Willie say thirty-one.

He raised the barrel and squeezed the trigger.

The hammer seemed to fall in slow motion. It struck the firing pin of the 9mm exploding round. Inside the Uzi, the gas cleared from the breach, ejecting the spent cartridge and sending it spinning through the air in a perfect arc. The bullet left the barrel at twice the speed of sound. It was impossible, but Chopstick's eyes seemed to follow it all the way. He looked down in amazement as his testicles exploded, leaving nothing but a gaping hole. Great chunks of flesh were missing from the top of his legs and his intestines hung from his belly in writhing coils.

He staggered and sat down.

Willie handed me the Uzi and turned to Pete. He bent down and drew the knife from the sheath on Pete's ankle, walked behind Chopstick, snapped back his head and slit his throat.

He wiped the knife on his pants, reversed it, and handed it back to Pete.

Pete took it without comment, inspected the blade, and slid it back into the sheath.

31

The winds of the approaching storm were beginning to moan through the trees, ripping off leaves and sending them spiraling through the air. Occasionally, a stronger gust bent the tops of the palms, rattling the fronds and blowing them out like streamers.

Using the speedboat, Snake Eyes and his band of murderers would be onboard *Temptress* in fifteen minutes. Somehow we had to find a way to stop them before they could put to sea.

We ran towards the garage and the four-by-fours. Pete got there first and wrenched open the passenger door.

Willie thundered past. "Fuck that, boyo," he cried, and headed straight for the two Harleys.

I grabbed Pete's arm. "Willie's right, it'll take us three quarters of an hour to get back to the marina by road. If we take the bikes to where we left the Jeep, we can run most of the way along the beach and be there in twenty-five minutes."

By the time we reached the Softail, Willie had the Fat Boy running and was backing it out of the garage. He revved the engine, bouncing a hellish roar off the walls and polluting the sea air with a thick plume of blue exhaust.

"Who are you riding with, Pete?" I shouted above the din.

Just then Willie dropped the clutch, lifted the front wheel, and left fifteen feet of burning rubber on the blacktop.

"Didn't want to ride with that crazy fucker anyway," said Pete and climbed on behind me.

It had been years since I had driven a motorbike, and Pete had never driven one at all. Between us we got the thing started and headed down the drive, tearing up ten yards of lawn and a flower-bed along the way.

Willie had Uzied the mechanism and the electric gate hung open. We rode through and hit the main road in time to see him disappear around the first bend.

The Harley was a handful on the pitted roads, but it could have been worse, it could have been raining. In a heavy downpour the roads of St. Peters flood. The potholes fill with water and you don't see them. Driving your car into a deep, water-filled hole gives you quite a jolt. Doing the same at eighty miles an hour on a motor bike will jolt you into the next world, leaving your nuts swinging from the handlebars like baubles on a Christmas tree.

In the distance, Willie swung hard right and pulled up at the end of the track leading to the beach where earlier we had parked the Jeep. He waited until we drew near then dropped the clutch, sending the bike slewing forward and a rooster tail of dirt high in the air.

The track ran straight for about a hundred yards then turned left and ran parallel with the beach, which lay beyond a high bank topped with scrub and sea-grape trees.

Willie ignored the bend and roared straight up the bank. At the top he stood back on the footrests and, knees bent, sent the six hundred and forty pound iron horse soaring over the scrub like a hunter after a fox. Free of the ground the engine redlined until he cut the gas and disengaged the clutch. As the bike slammed into the beach, he wound open the throttle and rode the back wheel all the way to the hard-packed sand at the water's edge.

Our leap wasn't as smooth. At the top of the bank the front wheel struck a chunk of half-buried driftwood and the bike stopped dead. The sudden deceleration tossed me onto the fuel tank. Pete slid up my back, pivoted around my shoulders, and crashed sideways onto the handlebars. Fighting for balance, he grabbed me in a headlock and twisted open the throttle with his knee. The massive intake of gas flooded the engine and it coughed, stuttered, and almost stalled. I had more or less untangled myself when the engine backfired, the bike came off the ground, and we somersaulted over the rear wheel into the dirt. Four hundred pounds lighter, the bike pawed the air with its front wheel and took off like a rampant stallion chasing a mare on heat. It covered a hundred yards then its heart gave out and it went down, spun around three times and lay still, the motor panting on tick over.

Pete was the first to reach the fallen beast. He crept forward, as if afraid it might leap up and mate with him, then sprang, shut off the ignition, and dropped to his knees in the sand.

I hobbled over and sat next to him. “Too old for this shit,” I offered.

“You speaking to me biker boy?” He spat, threw the bike a look of contempt, and went back to digging the sand out of his ears.

We could hear Willie powering away. The rumble of the straight-through pipes growing fainter until all that was left was the sound of the waves rolling up the beach.

Then, indistinct at first, the sound returned as Willie roared towards us along the surf line. The Harley was throwing spray high in the air. Above the roar, I could hear him letting out war-whoops. With the Uzi strapped across his naked back, and a bright red bandana cinched tightly around his head, he looked like something from the cover of a Heavy Metal album.

He spun the bike in a tight turn, circled us twice, and stopped.

We looked at him through the oily smoke rising from the wreckage of our bike’s smoldering engine.

Willie dismounted and poked the injured Harley with his foot. He slipped the Uzi from his shoulder, cocked it, and fired a round into the Soft Tail's crankcase. "Sorry, boss," he said, "but it's better to end her misery."

For the second time that day he began to cry.

32

Willie handled the Harley better with three on board than I could manage with just one.

We stuck to the water's edge, keeping our speed around forty miles an hour on the hard-packed sand. Pete sat behind Willie, with me acting as tail-end Charlie, holding on by squeezing the bike's mudguard with parts of my anatomy designed for a totally different function.

The bridge spanning the channel into the lagoon was less than a mile away when Willie de-powered and we shot down a narrow alley and back onto the coast road. Once we hit the blacktop, he wound open the throttle and we covered the distance to the final bend before the bridge in twelve seconds flat.

Willie began to cuss, his words, a mixture of English and Welsh, streamed over his shoulder like razorblades in the wind. He stomped on the brakes, throwing us forward, and brought the bike to a sliding stop.

Ahead the automatic barriers were down and the bridge was slowly beginning to rise.

We dumped the bike and threw ourselves under the barrier.

An inter-island freighter was halfway down the channel. *Temptress* was right behind her.

Someone in the freighter's wheelhouse was operating the ship's siren, which was faulty and sending out a continuous high-pitched scream that could shatter glass.

Two of her crew were shouting and gesticulating towards the bridge. Three more were pointing aft at the rapidly approaching bow of *Temptress,* from where Snake Eyes was firing a Kalashnikov assault rifle into the freighter's stern, sending chunks of rust and metal high in the air.

The bridge continued its slow rise. The control room was at the far side of the channel. Before the bridge hid it from view, I caught a glimpse of one of Snake Eyes' men working the controls.

The captain of the freighter had done the usual: cut in front of a yacht to remind the rich arseholes just whose island it was. Only this time he'd made a serious mistake.

A thick plume of black smoke shot from the freighter's stack as the engineer tortured the engine for more speed, causing the ancient ship to vibrate and rivets to pop. As it entered the narrowest part of the channel, it was caught in the strong ebb. For a moment the load came off the straining engine and she coughed out a jet of sparks. She was now moving faster than at any time in the last fifty years.

From our position on the road, the bridge was half-open; to the terrified crew of the charging freighter, it was half-shut.

The bow of the ship slid beneath the bridge but her steel foremast didn't make it and struck the edge of the span like a giant axe. It cleaved through the metal sidewalk, ploughed into the road, then sheared off and crashed down onto the freighter's deck.

The impact twisted one of the bridge's hydraulic rams, severing the pipes and sending a slashing stream of oil into the crowd from a nearby rum shop who had staggered out to join in the fun.

There was a screech of tearing metal, the bridge trembled and continued its slow rise.

Terrified, the helmsman jammed the wheel hard over in a desperate attempt to get the ship as far away from the fractured steel as possible. It was a good effort, but way too late. Caught in the strong current the freighter's port side slammed against the buttress, ripping off huge chunks of reinforced concrete. The impact splintered the wooden land-ties and hurled them through the air like javelins.

Unable to cope with the added load, the pipes carrying oil to the remaining hydraulic ram began to leak, and then burst.

As the freighter's wheelhouse scraped clear of the straining span, the bridge shuddered to a stop and dropped two feet.

The shock sheared off one of the rams.

Supported by only one piston, the bridge began to twist until the driving mechanism tore apart, and the nail—used years ago to replace the electric motor's troublesome fuse—finally melted.

The bridge groaned and dropped another foot.

Snake Eyes stopped firing as the bow of the motor yacht began to pass beneath the shattered steel of the bridge.

There was a moment of silence, followed by a shout. I heard the Harley roar to life and turned in time to see Willie crash through the flimsy wooden barrier. He was standing on the seat, aiming the bike like a guided missile. Powered by its 1340cc engine, it hit the ramp and hurtled up the bridge. As it shot off the end Willie leapt off the seat and dropped out of sight.

For a second the bike continued to climb. Scribing a perfect arc, it shot across the water and disappeared through *Temptress*'s wing-bridge door. Jammed at full throttle, its rear tire bit into the deck, causing the machine to wheelie as it ricocheted off the walls in the narrow confines of the wheelhouse. The front end caught the helmsman in the groin, tossing him over the chromed headlight and onto the handlebars, goring him like a rampaging bull.

Without losing speed, the bike roared across the wheelhouse and out through the opposite door. It tore through the thin aluminum of the wing bridge, disemboweling its rider and carrying him into the channel in a shower of blood and flaming gasoline.

With no one at the helm the motor yacht was out of control. The bow sheered to the left and there was a shriek of tearing metal as she dragged her port side down the shattered concrete.

Pete ran to the edge of the channel and looked for Willie in the swirling tide. I concentrated on *Temptress,* watching as she headed toward the rocks at the edge of the channel. When I thought she was sure to run aground, she turned wildly to starboard and struck the last bridge support, her stern slamming against it with such force that it shook the whole rickety structure.

Suddenly, Snake Eyes appeared on the aft deck of the yacht. He looked over the stern and fired a short burst at the water with the Kalashnikov. Then he turned and looked forward as *Temptress* swung towards the rocks. He shouted and sprinted for the wheelhouse. As he ran, he caught sight of me on the road and sent a burst of automatic fire in my direction.

I dove for cover as slugs tore through the galvanized rail inches from my head.

From somewhere, Pete's automatic barked a few shots in reply.

In the silence that followed, I heard the harsh grinding of a bow thruster, as someone at the yacht's controls fought against wind and current to keep the vessel on course.

Pete threw himself down next to me and together we peered over the rail.

The yacht was still close to the rocks but the bow thruster was doing its job. Between that, and careful use of the twin props, she was making her way back into deep water when suddenly she lost speed.

I grabbed Pete and dragged him to his feet, but already it was too late. As we watched, *Temptress* recovered and disappeared around the bend at the end of the channel. Ahead lay the gap in the reef and the open sea.

"Aw shit." was all I could say.

Pete grinned. "What did you think of Evil Kerfuckin' Knievil, then?" he said. And before I could reply, the devil himself began bellowing from the far side of the bridge.

Pete took a look and, shaking his head, flicked a thumb in the direction of the noise.

Willie was standing outside the control booth. He held a large chunk of wood in one hand and the limp body of a man in the other. As if on cue, the limp form raised its head, which earned it a verbal rebuke and a sharp tap from the chunk of wood.

In the brief moment of heads up, I recognized the limp form as the guy who had raised the bridge; Willie must have scrambled up the bank and grabbed him before he could jump onto the fleeing yacht.

Willie shouted and waved his club in the direction of the inner lagoon where the dinghy from the *Lady* was making its way towards us through the chop.

Pete grabbed my arm and together we slithered down the bank and stumbled onto the bridge's small maintenance jetty as the dinghy motored alongside. Toby Ascari was driving. His dreadlocks were sheathed in a red, gold and green woolen hat and he was grinning from ear to ear.

He stepped out of the inflatable and dropped a clove-hitch over a rickety bollard. When he was sure the boat was secure, he looked up at the twisted remains of the bridge. "Holy shit!" he said.

"That's not very original coming from a guy with a degree in music, but then, looking at that, it is rather poetic," said Pete following Toby's gaze.

There was another shout from Willie but his words were carried away by the rising wind. His prisoner was now sitting at his feet with his arms around his knees, all resistance thrashed out of him by the two-by-four in Willie's meaty hand.

Pete ignored the shout and turned back to Toby. "What are you doing here? You shouldn't be seen with us."

Toby dropped his gaze from the bridge to the swirling waters of the channel, where the remains of the helmsman had attracted a school of hungry fish. "Holy shit!" he stammered again.

Another shout from Willie broke the spell and we bundled Toby back into the inflatable.

Pete went to the engine and pulled the starter cord. The current was still running hard to seaward and Pete had to crab the boat sideways towards the opposite bank. As we came near, Willie lifted his friend off the ground by his hair and kicked him into the dinghy. Then he jumped in behind him and gave him another crack with the lump of wood.

Toby opened his mouth to speak, but Pete beat him to it. "Holy shit," he said, then laughed and jammed the dinghy into gear.

By the time we covered the short distance to the *Lady,* the word was out, and what appeared to be the entire drinking population of St. Peters was swarming over the boat and dock. It was like a high-season Friday night. The only thing missing was music, and that was soon taken care of when someone ripped the covers off the three 500-watt speakers and powered them up.

Pete ran the dinghy alongside and stopped the motor. Willie grabbed the painter and climbed onto the *Lady*'s deck. He forced his way through the mob and secured the line to a metal cleat.

The old schooner was rolling, and it was impossible to tell if the motion was caused by the approaching storm or the crowd on deck, who were now partying with a vengeance.

We bundled our prisoner onboard. Pete grabbed his arms, I grabbed his legs and, with Willie clearing a path through the revelers, we made our way along the deck towards the companionway steps.

No one took a bit of notice, but in the state they were in, why would they? In St. Peters, the sight of two men dragging another across a bar room floor doesn't mean much. It's just time out in the battle between booze and brain. And had we stood on the cabin top, swung him between us and launched him over the rail, it would have only raised a cheer.

Before we disappeared below, Pete acknowledged a wave from Sammy, his head barman, who was grinning and clutching a fistful of dollars in one hand while balancing a full tray of drinks in the other.

We maneuvered our prisoner over the combing at the top of the steps and I asked Toby to stand guard and make sure no one followed us down.

"Hey, Turpin, is that you?" The shout came from the far side of the deck. "Happy fucking birthday, mate!"

The salutation was followed by a choir of coconutters singing: "Happy birthday to you happy birthday to you, a bridge and a hurricane, happy birthday to you." The refrain went on and on until it was drowned beneath shouts and cheers and the gulping of lethal-sized shots.

Willie shook his head. "Hear that, Dick? There's a fucking storm brewing, the bridge is giving the world the finger, bodies are turning up all over the place and half the population are partying themselves to death. Is this a great country or what." He slammed the hatch, which reduced the din to an acceptable roar.

We hauled our friend backwards down the companionway, doing our best to keep his head from bouncing off too many steps.

Willie led the way into the saloon. Pete and I followed and, to our astonishment, so did Glokani, who appeared out of the shadows with a MAC-10 in his hand and a seething look of hatred on his face.

"Oh, look now," said Willie, "and there's I thinking there are no rats in the bilge of the *Lucky Lady* and one crawls out."

"Shut the fuck up you Welsh arsehole," screamed Glokani and punctuated his demand by shaking the MAC-10 in Willie's face.

Gone was the suave look of the superyacht owner with diamonds to sell and a country to buy. True, he was still wearing Armani, but now his clothes looked like they'd done a few rounds at the thrift shop. A ragged hole at the elbow of his cream linen jacket was crusted with dried blood. Half moons of sweat ringed his armpits. The once immaculate knees of his pressed trousers were caked with a mixture of grass and mud and what could have been old oil or dog shit. The gold doubloon was missing, but the chain was still around his neck. From its position against his Adam's apple, the medallion could be hanging down his back, perhaps tossed there during headlong flight. A vein pumped in his right temple and his hands were unsteady. From his voice, and the look of him, he was a man on the edge.

We were close enough to rush him but if we did at least one of us would not survive the machine pistol's lethal spray.

"You just broke the first rule of engagement," I said. "If you intend to shoot someone then keep your weapon cocked at all times." My voice was far calmer than I felt and I thought for a second he might fall for it. But a quick glance at the gun told him I was lying and, although his shooting stance was all wrong, his trigger finger was in the right place. He had assessed the situation and though still shaking with rage, was slowly bringing himself under control. This could work to our advantage; then again it could put the stamp on our death warrants.

From the corner of my eye, I saw Pete take a small step to the left. Glokani immediately swung the gun towards him. "Lay your weapons on the floor. We'll do it one at a time, beginning with you."

Pete pulled the automatic from beneath his shirt and placed it on the floor.

"Slide the gun towards me and then kneel and face the bulkhead."

Again, Pete did as he was told.

Glokani stepped forward and kicked me in the back of the knee. "You next, gun on the floor, then get down on your knees next to your black buddy and face the bulkhead."

I lowered myself down next to Pete.

Glokani had a serious score to settle with Willie and glared at him across the barrel of the gun.

Willie glared back.

"Now you, arsehole, on the ground." He was taking no chances with Willie, and took two steps back to open up his field of fire.

"Willie, don't say a word, just do it," I said.

Willie grunted and, with no weapon to dispose of, began lowering himself into a kneeling position on my right.

Without warning, Glokani drove his foot into the back of Willie's neck, smashing his face against the bulkhead with a sickening crunch. The kick spun Willie's head and the left side of his face took the impact. His cheek burst like a ripe tomato and with a long moan he slid to the floor, leaving a jagged gash in the mahogany and varnishing it with gore.

In the time it took Willie's head to spoil the woodwork, Glokani had leapt back into the middle of the cabin. "They still follow your fucking orders don't they, Turpin. Well, I'm giving the orders now. You say you kill people who hurt your friends. What about it, want to try your luck?

When I didn't reply, he drove a vicious kick into the belly of our prisoner who, until then, had been lying quietly by the table.

I risked a quick look and saw him place the muzzle of his gun against the man's head. The kick in the guts had brought him round or, perhaps like a good soldier, he'd been playing dead. Whatever his previous condition he was now wide-awake, gripping his stomach with both hands, and staring at Glokani in terror.

"If you listen, you might still get the boat and the diamonds back," I said, thinking it might stop him from shooting the guy.

It was a big mistake.

"I told you to shut up, Turpin. You fucked up my operation and you're on borrowed time. In fact take a look, so you know what's coming." He jammed his right foot across the guy's throat and with a quick downward chop, drove the muzzle of the gun through his lips, shattering his teeth and driving them back into his gullet.

The guy jackknifed off the floor and clawed at the gun. He was bleeding and choking, and as he thrashed about in agony, Glokani's foot began to slip. It gave him no option but to pull the trigger and finish it.

"If you kill him I swear you'll lose any chance of getting anything back!" I yelled and jumped to my feet.

"I told you to stay where you are," Glokani yelled back. He fought to control the writhing man but something in his eyes told me that what I said had registered. Suddenly, he yanked the barrel out of the guy's mouth, ripping apart a cheek with the open sight.

The wounded man hauled himself to his knees, spitting teeth and spraying a frothy mix of air and blood in all directions.

Glokani swung the gun around.

"Jesus," I spat, "you're a fucking animal."

"Just say your piece, Turpin."

"I'm saying nothing until you let us help Willie, and the poor bastard whose mouth you've ruined. Pull anymore stunts like that and you can wave your diamonds goodbye."

"This better be fucking good …" he snarled.

Before he could say more, Pete stood up and strode out of the cabin.

Glockani briefly tracked him with the MAC-10 then had second thoughts and pointed the gun at me.

Pete returned carrying a first aid kit and did what he could for gummy.

I went to help Willie. As I squatted next to him, he opened one eye. “Do I kill the bastard now, or later?” he hissed.

“Later,” I said, “we’re going after *Temptress.*”

33

Boots hammered along the passageway. On this Caribbean island, only those in authority wore boots. That they had managed to get past Toby without him shouting a warning meant serious friend or dangerous foe.

Glokani hid the MAC-10 behind his back. Pete scooped up the two pistols, tossed one to me and slid the other into his waistband.

There was a moment of relief as sergeant Ascari stormed through the door, but it was short-lived when Glokani whipped out the MAC-10 and Pete drew his automatic.

My reaction was a fraction slower.

The room froze.

Ascari took in the scene, his eyes flicking from the MAC-10 pointing at his head, to our pistols aimed at Glokani's. He glanced at Willie, and over to where the guy with the broken mouth was moaning and pushing his teeth around with his tongue.

There was the sound of breaking glass on the deck above. Someone laughed and the music cranked up a notch.

"Quite a party you're having, Dick." Ascari's voice was calm. He took a step forward, closing the distance between himself and the end of Glokani's gun. "Do you think we can lower the weapons, gentlemen?" No one moved, so he tried again. "Look, you haven't got long before the men and women of our gallant Defense Force are all over the boat."

Glokani slowly lowered the MAC until it was under Ascari's chin. Using the end of the barrel, he forced his head back, lifting him onto his toes.

I wanted to shoot the bastard, but all sorts of things could go wrong. I was six feet away and unlikely to miss, but even if I did manage to put one through his head, he could pull the trigger in a reflex action and we'd have two lots of brain omelet on the wall. Pete must have had the same thought, because he nodded, and together we lowered our guns.

Ascari, his head forced back at the end of Glokani's gun, saw us lower our weapons and wrapped the fingers of his right hand around the stubby barrel of the MAC-10 and coolly forced it down until it pointed at the floor.

We held our breath.

"So, now we're all being good boy scouts, when do we go after 'em?" said Willie, breaking the silence. He glared at Glokani then pulled the red bandana out of his pocket, wrung out the water, and began dabbing at the gash on his cheek.

"Go after them!" shouted Glokani. "Just how do you propose to do that? In your rubber fucking dinghy? They're gone, *Temptress* can motor at seventeen knots; she'll be twenty-five miles away by now going God knows where. You burned-out morons let her go."

Speech over, he slumped down on to the settee and stared at his feet. He dangled the gun between his knees, holding it loosely with both hands. He was the picture of misery, a man who'd gambled and lost—lost his son, lost his yacht, and lost his diamonds. With a bit of luck, the miserable shit would soon lose his life but for now we might need him, so we let him live.

"I think happy boy is wrong," said Pete, throwing a disgusted look towards the settee. "At one time the yacht might have been good for seventeen knots, but I don't think she is now. She hit something in the channel. My guess is that she clipped her port propeller on a rock at the edge of the breakwater. Dick and I saw her lurch and slow down. If she bent a blade, they'll have to stop the port engine or she'll shake herself to bits. One thing for sure, if the prop is damaged, there's no way they can outrun this storm."

While Pete was talking, Willie dug a bottle of rum out of a locker and poured a large slug into a glass. He crouched down and offered it to Gummy. Unsure of what was coming next, the injured man shuffled backwards like a lobster retreating under a rock. When he could go no further, he drew his knees up under his chin and sat there whimpering.

Willie hesitated then again offered him the glass. "Steady on, boyo. I only want your name," he said.

The man looked at him and spat gore into a handkerchief. He seemed to be working on a vicious reply then thought better of it and reached for the glass. "Fisher," he mumbled, "John Fisher."

The word came out 'Fither' but only Glokani laughed, which wiped more points off the animal's scorecard.

Fisher brought the rum to his lips.

"Go easy with that," said Willie. "It'll hurt like hell. But the chances of you seeing a dentist right now are pretty slim, so if I were you I'd rinse your mouth with half of it and swallow the rest."

Fisher nodded and tossed the rum into his mouth. He gagged then coughed and before he could get the handkerchief back to his lips, sprayed the cabin with rum, blood, and bits of teeth.

Once the coughing subsided he took another pull and swallowed hard. A long moan escaped his lips. He dropped the glass, clutched his forehead with one hand and twisted the other into a fist and jammed it against his mouth. We looked away as tears seeped between his fingers and ran down his cheeks.

Willie refilled the glass, gulped it down, and passed the bottle to Pete. Then he turned his icy stare on Glokani. "Before he died, Mohamed told us that Snake Eyes was heading for the Bahamas. That's over five hundred miles away. He had to know that somebody would track them down before they were even halfway there."

Glokani was forming a reply when Fisher began to mumble and twirl a finger in the air.

Pete crouched down beside him. Fisher spoke again, forcing the words out of the side of his damaged mouth.

Fisher fell silent and Pete stood up. "Helicopter. He says they never planned on taking *Temptress,* but the helicopter was low on fuel and they knew they'd never be allowed to refuel here."

"Then he's made a big mistake," said Sergeant Ascari. "Even if *Temptress* can make it to another island, no one will refuel the yacht or the chopper. And even if someone did agree to sell them fuel, all the harbors and airports in the area are locked down for the storm. There's nowhere for them to run. The Defense Force broadcast their description over an hour ago. Once the storm's over, every police and military vessel in the Caribbean will be looking for them."

Pete walked to the table and looked down at the chart that he'd unrolled earlier. He reached for a pencil and a set of parallel rules. All eyes were on him as he drew a line on the chart and measured it with a pair of brass dividers. When he was satisfied, he placed the open dividers against the latitude scale at the edge of the chart, keeping them opposite the line he had drawn to ensure accuracy. He picked up a notepad, did a quick calculation, and then wrote something on the chart.

Ascari moved to the table and looked at what Pete had written. They spoke for a few moments and Ascari nodded in agreement.

Pete turned. "Mexican Hat," he said. "They're heading for Mexican Hat."

Glokani shot out of his chair like he'd been jabbed in the scrotum with a cattle prod. "What good is that going to do them?" he roared. "What the fuck are you talking about? He didn't seem to know what to do with his gun, so he waved it about.

I gave him a look of contempt.

Then, to really piss him off, I told him.

34

Mexican Hat is a small, rocky island about seventy miles to the northwest of St. Peters. Approximately one mile long and three-quarters of a mile wide, the center of the island is dominated by a large bluff surrounded by tropical rain forest. On its eastern side, the bluff is shear and almost impossible to climb. However, on its western side, away from the prevailing wind, a track winds its way up to a small plateau a hundred and forty feet above sea level. On it stands the highest lighthouse in the Caribbean.

The Spanish discovered the island around 1520, and named it Los Pane de Sucre—Sugar Loaf Rock. By 1560, conquistadors had constructed a beacon on the plateau and established a settlement, complete with a platoon of soldiers and a priest.

The job of the priest was to take care of the spiritual needs of the troops and convert any passing Indians to the faith. The job of the troops was to capture passing Indians for the priest and keep the fire in the beacon lit, so that King Philip's ships could safely make their ponderous way carrying treasure from the New World to the old.

Legend has it that in the seventeenth century the privateer Edward Teach—or Blackbeard, as he came to be known—had marooned some of his cutthroats on the island after they fell out over treasure looted from Hispaniola. Over the years adventurers, using maps bought in bars or bequeathed in wills, have dug up huge tracts of the island, but nothing has ever been found.

When piracy followed Spain into decline, the island drifted back into obscurity, but not for long. The rise of the British Empire brought the tiny island to the notice of the High Lords of the Admiralty. Recognizing its strategic importance, they sent a company of engineers to Los Pane de Sucre, and in 1837 built a stone lighthouse and a small dwelling.

The Brits also re-surveyed the island and discovered it was nearly a mile from its charted position. Treating it as a new discovery, they renamed the island Mexican Hat.

The first lighthouse stood for fifty years before it was destroyed by the Great Hurricane of 1887. For two years, the lighthouse lay in ruins. Then, one night, a British warship attempting to fight its way into the Anegada Passage during a storm, ran on to the island and was lost with all hands. Within months of learning about the loss of his majesty's ship, the British Admiralty ordered the lighthouse rebuilt. They also built a substantial cottage to house a permanent crew, whose job it was to look after the new kerosene light with its state-of-the-art Fresnel lens.

By tradition, the lighthouse keepers came from the island of Anguilla, and were stationed on the island for three months at a time. Although often they were forced to stay longer if landing at the tiny cove on the island's southwestern tip was made impossible by heavy seas.

In 1990, the British Lighthouse Authority, Trinity House, sent a ship to the island during the calmer months of summer. Over a period of eight weeks, their engineers removed the cumbersome old kerosene light and replaced it with one powered by electricity.

They also built a helicopter landing pad at the base of the bluff.

When Trinity House sailed away, the men from Anguilla locked the cottage for the last time and sailed away with them, leaving behind the first fully automated lighthouse in the Caribbean.

By the time I finished my explanation; Glokani was standing next to Pete and looking down at the chart. "Nice fucking history lesson," he sneered, "but what the hell has it got to do with us?"

Looks told me that his use of the word 'us' instead of 'me' hadn't gone unnoticed; however, no one made a comment. Instead, Willie pushed Glokani out of the way and tapped the chart with his finger. "You should take more notice of what the teacher tells you, boyo. The light is fully automatic but contractors fly in every few months to service it. In case of emergencies, there's a supply of fuel there for the chopper. If Snake Eyes makes it to the island ahead of the storm, and can get ashore, you can kiss your diamonds, and the freak that makes them, goodbye."

Glokani started to speak but his words were lost in a burst of noise from the deck above. The party was spinning out of control, the rock 'n' roll was deafening, and whatever kind of stomping dance they had going was causing the yacht's old deck beams to creek and groan.

As usual, during one of the *Lady's* wild parties, the action was making its way below. Along the corridor, Toby was doing his best to convince a hysterical woman that her husband was definitely not in one of the cabins with two of her friends. He had just about persuaded her to rejoin the party when faintly, above the din, we heard the sound of an approaching siren.

The partygoers heard it, too, and the dancing stopped. By the multiple notes, it was obvious the siren wasn't alone. This was too much for the coconutters. They let out a mighty cheer and cranked up the music until they were stomping to more decibels than let rip by a Boeing 757 on takeoff.

Ascari made a dash for the door and ran into Toby coming the other way. "Which direction are they coming from?" he demanded.

Toby's face split into a grin. "East," he replied. "They're on the wrong side of the bridge."

Ascari squeezed past him, bolted along the corridor, and up the companionway steps.

Glokani leveled his gun and set off after him.

He'd almost reached the door when Willie stiff-armed him across the windpipe and wrenched the MAC-10 from his hands. Glokani clutched his throat and staggered around like a drunken man, then let out a stream of gurgling curses and fell to the floor in a heap. When he continued to curse and lash out with his feet, Willie threatened to let Fisher kick his teeth in. That shut him up and he looked nervously at Fisher who gave him an evil bloody grin.

The sound of boots announced the sergeant's return. "It's the Defense Force, they're at the far side of the bridge with three trucks, and there are more on the way."

"Where are the regular cops?" said Pete.

Ascari looked at me before he replied. "The whole island knows that Chopstick is dead. The cops won't be coming; those who aren't under arrest have fled. You're in the middle of a coup. The people are pouring out of the Meadowlands and our Defense Force is backing them. It's been a long time in coming, but we've finally had enough of the corruption. The government is no longer in charge, we are!"

For one giddy moment, I thought he meant Willie, Pete and me, but when Toby grinned at his father and produced an automatic from behind his back, something told me I could be wrong.

While his son kept us covered, Ascari pulled the handcuffs off his belt and strode towards me. "I am arresting you on suspicion of murder. Anything you say may be written down and used against you in a court of law. Do you understand what I am saying?"

"There you go," Glokani gurgled with glee. "You're a loser, Turpin, just like your friends. You're a fucking loser!" He was still howling when Ascari yanked him to his feet, spun him around, forced his hands behind his back and snapped the bracelets on.

After dragging the ranting Diamond King away and locking him in one of the cabins, Ascari strode back into the saloon and took charge. "I could just as easily have arrested you three cut throats; in fact the new government will probably demand it," he said.

He looked at each of us in turn and then went into a rapid explanation of what was going on, leaving us in no doubt that, for better or worse, St. Peters would never be the same again.

We listened and thought he had finished, but we were wrong. He whaled into us pointing out that, like most foreigners on the island, we had chosen to ignore what was going on and party ourselves into the ground instead.

I was about to deny it when two naked men sailed past the porthole and landed in the lagoon. A half-naked woman followed.

We stood there grinning while Ascari carried on in disgust.

He said we were little better than the scumbags who lived on the hill who, by the way, were all on their way to jail. Corruption was out, honesty was in, and the bent politicos were being given the choice: leave the island and your ill-gotten gains behind or face charges.

For one moment, I thought he was going to start punching the air and shouting Viva Zapata, but as quickly as it started, the speechifying stopped, and he turned toward us with a shrug.

"We've been planning this coup for over a year, but someone," he said, looking at Willie, "kick-started it by taking care of Chopstick. We were forced to act before the scumbags replaced him. We weren't ready but thanks to … whoever … there is no stopping it now."

Another naked drunk splashed into the water alongside.

Ascari walked to the porthole and looked out. When he turned back to face the room, I caught the ghost of a smile. "We do, however, have a problem that I think the three of you might be able to help us with. And in so doing, perhaps help yourselves."

"Where have I heard that crap before?" Willie mumbled.

Ascari ignored him and carried on. Talking quickly now, as though short of time. "We've had good people inside the government watching the Minister of Finance, Van Norte, for years. The minister's been siphoning off government funds and stashing it in offshore accounts. There's also a substantial amount of cash missing from the central bank and the treasury. Both were under Van Norte's direct control."

"What's a substantial amount?" I said.

He hesitated, looking at each of us in turn.

"Fifty million."

Willie let out a soft whistle as Ascari went on.

"We needed more time to get people in place before we toppled the regime. But it's too late for that now and unless we keep our heads there will be anarchy. If the new government is bankrupt from the start, then it's over already. Within months we'll have the same old corruption, or worse. When news of this coup gets out, it will kill our tourist industry unless we can control it and keep it low key. Without the return of those funds, we don't stand a chance."

"Why not get hold of Van Norte? He's the key to your problems," said Willie.

"Sorry, Willie's not usually as dumb as this; it must be the bump on the head." I said, and turned to Pete who was grinning widely.

"My guess is that Van Norte is on *Temptress*," said Pete. He leaned back against the chart table and folded his arms.

We all looked at the Welshman.

For once, Willie was lost for words. His only reason for going after *Temptress* was to administer his own kind of justice to Snake Eyes and the cutthroats responsible for Susie's death.

"There's no need to guess," said Ascari. We know for sure that Van Norte is onboard. If they make it to Mexican Hat, and refuel the helicopter, we'll lose him and the future prosperity of our island for years to come."

"What are you suggesting?" I asked, certain of what he was about to say.

"We … I mean, the new government that is, need a boat with a competent crew to go after him." His eyes were shining with hope, but when we didn't respond, he sank into a leather chair next to the chart table and stared at the deck overhead. More than a minute went by. Finally he stood and headed for the door. "Sorry. This is nothing to do with you; I'd no right to ask."

As he passed, Pete put his hand out and stopped him. "Wait," he said and threw me a look.

I knew that look and felt the familiar thrill. Even so, I felt obliged to say it. "It's your boat, Pete. There's a storm brewing and the *Lady* hasn't been to sea in those kind of conditions for years. We could wait for the storm to pass and then go."

Pete thought it over then nodded towards Willie. "What do you think?" he said.

"I say we get the sail covers off and the motor cranked up before you two old farts start looking for your pipes and slippers. We've a score to settle and fifty million bucks to find." He held out his hand.

Pete looked from Willie to me, then reached across and took the ignition key off the hook above the chart table and tossed it in the air.

Willie grabbed it in his fist, let out a war cry, and bolted for the door.

35

We had about two hours of daylight left if we were to make it through the reef before dark. In breaking seas, attempting the passage after dark would be suicide.

Anyone who has readied a yacht for sea will know how long the preparations take. Trying to get a one hundred and ten foot floating bar ready for sea in the face of a storm, while a full-on party is happening on deck, rewrites the book of seamanship.

During the tourist season the *Lady* goes to sea about twice a month, when Pete and Willie take a select number of guests to a small offshore island, where they dive or snorkel and enjoy a barbeque on the beach. This keeps the boat in sailing trim, although the insurance company insists they stay within five miles of the coast and avoid going out in winds above eighteen knots.

Every couple of weeks, Pete hires a diver from Willie's scuba shop to go under the boat and make sure the propeller and the bottom of the hull are clean. He does this all year round, so the boat is always ready to move.

The sails, however, are a different story. The main and foresail were still on the booms, but Pete had removed the jibs and stowed them in the forepeak ahead of the hurricane season. Each sail weighed around two hundred pounds, and we would need some help get to get them back on deck and hanked to the stays.

Before the jibs could be brought up from below, the giant deck awning and the strings of colored lights that hung between the masts had to come down. Ascari went below to get out of his uniform and into a pair of shorts and an Hawaiian shirt he borrowed from Pete. It was the only way he was going to get any of the coconutters to listen to him.

Pete found Sammy and together they press-ganged those who were not too drunk into joining the crew. The rest he sent ashore, having given them beers and bottles of rum and orders to keep out of the way. There was some argument when he unplugged the music but this quieted down once Willie got the engine running and the partiers realized we were serious about leaving the dock.

We talked it over and agreed to release Glokani and put him to work, although we warned him to stay well away from Willie and Fisher.

Everything loose was stowed or tied down. Cases of booze were thrown onto the dock then trundled away on carts and locked in the old shipping container. The sun awning came down with a run, burying half a dozen people who rolled around beneath it shrieking like kids at Hallowe'en.

Willie came up from the engine room wiping his hands on an oily rag and reported all was well below.

Next we hauled the sails out of the forepeak. Pete opened the hatch and fastened back the doors. Willie stepped over the combing and went down the ladder, taking the end of a halyard with him. He fastened the stainless steel snap-shackle to the lashing around the sail and then waved to Pete.

Pete threw a couple of turns around the capstan on the hydraulic anchor winch and kicked it into gear. With two people guiding it, the jib made its way smoothly up through the hatch and onto the deck. The volunteers then hauled the stiff canvas out along the bowsprit and hanked it to the stay.

After making sure that the sheets were led through the correct blocks, and the sail was securely lashed to the bowsprit, we maneuvered the staysail up through the hatch and hanked it to the inner forestay.

The sun was now low in the sky and the clouds on the horizon had an oily pallor that made you feel queasy. It was obvious by the fluttering of the tell-tails attached to the rigging that the wind had backed a point to the north, which meant the center of the storm was on the move.

According to Buys Ballot's law for finding the center of low pressure in the Northern Hemisphere, when you turn your back on the wind, the low is to your left. Mister Buys Ballot's rule is fairly accurate in higher latitudes but perhaps a bit shaky further south.

According to Pete's law for finding the center of low pressure, you listened to the local rock and blues station when it broadcast the weather on the hour. We left Ascari and Willie to take care of the stowing on deck and went below. Pete turned on the radio just as the latest weather update came through. Although island radio stations received their information from the hurricane center in Miami, it's comforting to know that the local announcers are facing the tempest with you. If a storm does go over the island then they get the shit kicked out of them too, and that makes everyone feel better.

This evening's announcer was a castaway from a famous rock and blues station in New York, and he played the best music around. The guy didn't know jack about ships and the sea, but he was good entertainment. Tonight he introduced the forecast by playing *Storm Warning* by Bonnie Raitt. As the music began to fade, he struck a match, inhaled deeply on a cigarette, and moved into the forecast. He gave the position of the storm—give or take a hundred miles—admitting he wasn't sure of where it was going because he'd lost the bit of paper it was written on, but he thought it might be heading north. He said that over the last few hours the central pressure had remained the same, so the storm had not intensified and things were pretty cool.

We heard him take another deep pull on whatever it was he was smoking.

"This is for all you sailor types out there, know what I mean," he said and exhaled as Dillon's *Blowin' in the Wind* crackled from the speaker.

We burst out laughing. "I think you might be right, Dick. We'll take our chances with Mr. Buys." Pete switched off the radio.

"You make everything a fucking game," said Glokani from the door. His voice, still raspy from Willie's punch, now matched his attitude. "You're about as much good as this wreck of a ship and that fucked up arsehole on the radio. How are you going to get through the bridge? Have you thought about that? The span is taking up half the channel, maybe you're going to limbo under it!" He tried to laugh but his damaged throat gave out and it ended in a fit of coughing.

Ascari pushed him out of the way and stepped through the door. He was wearing his service revolver over Pete's Hawaiian shirt, and he'd strapped on his boots. Toby stood behind him in his wooly hat. They looked at us expectantly and by their faces I knew there was hope for the island yet.

The light in the cabin had faded. We needed at least thirty minutes to get to the gap in the reef, and were now cutting it fine. Suddenly the engine changed note and the boat lurched forward.

"That's Willie checking the gearbox, I guess it's now or never," said Pete, and together we headed for the companionway steps.

36

The sky overhead was streaked with crimson mares' tails that streamed like firebrands from east to west. Long before the advent of satellites and long-range weather forecasts, mares' tales and the voodoo man's lumbago were the only warnings of an approaching tropical storm. I was wondering if the ache in my knee was trying to tell me something when a gust of wind moaned through the rigging, driving the hull against the old truck tires that protected it from the rough edges of the dock.

I made my way to the starboard rail and looked across the lagoon towards the mangroves on the far shore. Now the wind had backed to the north, it was far more erratic. From this direction, it could no longer flow smoothly over the mountains, but entered the narrow valleys where it accelerated before blasting across the lagoon in tremendous gusts. The time between gusts was impossible to figure. The lulls could last a few minutes or a few seconds.

We were now in a lull and the waters of the lagoon were calm. Yet even as I watched, the palm trees beyond the far shore began to bend as the leading edge of a violent downdraft roared out of a gully in the hills and landed amongst them. The wind charged across the abandoned sugarcane fields, flattening the pampas grass, before tearing through the mangroves at the water's edge and out onto the lagoon. Moments later it pounced on the *Lady,* slammed her against the dock and forced her over in submission. I staggered and grabbed the shrouds. As quickly as it arrived, the gust was gone, and the boat stood upright. Across the lagoon all was again calm.

I looked aft to where Pete stood at the wheel. Then walked across to the port side and watched as Willie mustered the crew. Ascari, I could rely on. Toby, I didn't really know, but he was Ascari's son, so I reckoned I could count on him, too. Against my better judgment, we were taking Glokani along, but only because he was familiar with *Temptress* and knew something about her crew. Glokani had his own agenda that he thought we were too stupid to know about. I would kill him if he stepped out of line.

We were also taking Fisher. There was something about Fisher that touched a chord in me. Perhaps, like the rest of us, he was caught up in something that had spun out of control and deserved another chance. I would kill him, too, if he proved me wrong.

Willie joined me at the gangway amidships. "Glokani's right. We might be ready, but how are we going to get the boat past the bridge?" he said.

"We're going to take your good friend's advice and limbo."

"What the fuck!"

"Trust me. Get as many people as possible off the dock and onto the boat, get Toby to help you. Tell them they have to be able to swim because once we clear the breakwater they're going to have to jump and swim to the beach. Give Sammy the key to the container and tell him there's an hour's free booze for anyone who helps. Tell him it's on me. Then get yourself into the dinghy and get ready to push our bows around when we cast off."

I thought for a second he was going to argue, but then he saluted, laughed, shouted something in Welsh, and sprinted down the gangway and along the dock.

I like to think that it was as much for the promise of adventure as the free booze, but within minutes we had about fifty people on the boat. Granted, half of them were too drunk to care, but as long as they could swim they would be okay.

Once our limbo crew had settled down, I hauled the gangway onboard then closed the door in the bulwarks and latched the cap rail in place.

Pete walked to the starboard side and checked that none of the naked coconuters were still paddling around. Satisfied, he gave the order to remove the fore-spring and shorten up on the lines.

Ascari tossed the spring onto the dock then jogged aft to pick up the stern line. He took a couple off turns off the cleat then, gripping the coils of rope in his left hand, turned and looked at Pete.

The boat was now held to the dock by just three lines. Pete walked to the port side and looked down to where Willie held the nose of the dinghy pressed against the bow. He waited for Willie to acknowledge his wave and then stepped back to the wheel. He placed his right hand on the engine control attached to the starboard side of the binnacle and looked across the water towards the mountains.

We waited for the order to let go, but Pete made a hold motion with his fist and a few seconds later a gust of wind slammed us against the dock. As the gust eased, he ordered Toby to drop the forward line. Immediately it was free the outboard motor began to rev—then labour—as Willie drove the inflatable against the bow.

Aft, Ascari acknowledged Pete's wave and let go the stern line. As soon as it was clear, Pete put the engine in reverse and backed down hard against the remaining spring. He increased the engine revs and the three blades on the fifteen inch propeller bit deep into the water, sucking down the stern. Under heavy load the engine blew out a stream of black exhaust smoke. Caught by the wind it curled over the rail and drifted across the deck in a sooty cloud.

At the far side of the lagoon the next powerful gust roared out of the valleys and across the cane fields. Pete watched it hit the water and pushed the throttle to the stops.

Our bows began to inch to starboard as our stern pivoted against the truck tires that hung from chains at the end of the dock.

The three-inch nylon spring reached its limit and groaned in anguish.

Two of the tires began to slip then shot upwards and the *Lady*'s stern ploughed into the dock. Pete kept the throttle wide open, increasing the pressure and sending wood splinters scything through the air.

I could hear the outboard screaming as Willie drove the bows further out. The gap began to widen, slowed, and then stopped.

The gust was less than five hundred yards away when Pete rammed the engine full ahead and screamed for Ascari to let go the spring.

Nothing happened.

Then, imperceptibly, the boat began to move. The sudden flow of water caused the rudder to grip and the stern slammed back into the dock. Low down, the jagged end of a steel piling snagged the transom and gouged a chunk of oak out of the hull. Pete heard it go but kept the throttle wide open. When he was confident the boat had enough way on, he put the rudder amidships.

We were picking up speed when the gust hit the starboard bow and the whole boat began to vibrate. The weight of the boat was enough to keep us moving but it wasn't enough to carry our bows through the eye of the wind.

There are times at sea when you have done all you can and then, like much in life, it comes down to luck. In the books you can find complex equations about speed and mass and force, but right now it was simple: we were fucked or we weren't.

Although the sound of the outboard motor was overpowered by the terrified shrieks from the crowd on deck, I knew for sure that Willie was still pushing.

The wind was now blowing from dead ahead and we were in danger of making sternway. If that happened we would be thrown against the dock with such force it would be a long time before the *Lady* went to sea again.

Tormented, the rigging began to shake and moan as the wind tongued one bow and then the other. Another massive gust swept across the deck. I felt the boat stagger and fall back. The coco-nutters began to panic. A guy launched himself at the rail and I tackled him and brought him down. It was like trying to control lemmings: one goes and they all go.

Maybe it was Willie's relentless pushing, or perhaps the 18O HP Gardner diesel finally won, for suddenly the shaking stopped and our bows passed through the eye of the wind. A great shout went up as the bowsprit fell away to starboard. Our stern kissed the dock for the last time and we were clear.

The whole episode had taken less than three minutes, yet it felt like an hour.

Now we had to maneuver around the bridge.

37

It was almost dark by the time we hauled Willie and the dinghy onboard and began edging our way down the channel towards the twisted remains of the bridge.

The torn metal looked quite artistic against the fading light. I wished the same could be said for the men of the St. Peters Defense Force who began tracking us with their guns the minute they had us in sight.

If our volunteer crew were scared before, they were terrified now.

Pete knocked the engine out of gear and came forward to where Willie and I stood next to the mainmast. We had about three hundred yards to go and, with the tide still ebbing strongly, less than a hundred yards before we were inextricably committed to passing beneath the bridge.

"You think they're waiting for the limbo show or are they going to blow us all to hell?" said Willie.

Ascari joined us at the mast. He had thrown off the glad rags and was back in full police uniform. "Just do what it takes to get us through the bridge and leave the rest to me," he said.

Willie took him at his word. "Show time," he beamed and went off to organize the dancers.

I stood alongside Pete as he carefully eyed the gap between the top of the bridge and the mangled concrete buttress on the left of channel. "Your idea is just crazy enough to work," he said. Then he bent down and pulled the K-Bar out of its sheath and pointed to the lanyards that attached the eyes of the rigging wire to the metal chain-plates along the starboard side. "Last resort, Dick. If you have to, cut the rigging free."

Pete made it back to the wheel just as the current took us in its grip. Now we had no place left to go but forward.

I heard Willie shout and turned to see our mob of human ballast rush towards the port rail. This gave the *Lady* a thirty degree list. Some of the gang couldn't resist and were mooning the cops. It was hardly the voyage out of the lagoon that I had envisaged on my birthday but it came close.

The moment the bowsprit drew level with the bridge, Ascari began addressing the leader of the troops up on the road in rapid Patois. He kept the conversation going by walking aft at three knots.

I took little notice of what he was saying and kept my eyes glued to the rigging on the foremast, which cleared the jagged edge of the broken span with less than a foot to spare.

Safely past the first hurdle I ran aft towards the main mast, passing a sour-faced Glokani along the way.

The main mast was higher than the foremast by almost eight feet. This put the rigging much nearer to the damaged span. It was impossible to gauge the distance in the gloom but I knew it would be close.

Ascari trotted by. He seemed oblivious to the danger and continued his shouted conversation with the officer on the road.

We were almost abeam of the buttress. I took a step back to get a better view and that's when I saw the end of the broken handrail at the very top of the bridge. Before I could slash through the lanyard, the jagged metal hooked the galvanized rigging and drew it out like a bow string. The mast began to bend and I knew it would snap. Suddenly there was a loud twang followed by a shower of rust, and we were clear.

Nothing could have prepared me for what came next: the Defense Force began to cheer. Their cheering was picked up by our human ballast and before long it was all you could hear.

Too surprised to join in, I ran to the rigging wire and gave it a pull. It was slacker than it should be but I couldn't see any damage. The rigging could be easily retightened by loosening the rope lanyard and then hauling it tight and re-lashing it.

Willie must have seen me heaving on the stay because he appeared at my elbow and handed me a pair of binoculars. I thanked him and brought them to my eyes. Starting at the crosstrees, I began a careful inspection, slowly working my way up until I reached the point where the rigging was secured to the top of the mast. I saw nothing unusual and by the time I lowered the binoculars, Willie had the lanyard undone and was re-tightening the stay.

It was almost dark as I pushed through the crowd and joined Pete at the wheel. He took the binoculars and, with a shrug, slid them back into the teak box at the side of the wheel.

We were approaching the outer end of the breakwater and the boat had taken on a slight roll. Pete waited until we had cleared the last of the rocks then turned to port, out of the buoyed channel, and ran the boat south parallel to the beach. He motored towards the shallows, going as close as he dare. When he could go no further, he brought the revs down to idle and knocked the engine out of gear.

I let our speed bleed off then opened the entry port for our volunteers. Hooting and hollering they tumbled off the *Lady* and swam or doggy-paddled towards the beach and another round of drinks. We waited until everyone was safely ashore then Pete turned the boat around and motored back towards the narrow channel leading to the pass in the outer reef.

The channel is dredged to thirty feet, and although well buoyed, you could never count on the lights working or all the marks being in place. Where the channel cuts through the reef, it forms a giant step that plunges straight down to a depth of sixty feet. In normal trade wind conditions, an occasional swell might roll in over the step. But tonight, with a storm offshore and the wind east of north, the swells marching in from the far ocean were being driven upwards and the step was a devil's cauldron of breaking seas.

38

When she was built, few wooden boats the size of the *Lucky Lady* would have been as strong. Perhaps there were some amongst those designed to sail through the ice of higher latitudes, but most of those are gone.

In the last few years, advances in restoration technology have saved many rotten and worm-eaten wooden yachts from the breaker's yard. The costs are astronomical and beautifully restored yachts are now the latest status symbol of the super rich.

Every year scouts for some wealthy wannabe classic yacht owner would corner Pete at the bar and offer him wads of cash for the *Lady*. Their appearance was cause for great celebration. Drinks flowed and invitations to fine restaurants followed, and Pete always took along his two trusted assistants who knew *everything* about the boat, and whose advice he followed to the letter. Of course, he had no intention of selling, but for a week we all ate well and his bar receipts went through the roof.

Some of the scouts even caught on to the scam but enjoyed themselves so much they came back every year. On their return they usually brought their wives or girlfriends. Pete would forge a hotel receipt and let them sleep in one of the cabins for free. Then for a week or more we'd all party ourselves stupid on their expense account.

When they left, Pete would laugh and go back to his island time yacht restoration, which entailed digging out patches of rot, chipping rust, and breaking every hour for a swim and a beer.

As we motored down the channel, I wished he'd left out the swim and the beer. Ahead, the entire horizon was an unbroken line of white water and if not for the buoys it would be impossible, in the dim light, to pinpoint the gap in the reef.

Further out the wind was stronger. It was blowing around thirty knots from the nor-nor-east and, with a quarter of a mile to go before we reached the open sea, the boat was already corkscrewing and plunging her bowsprit into the waves.

I had one arm around the starboard cap-shroud and was trying to identify the entrance when Willie tapped me on the shoulder. "Skipper wants us aft, boyo, he's about to play Blackbeard."

"How come you're so happy?" I said. "Have you taken a look ahead?"

"Yeah," he laughed, "but I'm low in the ranks. Shit like that's for the officers to sort out."

I followed him back to the wheel where the rest of the crew had gathered around Pete.

Pete cut straight to the chase.

"Dick, Willie, we've got to get some sail on. I don't want to run through the cut under engine alone. If we hug the starboard side of the channel then we should carry the wind on our beam all the way through. I'll keep her as far to windward as possible. That way we can free off a bit if we have to. Let's tuck a reef in the mains'l and hoist that first, then we'll run up the two headsails. She'll be pitching like hell until we clear the ledge and get into deep water, so I want everyone tied on."

Willie and I climbed on to the doghouse roof and moved towards the boom.

Pete pulled the throttle back and called Toby to the wheel. "Motor her slowly into the wind," he said. "Can you do that?"

Toby looked at the wheel and then gripped the spokes with both hands.

Pete waited until Toby was comfortable and then joined us on the doghouse roof and together we began throwing the gaskets off the mains'l. Once it was free, we hooked the first reef cringle over the hook by the gooseneck and then hauled the sail aft with the lower reefing line. As an extra precaution, Willie threaded one of the canvas gaskets through the reefing cringle on the leach and tied it under the boom.

The mainsail was now ready to hoist. Thank God it was Bermuda rigged; short-handed as we were, hauling up a heavy gaff would have pushed us to the limit.

I looked towards the bow. Sergeant Ascari and Fisher were on the bowsprit undoing the lashings holding the jib. There was no sign of Glokani, maybe he was below making the tea.

Toby was still motoring the boat into the wind. But once the sails were set, it would need a knowledgeable hand on the wheel, so Pete went back to steer and sent Toby forward to help with the grunt work.

We were well to starboard of the buoyed channel and approaching the shallows when Pete gave the order to haul. The mainsail was rigged with a wire-to-rope halyard that went to a massive winch at the base of the mast. The ancient winch was a notorious finger crusher, so when Toby leapt for the handle, Willie gently pushed him aside and began to crank.

Each turn of the geared winch-drum raised the sail eighteen inches; each turn of the drum required ten turns of the handle. By the time the head of the sail had risen twenty feet, Willie's face was slick with sweat and he was beginning to slow down. He raised it another two feet and then I took over.

In the stiff breeze, raising the last few feet of the heavy sail unleashed mayhem. With the boat head-to-wind, the flogging canvas boomed like thunder, the rigging shook and the masts pitched wild arcs across the sky. With eighteen inches still to go, Pete released the main sheet and the boom rose from the gallows. The flogging sail was deadly enough, but now it had a lethal weapon. I threw all my weight behind the winch handle. Three more turns and the luff was tight. I jammed on the brake and secured the drum.

Pete turned the boat away from the wind. There was a moment of silence, then the sheet blocks creaked, the sail filled, and the boat began to heel.

The sails on a yacht act like a wind vane: carry too much sail aft, and the boat is constantly trying to point into the wind. With only the mains'l set, Pete had to keep the engine at about a thousand rpm, and the helm slightly to port, just to hold the course.

By the time we made it back to the deepwater channel, Ascari and Fisher had thrown the lashings off the jib and were making their way back along the bowsprit towards the deck. We had done this so many times that no one was shouting orders and the second the two men were clear of the bowsprit, Willie and Toby began hauling up the jib. Unlike the main, the two jibs had rope halyards, which meant if you were strong, and fit, you could hoist them most of the way by hand. With two of them hauling, the jib shot up the stay like a greased snake. When it was as high as they could get it by hand, Willie threw three quick turns around the barrel of the halyard winch on the starboard side of the mast and jammed the handle in place. He gave the winch half a dozen turns then secured the tail of the halyard to the pin-rail and coiled up the slack.

The sail flogged then began to fill as someone on the port side tightened the sheet.

The flying jib was next. Willie did the hauling while Toby ran to the bow to make sure the sail didn't snag on the anchor windlass as it went up.

When it was set, the same unseen hands hauled on the sheet and soon both jibs were full and drawing as if forged of steel.

It was almost dark. Pete threw a switch and from their boxes in the rigging the red and green navigation lights bathed the foredeck with an eerie glow.

A channel buoy slid by twenty feet to starboard. Immediately it was clear, Pete brought the boat closer to the wind and turned our bows towards the gap in the reef and the open sea.

39

For all its dangers, the night was incredibly beautiful. A full moon rose over the mountains astern, laying a path of cold light down the channel for us to follow. The first of the shore lights were on and in the distance a pulsating blue and white strobe marked the control tower at the edge of the airport runway.

We were still close enough to the shore to smell damp earth and barbecue smoke. The early evening drinkers would be filling up the bars along the beach. It would take more than a coup to put a dent in happy hour and at least once I heard the tormenting strains of *Yellow Bird* drifting towards us on the wind.

If anyone bothered to look seaward, they would see the *Lady* as a dark shadow against the reef. A few more two-for-one drinks and she'd be little more than a memory.

Someone moved behind me and I turned to find Sergeant Ascari standing at the rail.

"You can't get it out of your system can you; that's why you do it, isn't it?" He nodded towards the bow and the unbroken line of moon-strafed surf that marked the reef.

"You don't know what we do," I laughed.

"You're wrong, Dick. I've been watching the three of you for years. When you're not holed up on St. Peters, you're on another island causing mayhem. The minute you arrive the body count goes up. But when you leave, you seem to leave a lot of good people smiling."

"Can't be all bad, then?"

"I've heard the stories. There have been arrest warrants issued for you on just about every island in the Caribbean, yet my sources tell me that other than the odd night in jail, not one charge has ever stuck."

"Mmm ..."

"Not one of you could do jail time, still you can't resist the danger that might put you there. If I was to ask each one of you where you'd rather be tonight, you'd all say anywhere but here. You'd all be lying. It's the only time you feel alive; when you're facing danger."

"What are you a cop or a psychologist?"

"Neither. Right now I'm a man who wants his country back and I'll do whatever it takes to get it."

We let that hover for a while.

"What did you tell the officer on the bridge?" I said.

"I told him you were a hero of the revolution and that we would probably build a monument to you in the square."

"Shit! What did he say to that?"

"He said you'd better return with Van Norte and the cash or you were going to jail with the rest of the scumbags."

"Jesus," I said, "you're as crazy as Willie."

The conversation carried us closer to the reef and, by the sound of the crashing waves; jail might be the least of our problems. I turned to go but Ascari stopped me with a touch on the arm.

"Thanks, Dick."

"What do you think of *Yellow Bird?*" I said.

"I kind of like it. Why do you ask?"

"No reason."

He laughed, and shaking his head, walked aft towards the wheel.

I watched him go then made my way to the foredeck. There was nothing to do now except work the sails while Pete drove the boat through the pass. I made sure he could see me from the wheel and then grabbed the inner forestay and looked ahead. From this position I could signal him to turn to port or starboard.

The wind was still blowing out of the nor-nor-east. It felt as if it had picked up a knot or two, although that could simply be the apparent wind caused by the forward speed of the boat.

Pete's voice carried towards me over the sound of the wind and sea. I looked aft to where he was pointing at the water on the starboard side. I leaned over the rail and watched another channel marker slip by; it was so close it almost bounced off the side of the hull. Pete was keeping the boat as far to windward as possible. Knowing it gave us a chance if we made a mistake.

Another marker slid by, it was the last one between us and the opening in the reef. Everyone was in position. Willie was standing next to Pete and ready with the mainsheet. Toby and his dad were on the port side within easy reach of the two jibs. If the shadow amidships was Fisher then I wondered where Glokani could be.

The reef stood ghostly in the moonlight and, with the ebb tide gripping our keel, approaching way too fast.

A dilapidated steel tower marks the opening at the right-hand end of the reef. At its base the coral drops straight down to a depth of sixty feet. The seabed then runs south for seventy-five yards until it comes up against a similar wall rising vertical from the bottom. This is the notorious ledge. It was blasted out of the coral during the Second World War, to allow American supply ships access to the seaplane base in the inner lagoon. If the Yank who lit the fuse had been with us tonight; we'd have taken turns at punching him for doing such a shitty job.

With no more markers to guide us, Pete was following a compass course from the last buoy in hope that one of us would spot the ruined tower ahead.

I pulled myself up onto the bulwarks and gripped the inner

forestay with my left hand. The tack of the inner jib was now almost level with my head and I had a clear view down the length of the bowsprit.

Pete had told us to tie ourselves on, but to hell with that. If it all went wrong, I'd have to move fast, and the last thing I'd need was to be tangled up in a length of rope.

All three sails were pulling hard and, riding the ebb, the boat was making about nine knots over the ground.

The stem plunged into the front of a breaking wave. Water surged over the bulwarks and swept my legs from under me. The force spun me around and as I fought to stay on the rail the wire forestay bit deep into my hand.

Our bows rose and the steel tower loomed out of the surf ahead. It was on the wrong side of the bowsprit and less than forty yards off. I screamed a warning and prayed Pete could hear me above the sound of the crashing seas. Instantly, someone eased the jib-sheets and the sails changed shape. With less than a boat length to go, the broken outline of the tower drifted across the end of the bowsprit and took up station on the starboard side.

We were on the ledge.

The bows dropped and kept on going. My feet lost contact with the rail and my stomach did a rollercoaster flip-flop and landed in my chest. I bent my knees against the impact. The end of the bowsprit disappeared beneath tons of water and continued down until it must strike bottom. Then buoyancy took over and with a sickening lurch the bows shot upwards, bringing with them an avalanche of water that washed me off my perch and tumbled me along the deck into the port scuppers.

The weight of water caused the boat to lose way and she came up into the wind. If she fell off on the wrong tack she would be driven onto the windward end of the reef.

I could hear the mains'l crashing from side to side, but that wasn't the only problem. Just inches from my head the jib sheets were thrashing the air in fury, and the demented sails were threatening to bring down the entire rig.

The bows began another corkscrewing descent when suddenly the sails cracked and filled and we charged off on the starboard tack.

I rolled out of the scuppers and crawled forward. Someone shouted; their voice reduced to atoms by the flying spray.

We were over the ledge where the depth dropped away. The outgoing tide was fighting for supremacy against the wind-driven waves of the storm. Between them they'd turned the pass into a maelstrom. This was the most dangerous part of the channel. If we could put three boat lengths behind us, we'd reach deep water.

Pete must have opened the throttle. I felt the deck vibrate and the boat pick up speed.

Another sea rose up to starboard and curled over the bow. This time I was ready and threw myself behind the anchor windlass and cursed myself for not tying on.

I raised my head above the rail and saw we had been driven to leeward.

Disturbed by the gap in the reef the wind had hauled around until we were motoring straight into it. The sails had been cranked in and were as flat as boards. They had lost all their drive and we were moving under engine alone.

Another wave rose over the bowsprit sending tons of water into the starboard bow and knocking us further to leeward.

Without warning the boat lost speed and her bows fell away from the wind. Perhaps the engine sucked in some dirty fuel or something had tangled in the prop.

I fought down panic as the sheet blocks screamed and the boat surged towards the reef.

Suddenly, the spotlight on the front of the mast came on, trapping me in its beam. Why had Pete hit the spotlight?

And then I knew. Without the engine we had to fight our way clear of the entrance under sail alone.

I grabbed a short lashing from a cleat on the anchor windlass then hauled myself over the bulwarks and out onto the bowsprit. The wood was slick. I wrapped my legs around it and dragged myself forward. One second I was looking at the sky and the next I was staring at the churning sea and up to my waist in water.

I dared not look back and risk being blinded by the spotlight. But I prayed someone was watching me from the deck or none of us would be going home.

The bowsprit was fifteen feet long. It felt like a mile. By the time I reached the end, my eyes were on fire and I was gasping for breath.

The boat burst through another wave and hurtled down into the trough. I grabbed the forestay, my hands fighting for grip on the wet steel. I held on until the bows began to rise then quickly stood, passed the lashing behind my back, and tied myself to the stay.

If the boat took another breaking wave on the starboard bow, the leeward coral would have us.

With so much white water ahead I knew it would be almost impossible to see the edge of the reef before we were on it. The spotlight destroyed my night vision, but if they turned it off they wouldn't be able to see me from the wheel.

Sudenly, the waves were no longer breaking. From trough to crest, they were soaring upwards, forming and reforming into towering peaks.

The bowsprit began to climb. At the edge of the circle of light a wave lost its translucence and became a solid shape.

We were on the reef.

I punched the air to my right. "Tack," I screamed, "for God's sake tack!"

The bowsprit continued its sickening climb and then the water fell away and I was looking down into hell. I tried to free myself from the lashing but the knot jammed. The boat began to shake as she clawed through the eye of the wind. Then the jibs crashed over and the spotlight went out.

I felt the keel strike. And strike again.

Someone had enough sense to back the jibs and slowly we began to heel. I counted: one, two, three … "Now!" I roared and the sheets were let fly. The sails swept across and were winched tight. The boat healed some more and slid off the reef back into the channel.

Through the darkness I could see Willie standing by the anchor winch. He was grinning from ear to ear. "Nice going, Dick," he shouted. "Ever thought of doing this for a living?" Before I could reply the spotlight blazed a warning and we charged through the breakers towards the reef on the starboard side.

We made two more tacks then, as rapidly as it had drawn ahead, the wind freed, the spotlight went out, and we were lurching from crest to trough in the open sea.

Around us the waves began to go down as the turbulence of shallow water gave way to the deep ocean swell. When I looked aft along the path of the moon, the reef was little more than a white line running away to port and starboard. If it hadn't tried to kill us, I would have called it romantic.

I stayed on the bowsprit for a few minutes and took a good look around; now was a bad time to run into some yachtsman desperately seeking shelter ahead of the storm. Satisfied, I tugged at the lashing holding me to the stay. The knot—that seconds before had jammed—fell apart without fuss sending a supernatural chill down my spine. I coiled the line, gripped it between my teeth, and slithered back along the bowsprit.

"Are you okay? You look like you've seen a ghost," said Willie as I jumped down to the deck. His hair was plastered to his head and his clothes were soaking wet. In the reflection of the green navigation light, he looked like the devil himself.

"Where were you while I was saving the ship?" I said.

"What," he laughed, "did I miss something?"

The blocks creaked as someone trimmed the sails. We were clear of the reef and the wind had swung back towards the north. That put us on a broad reach and the boat was barely heeling. Our present heading took us into the Caribbean Sea and soon we must alter course for Mexican Hat.

Above the masts the sky was still streaked with mares-tails but they had lost their fire and now hung like specters in the moonlight. As I watched, a jet laid a vapor trail from north to south and I wondered if the pilot was telling his passengers about the beautiful islands below. To the east, a black line above the horizon marked a bank of thick cloud. It might be nothing or it might be a violent squall.

I followed Willie aft to the wheel where the rest of the crew was waiting. Everyone was soaking wet. Toby had a deep cut on his finger and his father was muttering something about his musical career while wrapping the wound in a bandage. Pete looked a bit shaky but managed a grin when Fisher appeared from the deckhouse and offered him a steaming cup of tea. Maybe I was right about Fisher, the guy was in agony yet he had stood up with the rest of the crew.

Everyone was there except Glokani. Then I heard someone retching and spotted him hanging over the rail. It couldn't happen to a nicer guy.

We all had plenty to say but no one felt like talking.

Occasionally a wave crested alongside sending a dollop of spray pattering across the deck. But the seas had lost their vicious edge and although running high, the boat had an easy motion.

Something was missing and it took me a while to realize what it was: I could hear the wind and the sea but no chugging of the engine exhaust.

"What happened to the motor?" I said to no one in particular.

Pete shrugged. "Good question. All I know is it quit when we were over the ledge and almost killed us. Willie thinks it's a clogged fuel filter." He took a sip of tea then looked up at the sails. "Jesus, I thought we'd lost her."

"Can't drown them what's destined to hang," said Willie and disappeared towards the engine room.

It took us about half an hour to sort out the chaos caused by our wild ride through the reef and get the boat back into sailing trim. The waves sluicing along the deck had snatched some of the coiled halyards from the pin-rails around the masts and they were a tangled mess. The tail of the spare mains'l halyard had been washed out through the scuppers and I wondered if it had been sucked into the prop and stopped the engine. I quickly hauled the line onboard and was relieved to find it in one piece all the way to the fancy whipping that Pete insisted went on the bitter end.

It wasn't until I went below that I realized just how unprepared we were to go to sea. The cabins were bad but it looked as if someone had tossed a hand grenade into the galley. Lockers had burst open and tins and broken crockery were everywhere. No one had remembered to drop the catch on the fridge door and the floor was strewn with food. I rescued a bottle of Corona from the mess, wiped off the baked beans, and toasted the miserable bastards who never drink at sea.

Toby stepped through the door and found me sitting on the floor amongst the debris. My back was against the bulkhead and I was drinking the beer.

I wished Toby wasn't on board. He should be ashore playing his music and chasing the girls. Looking at him made me feel old.

I fished another beer out of the wreckage and offered it to him.

He shook his head. “Can I ask you something?” he said.

“Depends. If you want to know the meaning of life then you’ve come to the wrong guy.” I took a long pull of the Corona and wiped my mouth with the back of my hand. I was impressed, it had finally stopped shaking.

“Were you scared out there on the bowsprit?”

“Yes.”

“Willie told me that you were an officer in the Royal Navy and that he and Pete once served with you.”

“What else did he tell you?”

“He said you’d be scared out there but that I could count on you to keep us alive.”

I took another deep pull on the beer and when the bottle was empty used a kitchen knife to pry the cap off the one Toby didn’t want.

“How’s your hand?” I said.

He shrugged and held his hand up to show me that his fingers were all there. He turned and headed for the door, but he didn’t step through. “I never thanked you for what you did for me and my brother. I just want you to know that no matter what happens we’ll never forget that,” he said.

He was gone before I could reply, so I took another slug of beer and a moment later the bulkhead at my back began to vibrate as Willie coaxed the engine to life.

If this was a ship of war then we were back in fighting trim.

40

The island of Mexican Hat lies seventy miles from St. Peters, on a magnetic bearing of three hundred and thirty five degrees. The wind out of the nor-nor-east made it a close reach, but with a full moon we would have to allow a little more for the pull of the westerly current.

Finding the island shouldn't be difficult as the light on top of the bluff had a range of fifteen miles. However, this was the Caribbean and, like the traffic lights on St. Peters, there was no guarantee it would be working.

Pete had taken his departure from the sea buoy one mile west of the entrance to the reef. He had dialed the course into the ancient Robertson autopilot and the boat was now steering itself.

Fisher had swallowed a handful of painkillers and was asleep in one of the cabins amidships. Toby and his dad were on watch and Glokani was curled up aft within easy spewing distance of the rail.

Everything was running smoothly and the three of us went below and gathered around the chart table.

"We're averaging eight to nine knots," said Pete. He looked at his watch and wrote something on a notepad. "The *Lady*'s sailing well under this rig. If we can maintain the same course and speed then we should raise the island an hour before dawn."

I looked at the chart. "According to the Diamond King *Temptress* can motor at seventeen knots, but we're pretty sure she's only running on one engine. Even so, once they reach the island, they'll have to wait for daylight before they make a move."

"How do you think they'll work it?" said Pete.

"My guess is the pilot will fly ashore alone and the rest will take their chances in the dinghy. He won't want to weigh the chopper down with a load of passengers. In these seas lifting off from the back of the yacht will be difficult enough. To reduce the risk, they'll look for a decent lee, and that means running the boat in as close as they can to the old landing stage off the shingle beach. Once the chopper's on land, weight's no longer a problem. They can load up with fuel and whatever else they're taking and be on their way."

"I agree," said Willie. "Fisher said the chopper's tanks are almost dry, that means they'll need around a hundred gallons if they want maximum range. Even in perfect conditions, it would take hours to lug the fuel down to the beach and ferry it out to the yacht. Always assuming they have the containers to carry it in."

I looked at each of them in turn. "I'm counting on being right. Because when they touch down on the helipad, we'll be waiting."

We spent another half an hour going over the details then Willie went off to prepare the equipment and Pete and I joined the watch on deck.

The bank of cloud was still visible along the eastern horizon. It was no nearer but the towering thunderheads were now lit by the occasional flash of lightning. It was enough of a threat to keep the foresail furled on the boom but not enough to stop us shaking the reef out of the main.

We had to balance our speed against the risk of coming too close to *Temptress* or they might pick us up on radar. Our wooden masts and hull made a poor target, and once *Temptress* rounded Mexican Hat; her radar would be blocked by the high land to the east. But taking no chances; we lowered our radar reflector from its place at the head of the foremast and stowed it below.

After checking the course and the set of the sails, we explained our plan to the Ascari's. The plan was shaky but it was all we had. The Ascari's listened and were clearly unhappy with their role. So we went over it again, hammering away, until finally they agreed that it was the best we could do. It wasn't the way we would choose to go into battle—bad intelligence was worse than no intelligence—and there were so many things that could go wrong.

On his last trip below, Pete reported a drop in barometric pressure. A falling glass could mean the storm was moving towards us. He also pulled up a couple of floorboards and found more water in the bilge than usual. The electric bilge-pumps were keeping ahead of the flow but he thought it likely that we'd opened a couple of seams when the keel struck the reef.

On top of everything, we couldn't be sure that *Temptress* had damaged a prop or that Snake Eyes was even heading for Mexican Hat. Perhaps they were steaming north, or south, at full speed and now were hundreds of miles away.

I made a note to buy Pete a radar for his next birthday, knowing it would be like giving a Luddite a hammer. His painstaking restoration of the schooner didn't run to modern gadgetry. When he bought the boat it had already been converted into a floating bar by a carpenter whose only skills lay in the blade of a two horsepower chainsaw and the amount of rum he could drink. Pete's dream was to use the proceeds from the bar to return the yacht to its original glory. We'd stopped teasing him long ago about living to be a hundred and fifty, and the fact that the *Lady* could go to sea at all said something about his dogged determination.

An hour had passed since we cleared the reef and St. Peters lay ten miles astern. Old and tired as she was, this is what the schooner was built for and she surged over the waves with ease. Occasionally a rogue sea, stirred up by the nearby storm, ran across the existing wave-train and slammed into the hull, throwing sheets of spray into the jibs and soaking the deck. A skilled helmsman would hear the wave coming and ease into it by slightly altering course. But the old Robertson autopilot couldn't think or hear and if conditions deteriorated we would have to disengage it and steer by hand.

It was imperative that we get some sleep before reaching the island and that meant leaving the Ascari's in charge of the ship. They'd been around small boats all their lives and although they had limited experience on a heavy schooner, what they lacked in skill they made up for in common sense.

Ten o'clock. In five hours we'd be within fifteen miles of the island and, if it was working, the light on top of the bluff would guide us in.

The Ascari's had their standing orders: Keep a good lookout. Wake everyone up if you see a vessel or a light of any kind. Do the same if the wind picks up or if the weather shows any signs of changing at all.

Pete was uneasy and would have a hard time sleeping. Before going below he asked me to join him for a final look around the deck. We made our way up the starboard side, checking the sails as we went. At the bow we stopped and peered over the rail. Our navigation lights were off and the only illumination came from the moon, which shone wanly through thickening wisps of clouds.

We stood and listened to the bow-wave adding its voice to the endless rhythms of the sea.

"Everything is so beautiful tonight and here we are on our way to fuck someone up." Pete's voice was little more than a whisper above the wind. "I used to think about that when they sent us on a mission. We'd be going ashore in the Zodiac, the guys would be checking their weapons, and all I could think about was how beautiful the phosphorescence looked in the water."

"Why are you telling me this?" I asked.

Instead of a reply, he turned and walked to the winch on the port side and adjusted the jib sheet. He dropped the winch handle back in its holder then leant against the rail and waited for me to catch up.

"After the ops, we'd be heading back out to the sub. If it had been really bad, some of the guys would be crying or throwing up, and I'd be looking at the sea and thinking how lovely it was. All that killing and I never felt a thing." He pushed himself away from the rail and headed for the companionway steps.

"I once asked Willie what he thought about when he was going into action," I said.

He stopped and turned around.

"What did he say?"

"He said he thought about his granny's three-legged cat."

"Why?"

"Said it was beautiful."

"Guess we're all fucked up."

"Amen to that."

His grunt turned into a chuckle and he disappeared below.

41

After the fresh air of the open deck the cabins below were hot and stuffy. Before leaving the dock we had dogged down the portholes and closed the storm covers. Now, what little fresh air found its way in came through the Dorade vents, and the leeward side of the butterfly hatch over the saloon, which was cranked open half a notch.

Someone had cleaned up the mess in the galley and shoveled everything back into the fridge. I opened the door and reached for a Corona, thought better of it and grabbed a bottle of water instead. I made my way along the passageway and looked into the saloon. The smell of gun oil hung in the air and two watertight containers lay side by side on the floor.

Further along the passageway, I came to the first of the guest cabins. The door was open and Fisher was asleep on the bunk. He had a rag clutched to his face and a pool of watery red drool lay next to him on the pillow. The pills had taken effect and he was snoring loudly through his shattered teeth.

Glokani was in the second cabin. There was a bucket of vomit on the floor next to his bunk. He looked to be asleep, but I couldn't really tell. Just looking at him made my flesh crawl.

I slipped into the next cabin, pulled off my wet clothes and sat down on the bottom bunk. By the dip in the mattress above, I knew Willie was there.

Following the action of the last few hours, the rolling motion and the gurgling of the sea just inches from my head, acted like a soporific and within minutes I was fast asleep.

Willie's voice dragged me back to consciousness. "When we were together, she always spoke about you. Susie really loved you."

First Pete and now Willie. I felt like a father confessor.

"Go to sleep," I said.

"She was leaving you and going back to Africa. The island was getting to her, all the booze and the partying. You know what some women are like. She was missing the culture, said she needed art galleries and theaters."

He fell silent. I was hoping that was the end of it. But it wasn't.

"She was always crying, Dick. That's how I found her one day down by the old wreck on the beach. She was just sitting there, crying."

A wave slammed into the hull and the boat rolled to port. I hit the light button on my watch and squinted at the dial: 22:50.

"You don't have to explain. Get some sleep."

"Listen to me, Dick. She didn't want to hurt you. She was going to tell you about leaving when the time was right. You need to know. We talked and we walked on the beach, and sometimes she let me hold her. And yes, I wanted her but she never betrayed you."

"Have you finished?"

"No, you stupid fuck, why didn't you marry her?"

"That's enough, Willie."

"Mohammed was right about you, boyo … you don't know what you've got."

His words dropped onto my pillow like acid, igniting the feelings I'd forced aside since Susie's death. I gripped the edge of the bunk and worked my way through the anger and shame.

By the time I had come up with a suitable reply, Willie was fast asleep.

42

While lying in a soggy bunk, I have been tormented by all the childhood nightmares I ever had. It never happens ashore, only at sea. Even my dreams are more vivid. And while in that peculiar state, neither awake nor asleep, my mind conjures up the weirdest things. I can even program a dream and get right back into it after a visit to the head.

Erotic dreams are something else. And there are times, during a particularly difficult voyage with a mixed crew, when I've wondered what a shrink would make of my cerebral night time wanderings. My theory is that the constant motion, along with the damp and feral scent of unwashed bedding on an over-used bunk, triggers a primitive urge to mate. If only you could bottle and sell it.

"Come on, Dick. Wake up. What happened to all that military training bullshit; the instantly awake stuff?"

There was nothing erotic about Willie and had I a gun, I would have shot him.

"Toby thinks he's spotted the light on Mexican Hat. Come on, boyo, its action stations, or are you getting too old?"

"Fuck off!" I lashed out and missed.

"Here's some coffee, you ungrateful sod." He slammed a mug onto the side table and headed for the door.

As if to confirm the news about the light, the boat lurched upright and the sails began to flog as the crew brought her through the wind and ran her off on the port tack.

I dragged myself out of the bunk and pulled on my shorts. They were cold and clammy and I was going to have serious words with the cruise director about the valet service. I took a pull of Willie's coffee. The taste made up for my reeking clothes, though half of it slopped down my leg as I staggered up the companionway steps.

Pete was waiting on deck. He had the binoculars in one hand and a cup of coffee in the other. "Toby spotted the light away to starboard about ten minutes ago. He managed to get a quick bearing on it, that's why we tacked. If he's right then we're too far west and risk being spotted by *Temptress* on radar."

I took the binoculars out of his hand. "Has anyone seen the light since?"

"No. But Toby thinks he caught sight of it when we rode up the back of a wave. I want to continue on this course for fifteen minutes and then tack again."

I looked at my watch: 02:55. "Get everyone up and onto the bulwarks. If we don't spot that light again soon, we'll have no chance of finding the island before dawn."

The waves were running high, skittering across a long north-easterly ground swell. We were close-hauled on the port tack and the *Lady* was digging her shoulder into the seas, sending sheets of spray scything across the windward deck.

If Toby was right, the island should be somewhere off the port bow, making it impossible to spot from the starboard side of the boat. But if he was wrong, and he had seen the steaming lights on a ship, then the island could be anywhere to windward or leeward.

Pete checked the log and counted off the miles. Taking the distance run and the course he'd given the Ascari's to steer, he thought Toby was probably right and the island was close by.

I ducked under the jib sheet and made my way to the port

shrouds. With the boat hard on the wind, the sheets were bar-tight. I hauled myself up onto the bulwark and scanned the horizon. The moon was totally obscured by cloud. I concentrated, slowly sweeping the binoculars from left to right, searching for something solid against the liquid night.

"This is definitely above and beyond the call of duty, boyo."

My heart almost stopped.

"Jesus, Willie, don't you ever quit?" I looked up to where he was standing on the crosstrees of the main mast.

"Alleluia, brudder, I done seen de light." He laughed then slid down the rigging and landed on the bulwark next to me. "Check it out. It's around three-forty degrees. It's dim and not flashing like it should be, so it's hard to spot.

I hung the binoculars around my neck and began the steady climb up the ratlines to the crosstrees.

This was a part of sailing that I loved. I had no fear of heights and had worked on the yards of some of the tallest masts. But that was before I turned fifty and although the *Lady*'s main mast was fairly short, the going was tough. As I climbed, the motion became more violent until I was arcing across the sky like a man riding a demented metronome. I hauled myself up the last few feet to the crosstrees and rolled one arm around the mast. My legs were like rubber, my mouth full of spit.

I took a second to let my heart rate settle then looked down at the deck. Willie was grinning up at me and all I could do was laugh. Suddenly, the boat rose on a vicious wave, my legs went from under me and I swung out over the churning sea. I fought to hang on, clawing at the mast and losing my grip. The boat rolled the other way, pivoted me around and slammed me chest first into the mast. Vomit rose in my throat and I threw up to leeward. I was cheered by the thought of the spew hitting Willie, but caught by the wind it whirled off into the night.

Enough, I coiled myself around the mast like a boa constrictor and jammed the binoculars into my streaming eyes.

After the last big sea, the boat settled down. Perhaps there was some truth in the legend of the seventh wave. I looked through the rubber eyepiece and adjusted the focus as best I could. Then, using the built-in compass, I brought the binoculars around to three-hundred degrees and began a slow traverse towards the north. The binoculars were all over the place, first hitting the sea and then the sky. Was this what everyone else was seeing? On a wild night like this it was easy to mistake a wave for a reef; the moon for a sail; a star for a light. All sailors have done it.

A sea roared under the hull and before I could drop the binoculars and cling to the mast, something solid swung into focus then instantly disappeared.

Wave or boat, and where the hell was it?

Willie shouted from the deck, but I ignored him. I hadn't noted the bearing, but whatever I'd seen before the boat rolled had been between the shrouds of the foremast. I waited until we settled back on course then raised the glasses to my eyes. This time I found it on the first sweep: a dim light and beneath it the solid mass of a small island—Mexican Hat.

Just to show Willie that I could still do it, I grabbed a halyard and slid down it to the deck.

"What've you been eating, spinach?" he said and before I had enough breath to reply, added, "you saw the light?"

"Better," I gasped, "I saw the island. It's on a bearing of three-twenty degrees, and it's close."

43

Pete listened to the news and checked the course. He ordered the sails cranked in until they began to flutter and then eased them off a notch to maintain speed. Our course was taking us away from Mexican Hat, but we decided to hold it for three miles, hoping the next tack would bring us to the island's northern point.

Our plan was simple, which I liked. Willie noted it was also suicidal and, according to him, that added to the fun. If we made it back to St. Peters, I was going to get Willie some help.

The plan had its risks. There was only one place to get ashore on Mexican Hat, and that was difficult at the best of times. The tiny cove on the western side had been used by everyone since the conquistadores, and that is where Snake Eyes would land. He had no choice, and that meant neither did we.

Our plan was to sail as close to the northern tip of the island as possible and then launch the rigid inflatable boat. Once it was afloat, the three of us would swim to it and motor around the coast until we were in the lee of the land, staying far enough to the north to be invisible to anyone on *Temptress.* Although the island's north-western side was rocky, there were patches of sand between the rocks. It wasn't much, but it was all the help we were going to get. We had to get ashore without breaking any bones and with the weapons intact, and if we could save the RIB, that would be a bonus.

The *Lady*'s RIB wasn't quite standard issue. It had been modified for fishing, diving, and what Pete referred to as eco-tourism: entering and leaving an island at night without disturbing the wildlife. An extra layer of rubber, treated with a special coating, protected the inflatable tubes, and the underwater section of the fiberglass hull had been reinforced with Kevlar. Inside, the bottom boards were fitted with chocks and stainless steel eyebolts designed to hold weapons and ammunition boxes in place. The entire boat was black, including the outboard motor.

We went over the plan one more time, then walked over to where the RIB was secured to the deck on chocks. Willie reached in and clipped a three-part bridle to lifting points at the bow and stern. He made his way to the base of the main mast and unshackled the end of the spare halyard from the pin-rail. Having secured it to the eye in the bridle, he tensioned the halyard to prevent it from snagging on the crosstrees when the yacht rolled. That done, he climbed into the boat and checked the fuel in the tank. It must have been okay because he lowered the outboard motor and gave the fuel-bulb a squeeze. A 50 HP outboard is about the largest you can start with a pull cord; any bigger and you need battery ignition. Willie opened the choke and yanked the cord twice in rapid succession. Then he closed the choke and pulled the cord again. The motor roared to life. Without the deadening effects of the water, the exhaust note rattled the air like an AK-47 on full automatic. Willie gave the motor three quick revs then shut it down before lack of water could damage the rubber impeller in the cooling system.

He climbed out of the RIB and wiped his hands.

"Any problems?" I said.

"Big one." He pointed along the deck.

The noise of the outboard had brought Glokani from his deathbed. He looked like shit and stunk little better. I was wrong in thinking he was putting on an act, this was one seriously seasick sailor. His face was a mellow shade of green and I swear, looking at the hollows that passed for eyes, he had lost twenty pounds in the short time we had been at sea. The Diamond King and erstwhile owner of a million dollar yacht now looked like a wounded loblolly boy at the battle of the Nile. Had it been anyone else they would have earned my sympathy, but not a chance; I was hoping he would throw up again so I could laugh.

He didn't puke. He spoke. "I know what you're planning and I'm coming with you. If they are on this island, you have found them for me and your job is over. I will make sure you are well paid."

I was impressed. As sick as he was, the arrogant bastard still thought he was running the show, perhaps he'd once been a naval officer.

"You're staying aboard," I said. "In the state you're in you wouldn't last two minutes."

He took a step forward. I took a step back. His breath was rank.

"I'm coming with you, Turpin. What's on *Temptress* belongs to me and I intend to have it," he shouted.

"You're staying onboard to help sail the boat. You're implicated in murder and God knows what else. If you behave yourself, when we get back Sergeant Ascari might let you leave St. Peters with the rest of the dross."

"You think you're fucking clever, Turpin, but I haven't finished with you yet." He took another step forward and stopped dead in his tracks. His eyes focused on something behind me. Suddenly, he clamped his hand across his mouth and ran, dry-heaving, all the way to the rail.

I spun and found Willie shoving the remains of a bacon sandwich into his mouth. He had grease and ketchup running down his chin and I quickly turned away or he would have smothered me in it when he laughed.

"It's ready to load," he spluttered and nodded towards the RIB where two containers sat on the deck. I had worked with Willie long enough to know what they contained.

I checked my watch and looked around. Dawn was little more than an hour away.

The wind had increased and the gusts were hitting thirty-five knots. Finding the island in its path, the seas were high and confused, making the schooner's timbers creak and her rigging moan; a sound familiar to sailors for hundreds of years.

A feeling—half fear, half excitement—fluttered in my belly.

"It's almost time," I said. "Another ten minutes and we'll heave-to and launch the RIB. As soon as it hits the water, the *Lady* will tack away, and we jump. From then on, we're on our own. The Ascari's will sail back and look for us when they see a white flare. If they don't see the flare by ten-thirty, I've told them to head back to St. Peters and get us some help."

There was nothing else to say. Pete took a final look around the boat. He glanced at the sails, and aft to where Toby stood at the wheel, then turned and together we went below.

Five minutes later and we were back on deck, each of us wearing a ten-ounce wetsuit. The wetsuits would give us some protection should we end up in the water amongst the rocks.

The northern tip of the island was now visible off the port bow; a dark mass against the turbulent sky. A jagged white line marked the shore and the sound of breakers rolled towards us like thunder. Above the roar, I heard an occasional whoosh as the sea forced its way into a hollow rock and shot upwards like a geyser. We were so close we could no longer see the light on top of the bluff. The proximity of the land was playing havoc with the wind and if we waited much longer it would be too dangerous to heave-to.

The boat was on the starboard tack, heading straight for the island. Pete judged it to the second and gave the signal.

Toby put the helm alee.

The *Lady* came up into the wind and with a crashing of blocks and canvas, fell off to starboard and lay quietly hove-to. After pounding through the seas, the silence was eerie. The schooner rode the waves, allowing the swell to go under her while slipping sideways into the calmer waters of her own lee.

We kept our voices low, not from fear of being heard from the shore but because in Special Forces you equate sudden noise with action. Some call it unique training, others, brainwashing. We spent endless hours in the mess swilling beer and arguing the subject. To prove a point, Willie once dropped a metal serving tray behind an SAS training officer, and although you weren't supposed to carry weapons in the mess, he woke up on the floor with enough hardware pointing at him to start a war. The prank cost him a month's leave, and he was ordered to run up and down a nearby mountain in the freezing January rain in full kit every day for a week. It did nothing to endear him to his officers and simply made him crazier.

"You all set?" Ascari asked. He was standing at the base of the mast along with Fisher, who had one hand on the halyard winch ready to hoist the RIB. I still wasn't sure about Fisher but if nothing else he would keep Glokani in line.

Willie gave the RIB a final once-over, nodded, and handed Pete the bow-line.

"Do it," I said.

Ascari and Fisher began cranking the winch.

Willie steadied the dinghy as it rose from the chocks. When it was high enough, he walked it to the side of the boat and swung it out over the rail.

I waited until the *Lady* rode over the next wave then ordered them to release the halyard. The dinghy hit the water and surged up the side of the hull. Willie reached down and quickly unclipped the shackle and dropped the lifting bridle into the boat. Free of the bridle, the RIB rapidly drifted astern. Pete kept pace with it; juggling the painter around the rigging until he reached the aft deck, where he secured it to a cleat.

The RIB was now trailing fifty feet astern. It was plunging violently, in danger of flipping over or ripping the painter out of its fitting in the bow.

As usual, Willie was first to go. He leapt over the rail and swam, cutting through the waves with powerful strokes.

He reached the boat, hauled himself up onto the edge of the tube and rolled aboard. He tried to stand but the violent motion knocked him down. He staggered to his feet, flung himself at the outboard and pulled the cord. The engine fired. He made a quick cutting motion with his hand, and Pete untied the bow-line from the cleat and let it go.

Pete and I went over the rail together, and by the time we broke surface, Willie had the bow-line safely onboard and was powering towards us, closing the gap with short bursts of speed.

Because the RIB was no longer tethered to the yacht, it was much easier for us to climb aboard. It took less than a minute to sort everything out. Pete took up position in the bow while Willie checked the equipment to make sure nothing had been lost during the launch. I moved to the stern and sat on the port tube, my right hand clamped on the throttle.

We heard flogging canvas as the crew of the *Lady* let fly the sheets and got underway. For a moment the schooner rode above us like a phantom, then she was swallowed by the night and we were on our own.

Another wave hurled us skyward and I saw the island ahead. As we slid into the trough, I put the engine in gear and eased open the throttle.

Following the coast, I threaded the RIB through the mountainous seas.

44

Mexican Hat has a notorious reputation for drowning men even on calm days.

Tonight the seas were rolling in from the storm and, finding the island barring the way, curling back on themselves only to be driven forward again by the relentless power of the wind.

The closer we came to the shore, the greater our risk of capsize.

As we approached the northeastern tip of the island, the seas increased. Losing much of their lee, the waves now took the full brunt of the wind and, galvanized by the current, picked up speed as they hooked around the point. It was like maneuvering inside a washing machine.

There was nowhere to land.

In the darkness each promising patch of sand turned out to be a sheet of rock, encrusted with barnacles as lethal as iron spikes.

The sensible thing to do was to wait until dawn, but by then it would be too late. We had to be at the helipad before Snake Eyes, and once ashore we still had to hack our way through the jungle.

Pete was the first to see it: a depression in the coast trimmed by a thread of silver that covered and uncovered with every wave.

Taking care to stay beyond the line of breakers, I took the RIB in for a closer look.

From our position a hundred yards out, the inlet appeared as a narrow funnel protected on each side by jagged fingers of rock. The entrance was about two boat lengths wide. Beyond the entrance, a steep shingle beach led to a scrap of sand. The seas were losing some of their force as they struck the rocks on either side. But the occasional rogue wave found its way in and broke right up the beach, dragging tons of shingle and seaweed along with it.

We should have gone for it straight away but, like idiots, we motored along for a quarter of a mile looking for somewhere more protected. All this did was use up valuable time. Nothing was protected on this savage coast and after fifteen minutes we turned back.

Finding the inlet again wasn't easy and when we did it looked even more dangerous than it had before. Maybe the wind had shifted or the tide had turned because now the rocky outcrops offered little protection and the seas were curling in.

I took the RIB as close to the edge of the breakers as I dare then ran parallel with the shore. It would be suicide to try and land bow first. The second the boat hit the beach, it would be swamped and rolled over. This meant picking the right wave, riding it to the very edge of the beach and, just before impact, spinning the boat around until it faced the sea whilst at the same time tilting the outboard motor. If I got it right, Pete and Willie would be able to jump out in shallow water and hold the boat into the waves until I got out, then together we could drag it up the beach. We had carried out this maneuver many times and it always worked.

We motored past the inlet a couple of times and then stopped opposite the entrance.

Surfers wait and go on the wave's leading edge. That would get us killed.

I let three waves roll by and was ready to go on the fourth, then, as we rose, I noticed the inlet was no longer directly ahead, but slightly to port. I tweaked the throttle and brought us back into line.

Two more waves rolled in. We were beam-on to the shore and

opposite the scrap of beach. "Here we go," I said.

The RIB slid down the back of the wave and into the trough. I wound open the throttle and the boat stood on end. Pete and Willie threw their weight forward. The boat accelerated, slewing from side to side, as we roared off in pursuit of the fleeing wave.

We shot through the narrow gap. Rocks flashed by, foaming and snapping like rabid dogs.

Willie and Pete were yelling but their voices were overpowered by the sound of the waves smashing on the beach and dragging tons of shingle back to the depths.

The next sea burst through the entrance.

I kept the throttle open ready to power the boat around.

Ten yards from the beach the propeller hit a rock, the engine crashed to a stop and the motor shot upwards.

Pete and Willie flew over the side and were instantly taken by the sea.

Caught in the undertow, the RIB was thrown on its beam and hurled backwards.

I fought to get the outboard down and the engine started but the next wave pounced, driving the boat upwards until it was vertical and then hanging upside down beneath the curling crest.

The wave hit the shore with the force of a runaway train and my world went black.

Driven down, the RIB slammed into the liquid shingle and exploded, trapping me between the weapons box and the Hyperlon tube. My fear of drowning was overpowered by the terrible noise of the shingle. Senses awry, I couldn't tell if I was being dragged towards land and salvation or death at the bottom of the sea.

Suddenly, the RIB broke free and, with a final bone-jarring crash, came to rest high up the beach. Its moment of glory over, the wave rolled back. It made a weak attempt to take the shattered boat with it but, full of sand and pebbles, the RIB refused to move.

I fought my way out of the wreckage and fell down amongst the seaweed. My right eye was swollen and I could taste blood. After a few gagging mouthfuls of sweet sea air, I was able to push myself up and look around.

Another wave rolled up the beach but its fingers couldn't quite reach the mangled RIB. As it retreated, Willie and Pete rose like Neptune from the sea and staggered ashore.

We stripped off our wetsuits and stowed them above the high water mark, then began digging the boat out of the muck. The tubes at the back still held air but the front chambers were flat. One propeller blade was bent but when I pulled the starter cord the engine turned over. With some work it would probably run.

Best of all, the weapons box was still in place.

"After this shit, I'm going to shoot somebody," said Willie. He ripped the Uzi out of the box and looked at me.

I raised my hands. "Okay, but that maneuver usually works, and how the hell was I to know there was a bloody rock in the way? Anyway, Pete was supposed to be lookout."

Pete threw up his hands. "Blame me. Everybody blames the Americans."

Willie switched his gaze. "Bloody American outboard, too. A British outboard wouldn't have quit."

"Limeys don't make outboards," said Pete.

"Bloody right they do," said Willie. "What about the British Seagull. Now there's engineering for you."

"What," spluttered Pete, "the only moving part is the man with the string."

They carried on trading insults and checking the weapons. After a few minutes, they fell silent.

"Ready?" I said.

They nodded.

Willie slung the Uzi over his shoulder and handed me a 9mm Glock, then he tossed me the Mossberg pump action shotgun he'd taken from the guard whose brains now decorate the wall at Mohamed's house. "I figured you'd want the shotgun," he said. "It's carrying a full load of slugs and there're more in the pouch."

I secured the weapons then checked my watch and the small compass attached to the wristband.

There was a smudge of light in the east as we left the beach and moved into the jungle.

45

Perhaps jungle is too grand a description for the vegetation on Mexican Hat. But, since few people had lived on the island, it was virgin growth and a tangle of trees and vines grew all the way to the beach.

Pete led the way, swinging a machete honed to a razor's edge. For the first fifty yards the terrain was flat and then, gradually, it began to rise. I knew that if we kept on climbing, we would eventually come to the path leading from the helipad up to the light on top of the bluff.

Pete hacked away for twenty minutes before handing the machete to Willie.

Then it was my turn.

We climbed steadily, the going becoming easier as the tangled brush of the lower slopes gradually gave way to old growth trees.

I stopped and glanced at my watch in the gloom. The sun had risen but it would take a couple of hours for the light to penetrate the dense canopy of the rain forest.

We traded stealth for speed, doubting all but the birds would hear our approach above the soughing of the wind.

The ground ahead suddenly steepened and, using exposed tree roots for handholds, I scrambled up a short vertical bank. At the top, twenty yards to the right, the rutted track leading to the lighthouse disappeared beyond a bend. The helipad was in the opposite direction, about a quarter of a mile downhill. A recent heavy rain shower had turned the surface of the track to mud. There was no sign of recent footprints.

I heard Willie and Pete clambering up the bank and seconds later they appeared at the edge of the track.

The sun had barely risen yet the temperature was stultifying and the humidity had us dripping with sweat. In addition to the Uzi, Willie had a coil of rope. Pete had a Glock, his K-Bar, and a pack containing emergency rations and field dressings. Along with the shotgun, I carried a pistol, spare ammo, and the flare gun. We had spent weeks trekking through thick jungle carrying eighty-pound packs, but that was long ago before too much beer and rum.

"Fit then?" I wheezed, and before they could reply, set off jogging down the hill.

After a couple of hundred yards, the track widened, and to the right we caught an occasional glimpse of the ocean through the trees. From what I remembered, the helipad was around the next bend.

I made a slowing motion with my hand, then signaled Pete and Willie to follow me into the trees. A hundred yards in, we came to the edge of the helipad and crouched down behind the rusty remains of a Massey Ferguson tractor.

To make way for the helipad, the builders had cleared an area of forest about the size of two tennis courts. A small stone bunker containing tools, engine oil, and a portable hand operated fuel pump, stood off to one side. Next to the bunker, the fuel for the helicopter was kept in a steel tank raised off the ground on cinder blocks. Across from the tank, where the narrow paved road leading from the beach entered the clearing, engineers had levelled the ground and laid a square of reinforced concrete. The only thing that had changed since my last visit was the art work on the helipad: where the prerequisite 'H' should be, someone had painted a giant smiley face sucking on a spliff.

Apart from the occasional shriek of a bird going about its morning ablutions, the clearing was quiet. I sent Pete to check the road leading down to the old quay and, while Willie covered us from the tractor, jogged over to inspect the fuel bunker.

It was obvious that no one had been to the island since the last maintenance visit. The padlock securing the bunker's heavy steel door was intact. A look at the sight-glass fixed to the side of the fuel tank showed it was three-quarters full.

I ran a quick circuit of the clearing and then made my way back to Willie.

A few minutes later Pete appeared at the top of the road. He looked around then, staying close to the trees, made his way towards us and threw himself down behind the tractor.

"I followed the road all the way to the beach. There's no sign of *Temptress*. The old dock is empty and there's nothing in the bay. They're not here, Dick."

We lay with our backs against the old machine and watched as the shadows in the clearing were slowly driven back by the sun. We all had our own theories but no one wanted to put them into words.

After an hour Pete went to take another look at the bay.

After twenty minutes, he was back.

"Well?" I said.

"Nothing. And the weather's getting worse."

Willie looked at me.

I shrugged.

Time was running out. If we didn't signal the *Lady* before 10:30, they would leave and, like Blackbeard's pirates, we'd be marooned on god-awful Mexican Hat.

Another hour went by. Pete reached into his backpack, took out some oatmeal bars and handed them around. A cloud passed across the sun. He was about to speak when the wind rattled the trees ahead of a vicious rainsquall.

We hunkered down beneath the tractor and chewed.

"Jesus Christ," hissed Willie.

I followed his gaze. Snake Eyes was standing at the edge of the clearing. He looked towards the tractor and then at the fuel tank. Moments later Debbie, Van Norte, and a guy who fit the description of Andropof, appeared beside him.

No one moved.

Lightning flashed and was immediately followed by a rumble of thunder. We used the cover of the sudden squall to slither backwards into the forest.

As quickly as it had arrived the rain eased, and then stopped, leaving just a few tendrils of cloud hanging like spider webs amongst the higher branches of the trees.

When I looked, Snake Eyes was halfway across the clearing, cautiously making his way towards the fuel tank. He was wary, like a large cat, and he kept stopping to sniff the air as if he knew something was wrong but couldn't quite figure out what.

He was wearing khaki battle fatigues and carrying an AK-47 with the stock folded back. A pistol in a shoulder holster sat snuggly beneath his left arm. Had I been recruiting for Mercenaries R Us, I'd have hired him on the spot.

Debbie left the two men by the side of the road and wandered over to the tractor.

She looked at the ground and glanced quickly at Snake Eyes.

Pete slipped the K-Bar from its sheath and slithered forward. I put out my hand to stop him. Debbie picked something out of the dirt at her feet and put it in her pocket. She turned and walked towards the bunker.

Pete took a deep breath and the tension went out of his body.

Snake Eyes watched Debbie approach. He said something and rattled the padlock on the steel door. Certain he couldn't open it by force of will; he hung the AK over his shoulder and drew the pistol from its holster.

Two rounds destroyed the lock and the door swung open.

I waited for him to twirl the gun around his finger and blow across the end of the barrel, but the miserable bastard simply shoved it back into the holster and unclipped a portable VHF radio from his belt.

"He's calling the chopper," said Pete.

Snake Eyes waved towards Van Norte, and he trotted over and followed him into the bunker. They reappeared pushing a refueling trolley that carried a hose coiled around a metal drum, and a portable hand pump. While Snake Eyes connected the pump to the tank, Van Norte unrolled the fuel hose and dragged it backwards towards the helipad. When he reached the edge of the concrete, he laid the nozzle down in the grass.

Nearly fifteen minutes had gone by since they entered the clearing.

I turned to Willie and Pete. "If the chopper makes it, we'll wait until they're pumping fuel and then make our move. Try and keep Van Norte and the woman alive, unless they're a threat, then take 'em out."

Across the clearing, Snake Eyes pulled a cigarette from his pocket and lit up. He was calm but he never stopped looking around, and a couple of times he stared towards the tractor as if he sensed we were there. In comparison, Van Norte couldn't keep still and paced backwards and forwards making impatient gestures with his hands.

Snake Eyes ignored him and blew a stream of smoke into the wind.

Pete nodded. "That guy's good, we could have used him in special ops. If I didn't know better, I'd say he was on to us—"

"Shhhh," Willie spat. "Here it comes." He cocked his head to one side and pointed towards the west.

Seconds ticked by, then I heard the unmistakable sound of rotors beating the air. The noise grew louder ... faded ... grew loud again, closer, reaching a crescendo as the helicopter rose above the trees.

The pilot was taking no chances and slowly skirted the edge of the clearing before starting his descent towards the landing pad.

Blasted by the downdraft, a tornado of dead leaves took to the air. In the turmoil we moved off through the trees, heading for a small rise overlooking the smiley face and the spliff.

We made it just as the helicopter leveled out over the pad. The pilot lost height until the machine was hovering six feet from the ground, turned into the wind, flared out, and gently set it down.

Snake Eyes and Van Norte ran to the helicopter. Snake Eyes pulled open the right-hand door. He shouted to the pilot and then sprinted across to the fuel pump and grabbed the handle. Van Norte quickly jammed the nozzle into place before too much fuel could splash on the ground.

I'd counted on them shutting down the engines but Snake Eyes was spooked enough to risk fueling with them running.

"What the fuck!" Pete's cry was followed by a shot.

Van Norte let go of the nozzle and dove out of sight.

The next round punched a hole in the helicopter's windshield. The engines roared and the machine left the ground.

Snake Eyes didn't hear the shots but the howling turbines got his attention. He stopped pumping and spun around. It took him a moment to work it out then he reached for the assault rifle and ran.

He ran straight towards the helicopter, which was already well clear of the ground. He danced left and then right, trying to work out which way the pilot would turn. The left-hand door of the helicopter swung open. Snake Eyes saw it and lunged forward, zigzagging to avoid the bullets ripping into the dirt at his feet.

The helicopter tilted and continued to rise.

Another burst of automatic fire erupted from the trees. The gunman was closer and we managed to pinpoint his position above the sound of the turbines.

"Holy shit," roared Willie as Glokani stepped into the clearing like an apparition from hell. The maniac was covered in blood and is clothes hung from him in rags. The bastard had guts to swim ashore, but he'd paid the price. His left shoulder was twisted at an impossible angle and his arm hung limp at his side.

We watched as he shook the empty magazine from the automatic. Gripping the gun between his knees, he fished another magazine from the remains of his pocket and rammed it into the butt. He staggered then brought up the gun and looked around for another target.

Van Norte was back on his feet. Glokani saw him and fired two rounds in his direction. It was too much for the finance minister and he bolted for the road leading down to the beach.

There was no sign of Debbie or Andropof.

"Come on," I shouted, "let's end this."

"Why? This is better than the movies," laughed Willie as Snake Eyes took aim at Glokani and opened up with the AK-47. His first burst went high and wide and ripped the branches from the trees above his head. If Glokani had had his wits about him, he could have dropped Snake Eyes with his next shot, but he'd seen Willie and fired at him instead.

Snake Eyes looked to see where the shots were going, and for a second we locked eyes. With so many people to kill, he didn't know who to shoot first, but one thing I will never forget, the evil bastard smiled.

The helicopter gathered speed. Gaining lift and forward momentum; it turned and headed for the gap in the trees. It continued to climb and, like a pink umbilical cord, the fuel hose climbed with it. Whether the hose was caught on the skids or the nozzle had jammed in the fuel port, it wasn't the way a gas jockey usually does business.

As the helicopter cleared the road it banked sharply to the left, dragging the hose across the clearing and knocking Snake Eyes off his feet.

Glokani let out a whoop of joy and loped towards him like a demented ape.

He had less than twenty yards to go when the fuel hose reached the end of the drum and the helicopter jerked to a stop.

The pilot might have got away with an emergency landing. Instead, he hauled back on the collective and the chopper shot straight up. For a moment the hose slackened, then stretched to its limits, and with a mighty crack, tore the fuel pump off its trolley and catapulted it into the air.

Glokani watched transfixed as the helicopter began its dance of death. Out of control, it tipped forward and sucked the hose into the thrashing blades. I screamed at him to run but the stupid sod fired wildly in my direction and then took aim at the chopper. He pulled the trigger until the magazine was empty then hurled the weapon through the air.

The helicopter cart-wheeled into the ground at his feet and the Diamond King vanished in a seething ball of flame.

The explosion ripped through the clearing. Burning aviation fuel engulfed the bunker and it blew up, sending a roiling cloud of smoke and flame into the sky.

I rolled over and over as metal and flaming leaves peppered the ground. The smoke was thick and choking and I kept on rolling until it began to thin. I had lost the shotgun, so pulled the Glock from its holster and hit the safety.

Pete shouted. His voice came from the left and was followed

by a rapid burst of automatic fire. My eyes were stinging and my throat was raw. I tried to shout but it came out as a croak.

Another burst of gunfire, this time the unmistakable rattle of Willie's Uzi.

Suddenly the firing stopped and the only sound was the burning helicopter as it twisted and spat amidst the leaping flames.

The smoke was clearing and I needed cover. I had no idea where anyone was, so I ran towards the safety of the scrub at the edge of the trees. The action had been fast and lethal and the adrenaline was coursing through my veins. At moments like this you risked being taken out by friendly fire. Pete and Willie were good, but in similar actions we'd all made fatal mistakes.

Through the smoke I saw the old tractor on my right. I kept going, dodging from tree to tree, holding the Glock in a two-handed grip until I reached the rise overlooking the helipad.

From the top of the rise I could see all the way across to the fuel bunker. Nothing moved.

Having consumed the fuel, the flames were dying down and, apart from the remains of the helicopter, the clearing was empty.

I backtracked, keeping to the trees, and made my way to the road leading down to the beach.

Silence—no gun fire, no voices—nothing.

I stepped onto the road and looked down the hill. Ten yards away, Willie was kneeling over Pete and pressing his blood-soaked hands to his chest.

Willie looked up. "Shit! What a fuck up. The flare, Dick, fire the fucking flare. We need the *Lady* here, *now!*"

I pounded down the hill and threw myself down next to Pete. He'd taken two rounds. One had gone right through the fleshy part of his thigh without hitting the bone. The wound was clean and hardly bleeding. The other bullet had struck him in the chest just to the right of his heart.

He was conscious.

I shook off the backpack, ripped out the heavy Very pistol, cocked it, and sent a white flare into the sky.

Pete moaned. "They won't see it, were on the wrong side of the island."

"They'll see it, arsehole, just stay with us," said Willie.

Willie grabbed my hands and forced them down onto the field-dressing covering the hole in Pete's chest. Then he took off down the hill.

"Willie, wait. Aw shit ..."

"He called me an arsehole!" Pete gasped and tried to stand up. I held him down as he started to cough. He wasn't bringing up blood, so the bullet had missed his lungs. And when I felt his pulse, it was weak but steady.

"Listen to me, Pete. The bullet's still in there but I see no sign of internal bleeding." The field-dressing on his chest was already bright red, so I grabbed another and ripped open the packet with my teeth. "I'm going to change the dressing and I want you to press it to your chest with the heel of your palm, we've got to get the bleeding under control."

" ... I'll try," he said through the pain.

He raised his hand and I guided it to the dressing. "Good man, hold it tight, the cavalry's on its way."

When I was sure he could hold the dressing in place, I broke open the Very pistol, ejected the spent 26.5mm aluminum cartridge and replaced it with a new one from the backpack.

Pete moaned as blood ran between his fingers. "It's bad, isn't it?

"Bad, yes, but we've both seen men survive with worse."

I cocked the Very pistol, warned Pete, stood, and fired.

We had a pack of one-time use morphine syringes in the medical kit. I dug them out and ripped open the pack.

"Dick, no," he groaned, "not yet. If the bastards come back, I can still hold a gun. That shit will knock me out."

Willie came storming up the hill. "They're long gone. Someone was waiting offshore in the big tender. By the time I got there they were out of range. I watched them board the yacht. They went south, heading God knows where." He knelt down and squeezed Pete's arm. "How yer doing, boyo, ready for a trip round the bay?"

Pete tried to smile then closed his eyes.

Willie stood and beckoned me to the side of the road. "The *Lady*'s already in the bay, but you're not going to like it. Sergeant Ascari's dead. That bastard Glokani slit his throat before he swam ashore."

"How do you know?"

"Fisher's down by the jetty in the clinker pulling boat. Toby's sailing the *Lady* backwards and forwards across the bay, staying about half a mile out. It's frigging wild out there and Toby's a mess, Fisher says if we're going to get off this fucking rock we have to go now, before Toby falls apart."

We quickly checked the field dressing on Pete's chest, then wrapped a bandage around his upper body and buttoned his shirt to keep it in place. Before he could protest, I snapped the end off a morphine ampoule and jabbed it through his clothes into his thigh. Then we picked him up and, half dragging half carrying, set off down the hill.

The sight from the granite jetty was not what I wanted to see. The wind had strengthened and veered towards the east, turning the waves into a tumbling mass as far as the eye could see. But there was some good news: the veering wind had put the cove in the lee of the northern point and although the waves were still rolling in, they were no longer breaking.

I looked down from the edge of the jetty to where Fisher, a

superb oarsman, was having little trouble keeping the pulling boat on station. Perhaps I was right about him, or why the hell would he be there?

Pete looked out to sea and groaned as Toby turned the *Lady* through the wind and sent the sails slamming across the boat.

"Shit," said Willie. "Did you see that? Fisher's right, Dick. He'll have the sticks out of her if we don't get out there soon."

We hurried Pete along the jetty and laid him at the top of the steps. A massive surge was running up the wall and I wondered just how the hell we were going to get off.

I left the two of them and ran towards the end of the jetty. Fisher rowed towards me and stopped about ten yards off.

"Do you have the second set of oars with you?" I shouted. He nodded towards the bottom of the boat. His shattered mouth must have been giving him hell. "You'll have one shot at it. You have to take all three of us off together. Don't hesitate. When you think the waves are right, come straight in. Once we're aboard, Willie will take the other set of oars while I take care of Pete."

He nodded and bent to the oars.

I ran back to the steps and told Willie and Pete the plan.

We secured our weapons and tightened the straps on the back-packs.

"Ready? I said.

Willie grunted and took Pete's legs, I took his arms, and between us we carried him down.

The sea was sweeping over the steps. They were covered in razor-sharp barnacles and slick with weed. It was like running on oiled glass.

Willie cussed and went down, taking the two of us with him.

The sudden jolt wracked Pete's body and he cried out. But there was no going back. The boat was almost abeam and Fisher was turning the bows towards the waves. He hauled on the starboard oar while backing the one to port, and slowly the boat came around until it was pointing at the jetty. His timing was superb. He let the boat ride over the waves until he was directly opposite the steps. He let another wave roll by and then pulled for all he was worth. At the last second he spun the boat around until it was parallel to the jetty, then dragged the starboard oar out of the rowlock and came alongside.

"Down, Willie, go down," I screamed.

The boat was driven sideways and smashed against the granite. Her stern rose and her bows swung away. Willie threw himself over the transom, dragging Pete and me with him. We hit the bottom boards in a tangle of arms and legs. I tried to stand. Pain shot through my right knee and my leg buckled.

Willie trampled over me and grabbed the second set of oars.

Pete had landed face down in the bilge water, turning it red. I dragged myself forward and rolled him over. The boat surged and slammed against the jetty. Fisher was thrown forwards and lost his grip on the oars. The next wave carried us towards the rocks at the head of the cove. Then Willie was pulling, Fisher was back on the thwart, and together they dragged us clear.

My right knee was locked and useless and I was almost retching with pain. But Pete was far worse. The minute he could leave the rowing to Fisher, Willie stumbled aft and we went to work. Pete was incoherent. The compress had been torn from his chest and he was hemorrhaging. We worked quickly—not knowing how much blood he'd lost and afraid he'd go into shock and die. Willie pulled the K-Bar from the sheath on Pete's ankle, carefully sliced through Pete's shirt and pulled it off.

I tore open a new field-dressing. Everything was soaked, but we managed to get another compress on him and a bandage in place. I checked the hole in his leg; it wasn't pretty but it would be okay, at least until we got him strapped to a bunk onboard the

Lady.

When we had done what we could for Pete, Willie turned to me. “Am I going to do it, or you?” he grinned.

“You sadistic fuck,” I said, and lowered myself down next to Pete in the bottom of the boat.

Willie put one hand on my knee and gripped my ankle with the other. “Don’t faint on me this time you fucking sissy.” He laughed, and with a sudden twist, snapped my knee back into place. The relief was instant but the crack was sickening, and I stumbled to relieve Fisher at the oars before I threw up.

How had Fisher rowed the boat alone in these appalling conditions? I looked aft to where he was now cradling Pete’s head in his lap and doing his best to keep him from rolling around in the heaving bilge. If we ever made it back to the island, I would make it my job to find out what role Fisher had played in all this. But now wasn’t the time to dwell on it. At the moment it was taking all my strength and concentration just to row.

Willie slid onto the aft thwart, adjusted the rowlocks, and a moment later we were pulling together towards the open sea. It was backbreaking work and after a few dozen strokes the loom of the oars had stripped the skin from my hands.

The end of the jetty slipped by to starboard and the wind slammed into us like a fist.

I risked a quick look over my shoulder and saw the *Lady* heading north. Toby had managed to drop the stays’l, but in the stormy conditions she was still grossly over canvassed under jib and main.

Toby must have seen us round the end of the jetty, for suddenly the schooner crashed through the eye of the wind and headed inshore on the port tack.

There was now more water in the bilge than we could possibly have shipped over the bow and I reckoned the boat had been damaged when it slammed against the steps. Fisher noticed it, too, and abandoned Pete in favor of the bailer.

The height of the waves, along with the bilge water surging across the boat, meant the oars were spending more time in the air than in the sea. "Willie. Stop rowing," I shouted. "We can't go much further without swamping her. Let Toby come to us."

We rested on the oars and let boat the drift beam-on to the wind.

"Not sure I like the look of this," said Willie. "The *Lady*'s difficult enough to handle with a full crew."

We watched the approaching one hundred and thirty ton schooner like Snake Eyes had watched the helicopter, not knowing if it was going left or right.

The *Lady* came towards us as if on rails.

For once, Willie was the first to lose his nerve. "Shit, he can't see us from the wheel …" he bellowed and threw himself against the oars.

He hadn't taken a stroke when beneath the din of thrashing canvas the yacht rounded-up and hove-to.

"Oh ye of little faith," I chortled and relaxed my terrified grip on the oars.

My joy at Willie's panic was cut short when Toby's ravaged face appeared at the rail. He looked down into the boat then quickly released the catch and swung open the entry port.

Before the *Lady* could drift away, Willie bent to the oars and brought us along side.

The moment our topsides touched, I scrambled aboard and thrust the bow-line into Toby's outstretched hand, then reached down and helped Willie and Fisher haul Pete onto the deck.

"What about the pulling boat?" Toby shouted.

"It's over," I said. "Let it go."

46

We ignored Toby's grief to take care of the living. Pete was semiconscious. We carried him below to the captain's cabin, undressed him, and lowered him onto the bunk. His wounds had stopped bleeding and, thanks to all the salt water flying around, were clean.

Willie packed Pete's wounds with antibiotic powder from the ship's first aid box and reapplied the dressings. Then we surrounded him with cushions and dropped the bunk-boards into the slots to prevent him from rolling out. I wanted to give him another shot of morphine, but he was lucid enough to say no, so I let it go.

A few minutes later Fisher appeared with a mug of warm cocoa and dribbled some between Pete's lips. He offered to stay and nurse him, but I shook my head.

We climbed back to the deck and Willie and I made our way aft to the wheel.

I laid my hand on Toby's arm.

Toby gripped the wheel and stared straight ahead. Tears ran down his face. "Dad was steering while I went down to look at the chart. I thought Glokani was sick ... I didn't know. I should never have left him, I—"

"Where was Fisher? Could Fisher have done it?" I said.

"What?"

"Fisher. Where was he?"

"I … He was up in the bows. We'd just tacked and he was sorting out the sheets."

"Where's your dad now, Toby?" I asked gently.

He wiped his eyes with the back of his hand. "We carried him below and laid him in the forepeak."

"Stay here and watch the wheel."

His fingers latched on to my arm. "Where are you going?"

"Below, we need to look at the body."

"I won't let you throw him overboard," he sobbed.

"Easy, Toby, no one's throwing your dad overboard. This will only take a few minutes, just stay here and steer the boat."

I thought I was going to have to pry his fingers open, but after a few moments he let go of my arm and took hold of the wheel.

Willie followed me down to the forepeak.

"Aw shit, is there no end to it?" he said as I opened the forepeak door.

Toby and Fisher had cleared a narrow space amongst the spare sails and laid Ascari's body on the floor boards.

Willie knelt down next to the corpse. He lifted Ascari's head and moved it from side to side. There was little blood and the slash in his throat was hardly visible.

"This wasn't done with a knife," he said. "The wound goes all the way around. It's a wonder his head's still in place. This was done with a cheese cutter—a garrote, a lot of lads in the regiment carried them."

He lowered Ascari's head and covered his face with a piece of sailcloth.

"What are you thinking, Dick?"

"Glokani," I said. "Would he know how to use a cheese cutter?"

Before he could answer, I heard a noise and turned to find Fisher staring at me. I had no idea how long he had been there.

"I've just copied down the latest weather forecast," he mumbled. "I think you should take a look."

I stood and followed him down the passageway. Behind me, Willie closed the forepeak door.

Fisher led us to the chart table in the main saloon. He had written the forecast on a yellow legal pad in large capital letters. I didn't like what I saw. According to the meteorologist, upper level winds had affected the track of the storm, causing the center of low pressure to accelerate to the nor-nor-west. I reached across and tapped the face of the barometer and was rewarded with a slight rise. The rapid movement of the low would account for the wind shift that made it possible for us to get off Mexican Hat. However, the new track put us closer to the storm's dangerous quadrant, where the seas were at their worst.

I had to discuss this with Pete. The *Lady* was his. If he could, he should make the decision.

Willie and Fisher headed for the deck with orders to keep the boat heading south until we had a definite plan. I waited until Fisher reached the companionway steps and called Willie back. "See if you can get Fisher to talk," I said. "Find out if he was in the military."

Willie nodded. "You don't trust him, do you?"

"Don't know. There's something about him that doesn't quite fit. He's a hard case, I know that."

"I could kill him. Solve the problem."

He grinned at me.

I glared back.

"Sorry …" he said on his way out.

Pete didn't look good, but then neither would I with two bullet holes in me. I thought he was unconscious but as I approached the bunk his eyes flew open. I pulled back the blanket and looked at the dressing on his chest. It was stained deep red but the bleeding had stopped.

"Pete, can you hear me?"

He didn't respond, so I took the damp cloth from the table next to the bunk and wiped his face. He was feverish and rivers of sweat ran down his body, soaking the sheet. Five minutes became ten, and his eyes remained unfocused. I prayed he was still reacting to the morphine and not going into shock.

"How is he?" Willie said from the door. "Sorry, Dick, but we need you up top. We're out of the lee of the island. Toby's dead on his feet and Fisher's no better."

"Give me a few seconds," I said.

He walked to the bunk and looked down at Pete. "Aw shit, how much blood has he lost?" He reached down and felt for a pulse, then shrugged and looked at me.

"Pete. You don't have to talk, just listen." I took his hand and told him about the storm. His eyes never focused, leaving me no idea whether he understood or not. There was little more we could do, so I pulled the blanket over him and turned towards the door.

"Don't sound so worried, Dick … I won't leave you alone with crazy Willie …" Pete's voice was a gravely whisper.

Willie touched Pete's face. "Die now you bastard and I'll tell everyone that you spoke my name as you croaked. Wouldn't do, boyo, to have the lads thinking you fancied me."

Pete chuckled, his eyes flickered, and seconds later he was asleep.

Battlefield humor, rough yet poignant. Even if he died, Willie knew it's what Pete would have wanted to hear.

We reached the deck to find a halo of bilious cloud around a low sun the color of dishwater. A dark squall was building along the southern horizon. As we watched, the finger of a waterspout appeared below the clouds and slowly spiralled down towards the sea.

Mexican Hat was falling astern and there was work to do if we were to survive the night. One look at Toby was enough; he was exhausted and gutted by grief. For the next few hours he would be useless, so I sent him below with orders to find some food and then get some sleep.

Fisher wasn't in much better shape, but I didn't want him below with Toby, so gave him some guff about being constantly ready and told him to catch some sleep on the pilot berth in the deckhouse.

It was a relief to have the deck to ourselves; now Willie and I could get on with nursing the ship through the night. We discussed raiding the medical kit for amphetamines to keep us awake but decided to make do with coffee and cocoa instead.

Most of the work of stowing had been done before we left St. Peters, and all the heavy equipment was lashed down. This left the engine and sails. The sails were the priority. A well-found yacht facing a storm at sea has little use for an engine, so the next hour was spent inspecting the canvas and rigging. After tweaking the autopilot and checking the lashings holding the foresail to the boom, we climbed onto the roof of the deckhouse and lowered the mains'l as far as the second reef. Without the extra hands it was brutal work.

We worked in silence, beating the salt laden canvas into submission and lashing it in place. As we tied off the last of the reef pendants, I found myself facing Willie across the boom.

He stared at me in silence.

"It was complicated," I said. Willie tied the final knot and punched the sail for good measure. I waited for him to speak but he remained dumb. "You think Susie died in that cellar. Susie died in South Africa. You saw the way she reacted to Chopstick. Sometimes, when she went away for weeks at a time, she was in the States seeking help. She'd come back and for a while everything was okay. But it never lasted, something would trigger the memories and the nightmares would start all over again."

A wave slammed into the hull. The boat heeled and a curtain of spray swept across the deck. We steadied ourselves against the boom until the boat straightened up, then jumped down off the deckhouse. Willie ran to the wheel and I leapt towards the winch on the mast. I waited for him to turn the boat into the wind and threw my weight behind the winch handle. After a few seconds he ran forward and together we re-hoisted the main.

Willie hadn't spoken since we climbed onto the deckhouse and his silence was pissing me off. I slammed the coiled halyard into his chest. "Secure that to the pin-rail," I said and pushed him out of the way.

"She was having your baby."

I stopped.

"What did you say?"

"I said Susie was pregnant, she found out over a week ago. She told me on the night we sprung you from the old prison."

"You knew about the baby when you saw what Chopstick had done to her?"

"Yes."

"Jesus, Willie."

He stepped forward.

"I had to save you from that, Dick."

"And now?"

"You have a right to know."

"Did Pete know?"

He shook his head. "No. Just me."

A gust of wind struck the boat. It was too much for the autopilot and she edged closer to the wind, causing the sails to shake.

"After she told me about the baby, I knew we could never be together. If she couldn't have you, she didn't want anyone."

"It didn't stop you loving her, though, did it?"

"No."

"I'm so sorry, Willie."

"All these years, Dick, and what the fuck has it brought us? You, me, Pete, look at us. We should've stayed in the regiment." His hair was plastered to his head and spray ran down his face. He was as angry as I'd ever seen him and I took a couple of steps back to get out of his way. "If we ever get this floating wreck back to the island, any island, then I'm gone. Going where there's decent beer and the only pirates are on stage in Pen-fucking-zance. God'amn Caribbean."

Another gust hit the starboard side. This time the boat rounded-up and stayed there, her sails flogging.

We ran aft. I disengaged the autopilot and spun the wheel to leeward, hoping the boat still had enough way on to turn. The *Lady* hesitated and then slowly fell back on the starboard tack.

"That was close. It's going to be a long night, Willie. Why don't you get your head down for a few hours, I'll call if I need you."

He looked at me and the anger had gone from his eyes.

"Cocoa?"

"Eh?"

"Cocoa."

I stared at him.

"Sure. Why the fuck not? Brits answer to everything, tea and bloody cocoa."

He put his hand on my arm "Dick. You and me. We're okay, aren't we?"

"Always, Willie."

He waited until he saw the grin then disappeared below and returned a few minutes later carrying a steaming mug. "I looked at Pete. He's hanging on, but only just. This is the last time I go to sea on this hulk unless he gets a radio transmitter and radar. It's like sailing in the eighteenth century, for Christ's sake."

I took the cocoa and brought it to my lips. It was thick and sweetened with half-a-pound of sugar. The steam caught in my nostrils and I inhaled the strong smell of rum. "Welsh cocoa," I said. But Willie had already gone below.

It had been a long time since I stood watch alone at sea. Usually it cleared my mind and helped put my chaotic life back into perspective. But not this night. This night everything had changed. My thoughts were about Susie and our unborn child, and how we'd shared so much yet ended up strangers. I tortured myself with that until I heard Mohamed's voice whispering in the rigging. And just as his agonized mumblings faded away, my friend the sergeant staggered up the companionway steps, wearing a sail-bag for a shroud.

All this death and destruction for a few pretty pink stones that weren't even real.

I was drifting between food and the erotic when the sound of heavy gunfire broke through the fog in my brain and I woke up lying on the deck with the sails flogging themselves to death overhead. A sheet of cold spray did the rest and I staggered to my feet.

In the early days of the Royal Navy, falling asleep on watch meant death at dawn. Right now on the *Lady* there was only Willie to care and we decided long ago not to kill each other—although recently we'd come close.

I spun the wheel and watched the compass needle swing through twenty degrees. The path of the storm made it possible for us to follow a course roughly between St. Peters and the Virgin Islands. On a night like this, I'd be surprised if any other ships were out here, but I'd fallen asleep, so needed to look around.

I re-engaged the autopilot and made my way forward, checking the sails as I went. As I drew level with the mainmast, the shadow of a man fell across the anchor windlass. Unnerved by my hallucinations, and no longer sure that what I was seeing was real, I crept forward, staying low and close to the rail. My approach was hidden by the sound of the wind. But, as I came near, some sixth sense made the apparition turn. He was quick, but his hand didn't quite reach his pocket before I had him by the shirt and drove my knee into his balls. The impact spun him round. As he went down, I grabbed his head and rammed his face into the cogs on the windlass. His hand shot up to protect his damaged mouth. The hand held a piece of wire attached to two wooden pegs.

Fisher didn't resist when I plucked the cheese cutter from his hand. I gave him plenty of time, hoping he would give me an excuse to kill him, but he was too busy dabbing at his bleeding lips.

A sheet of spray blew across the deck, thinning the dripping blood and washing it out through the scuppers.

"What we got here then, boyo?" Willie had come up the windward side and was now towering over Fisher, who was jammed in a corner with his back against the winch.

Willie took the cheese cutter, gripped a toggle in each fist, and snapped it open. Following our earlier conversation, I didn't know how he would react. Willie was no stranger to the killing device, so I was surprised when he reached down and helped Fisher to his feet. "Come on, Dick, let's get him back to the wheel, we can talk there." Shunning a reply, he placed his arm around Fisher and walked him aft along the deck.

I watched, expecting Willie to suddenly snap Fisher's neck and throw him overboard, and felt cheated when they carried on walking and disappeared from sight.

Uneasy, I pulled myself up onto the bulwark and scanned the sea.

A line of jagged waves reached to the horizon; night had fled and dawn had come.

47

There was little joy in the voice of the weather forecaster as she relayed the latest news of the storm. The castaway from New York had gone, no doubt leaving her to deal with a studio full of discarded pizza boxes, empty beer bottles, and cigarette butts. Then again, perhaps the storm was heading her way and she was simply worried about the roof.

Willie marked the storm's position on the chart. It was to the east-south-east and threatening to strengthen into a hurricane.

"What do you say we hold this course, Dick?" Willie slid the dividers across the chart and I followed the line with my eyes. "It takes us to the west of St. Peters, but once the storm moves on it puts the wind behind us for a fast run home."

I looked at him. "This is the safest course to follow," I said, and drew my own line across the chart. "It puts more miles between us and the eye of the storm. If the damn thing does turn into a hurricane then every mile will help."

We glared at each other. Someone had to make a decision. If we survived the day, Willie's course would get Pete to a doctor within twenty-four hours. My course would keep the boat safe, but take us far from land, facing a long beat home once the storm moved away.

Willie threw the dividers down on the chart and folded his arms. "Glad I'm only a sergeant. It's your call."

"And if I call it wrong, we've all got to die sometime, right?"

"Aye. Something like that."

I picked up the dividers and walked the various distances off against the latitude scale. "Set your damn course Willie. Then get Toby and Fisher on deck. I'm going to talk to Pete again."

I handed him the dividers and made my way forward. The motion of the boat was much more noticeable, especially in the confines of the narrow passageway.

The door to Pete's cabin was open; he was lying on his back, his empty eyes staring at the deck above. I ran towards him and almost sobbed with relief when he coughed. His eyes went to a bottle of water jammed against the pillow next to him. I reached for it, unscrewed the cap, and brought the bottle to his lips. The first mouthful made him retch. Then he managed to swallow some down.

He gasped a few words but I told him to wait until I looked at his wounds.

The dressing covering the hole beneath his heart was only slightly bloodier than before. I put my ear to his chest and this time heard a deep wheezing in his lungs. "You're doing okay," I said, keeping the bad news to myself. "Now you can talk, but only for a few minutes.

"You make a better assassin than nurse. You thought I was dead when you came through the door." He started to laugh but the breath caught in his throat and his eyes clouded with pain.

"Glad you still have a sense of humor," I said.

"Tell me you haven't left that crazy Welshman in charge of my boat," he wheezed.

"Sort of. I left him arguing with the autopilot, it could be love."

He smiled and I raised his head and brought the bottle of water to his lips. He took a few more sips and then lay back.

I waited for his breathing to settle down and then told him the plan. He listened for a few minutes but cut me off before I could finish. "No, Dick. Willie's wrong, don't listen to him. Steer away from the storm. You know the rules. We fight for the safety of all, not for the safety of one. I'm no fool, so stop treating me like one. My chances of surviving are slim. Shit, with a wound like this, I should be dead already."

"If you die, Willie will tell everyone the boat's his."

"You bastard," he groaned.

"I know."

Shouting filtered down from the deck above. The sails began to flog and I heard the rattle of the sheet winches as Willie settled the boat on its new course.

Pete rolled his head to one side. "Sounds like you've already made a decision."

"Yes. And I don't want a mutinous Welshman on my hands, so I'll let it stand."

"Since when have sergeants given the orders?"

"How far back do you want to go, Waterloo?"

"You're a fool, Dick, steer away from the storm, I'm finished and you know it ..." He tried to say more but the effort was too much and after few seconds his eyes fluttered and he drifted off.

I checked the bunk-boards and rearranged the cushions to prevent him from moving about. I prepared another shot of morphine, then decided against it and put the syringe back in the pack. He hadn't asked for one, but then the tough bastard never would.

"Dick, you need to come up." I looked around and found Toby in the doorway. He threw a glance at Pete and covered his eyes.

"It's okay," I said. "He's asleep."

He moved across to the bunk and put his hand on Pete's forehead. Reassured, he delivered his message. "There's a black line from horizon to horizon, Willie says it's a bad squall and we're heading into it."

I followed him along the passageway and up the companionway steps. As we emerged into the sultry air the boat lurched and heavy rain spattered across the deck.

Willie and Fisher were by the wheel. Willie was steering, leaning to windward and gripping the spokes with both hands. He raised his eyes from the compass and nodded towards the bow.

The squall was about a mile off, spiraling upwards from the sea and filling half the sky. Judging by how the water was blowing from the wave tops, I estimated the wind at around fifty knots.

"Toby, I want you on the foredeck and ready with the jibs. Make sure you're tied on and keep your eyes aft, you won't hear me above the squall, so we'll use Fisher here as a runner. He'll bring you my orders. Willie, you watch the mains'l. Take a little weight on the topping lift and then stand by the main halyard. If I can't leave the wheel, then you'll have to control the sheet as well. You know what to do."

Another curtain of rain slashed across the deck. When it cleared the hard edge of the squall was less than a quarter of a mile from the bow.

"I'm going to bring the boat closer to the wind and try and sail through it. There'll be a hell of a noise from the sails. I'm counting on the wind easing as we get through the squall's leading edge, so just keep your eyes on me and hold on."

Willie stepped away from the wheel and I slid in behind it.

"Bring the mains'l in a tad, let's see if she can handle it," I said.

The mainsheet screeched in protest as Willie cranked the winch, bringing the boom further amidships. The second it was secure, I turned the wheel, forcing the *Lady* closer to the wind.

Our bows entered the rain at the edge of the squall. For a moment the wind died and the boat seemed to shudder with relief.

Fooled like sailors before him, Toby forced a grin and waved from the bow.

Then it was on us.

"Sheets. *Sheets!*" I screamed, and snatched the cutlass from its sheath alongside the steering box.

Too late. The wind tore across the starboard bow forcing the ship on to her beam ends. Pinned by the sails, the angle of the deck increased until the lee rail went under.

Rain scythed through the air, making it hard to breath and impossible to see. The wind and seas beat us down, submerging tons of teak and oak.

The rudder was useless and the wheel dead in my hands.

I clung to the spokes.

Water roared across the deck, sweeping all before it, seeking a way below.

The masts reached for the wave tops and we began to founder.

I let go the wheel and swung the cutlass at the mainsheet, missed and swung again.

There was an almighty crack and the boat staggered upright.

Tons of water sluiced out through the scuppers and the *Lady* came up some more. As she rose, she began to round-up until her bows were facing the wind. The mainsheet was still tight, but someone had saved the ship by freeing the jibs and, seeking retribution, they were flogging themselves to death on the stays.

The wheel kicked and I threw myself against the spokes and forced it down.

With no way on, the boat climbed the face of the next wave until the deck was near vertical and the bowsprit pointing at the seething clouds. The bow punched through the crest, the wave collapsed and the yacht fell, plowing her stem into the waiting trough. Her bowsprit disappeared and the bulwarks went under. A wall of water thundered aft carrying a man with it. Caught by the force of the wave, the body slammed into a stanchion and came to rest in the scuppers.

Another wave rolled towards us. The boat began to climb until our bows were hovering above the crest and we were at the mercy of the sea.

All headway gone, the *Lady* slid backwards down the face of the wave. As she fell, she corkscrewed, offering her starboard side to the squall. The movement saved us. Instead of falling back, the wind drove the boat hard to leeward and, before the next wave could claim its prize, the mains'l filled and the wheel bucked in my hand.

To survive we must have speed. I pushed the helm down, forcing the boat away from the wind. I was talking to her, urging her on.

The *Lady* began to move, creeping forward.

I brought the wheel amidships—held it there—then gave it three spokes to port. The old girl responded, staggered drunkenly over the next crest, taking the brunt of the sea on her shoulder and throwing whatever water came on board out through the scuppers.

Lightning struck the sea to starboard, painting the waves with sickly light. Then, with the same speed it began, the wind eased.

We were back under control, sails pulling, but would it last?

I gave the wheel two more spokes to port.

Willie and Toby stumbled past, their voices muffled by a distant peal of thunder.

The sea had almost forced Fisher out through one of the freeing-ports and, by the way his head rolled from side to side, I knew he was dead.

They lifted his body and brought it forward. Willie raised an eye and nodded towards the rail. It was the sensible thing to do; we already had one corpse in the forepeak and soon the stench would make going below unbearable.

Then there was Pete.

The wind had dropped to around twenty five knots, it was holding steady and, if anything, veering towards the north. That could mean the low pressure was on the move or another squall was building.

"Put him over," I said.

"No!" We looked at Toby. "Put him below with my dad."

"It might be days before we reach land, Toby. It's best he goes over the side." I said it with authority, but the look on the lad's face told me he wasn't going to do it.

Willie gently pushed him aside and hefted Fisher onto his shoulders.

"Don't throw him in the water." Toby forced himself between Willie and the side of the boat.

Willie's face flushed with anger. Even with Fisher's body across his back he would think nothing of knocking Toby aside.

We both knew what the smell of death did to men on the battlefield, but what right had we to enforce our military code on a frightened kid who'd just seen his father garroted.

The *Lady* gave a lurch and Willie did a little dance with the dead man. He flashed his eyes in my direction and I knew his next move would erase Toby from the equation.

I looked from Toby to Willie and shook my head. "Okay, we'll keep him for now, but not below. Take him as far aft as you can, then get some sailcloth from the locker, wrap him in it and lash him to the stanchions. Can you do that, Toby?"

For once, Willie didn't argue. He laid Fisher down on the deck, told Toby to take his feet, and in silence they carried his body to the stern.

A few minutes later Willie was back at the wheel. "In a couple of days he'll beg us to throw the body over the side, same goes for his father."

"It's Pete," I said. "He's thinking about Pete. He wants his friends and family in the ground, not out here in this godforsaken ocean. You can hardly blame him for that."

"And me Dick, what if I was laying dead in the scuppers, would you put me over the side?"

"Have to, Willie. No dumpsters out here."

Just then Toby walked by carrying the sailcloth.

I left Willie trying to explain why we were laughing and made my way below.

48

I heard it the moment I reached the bottom of the companionway steps: running water and lots of it. I grabbed the bronze lifting-ring in the nearest inspection hatch and pulled. The hatch came up to reveal eighteen-inches of filthy water surging through the bilge.

The water could have found its way below when we were knocked down, or come through a broken porthole somewhere, but I didn't think so. This water was still coming in, which meant we had sprung a plank or were holed.

I left the hatch open and moved forward. The next hatch was jammed, so I ran to the galley and grabbed a knife. I worked the blade between the floorboards and the edge of the hatch and after a few seconds it was high enough to squeeze my fingers underneath and force up. More water, but thanks to the rise in the forward section of the hull, not as deep.

I shoved the hatch to one side and sprinted aft towards the engine room. As I ran the noise of water grew louder, and when the boat suddenly rolled I heard it slosh up the inside of the hull.

The *Lady's* engine room takes up the full width of the yacht. It houses the one hundred and eighty horsepower Gardner diesel, which is bolted amidships on two massive timbers that run fore and aft. Two zinc-topped workbenches flank the engine, one on either side. On the wall above each bench, pegboards carry a selection of tools held in place by stainless steel clips. Most of the tools are modern, but some are over a hundred years old.

The suction pipe from the manual bilge pump on deck runs down through the engine room and disappears into a deep sump beneath the engine oil-pan. The sump was full, the gearbox was already under, and water was lapping at the hole that held the engine dipstick.

The *Lady* has a number of electric bilge pumps located in various places throughout the boat, but by the depth of water I knew they were either overwhelmed or not working.

I slammed the engine room door and ran back along the passageway. My first shout brought Willie to the top of the companionway steps. "Never mind putting the stiffs in the sea," I roared. "If you don't get down here quick, we'll be going with 'em."

Willie launched himself down the steps, glanced at the open hatches, and ran aft towards the engine room. I followed, taking a quick look into the bilge where the water was steadily rising.

The air in the engine room was rank with fumes as the water in the sump mixed with old oil and years of accumulated sludge. Willie went straight to the starboard workbench and pulled open a drawer. He took out a bag of tapered ash plugs of various sizes, selected one of the smallest, and grabbed a hammer. Fighting the motion of the boat, he staggered to the engine, yanked out the dipstick, and with three sharp blows drove the plug into the hole.

"Too late for the gearbox, it's under. Let's pray the baffles in the vent have kept the water out," he said.

"You've got to get it running, Willie. My bet is the electric pumps have flattened the house batteries, if we can get some power into them then we might have a chance. Do what you can while I heave-to and get Toby on the bilge pump."

I ran down the passageway and climbed to the deck.

Toby was at the wheel. His face was a mask of shock, he was on the edge of panic. "We're sinking," he cried, "I know we are." He tried to dodge around me.

No more compassion; if he wanted to live then he must listen. I got right in his face, my eyes inches from his. The trick was to make him angry, so I grabbed the front of his shirt and slammed him into my chest.

He took a wild swing.

Good. I stepped inside the blow and slammed him hard against the wheel. "Toby, listen to me. We're out of time. There's a good chance you're going to die. The ocean Toby, take a look." I forced his head around until he was looking at the line of marching waves. "Immutable, Toby. The sea doesn't care if you live or die. We're on it, and soon we'll be in it, and maybe you're the one who can prevent it. Are you listening?"

He threw a weak punch. His fist slid up my arm and the fight went out of him. I pulled him to me and held him while he sobbed; waiting, knowing the sea was pouring into the boat but not daring to let him go.

Suddenly, a familiar tremor ran through the deck. Willie had managed to start the engine. Toby felt it too, and it seemed to calm him. "What can I do?" he stammered.

I took a step back and made him look me in the eye. Perhaps we would never again be friends, but at least we might survive. "Come on," I said. "I'll show you."

We worked the sails, brought the boat into the wind and hove-to. Then I bundled him forward to where the ancient double-throw bilge pump was bolted to the deck. "Keep your eye to weather and call me if you see another squall. If the wind doesn't increase too much then we should be able to ride it out. But if we can't get the water out of her it won't matter either way, so keep pumping. We won't abandon ship until we're forced to step up into the life raft, maybe not even then. Knowing Pete, that life raft hasn't been serviced in ten years." I thought I'd gone too far by mentioning the life raft, but on hearing Pete's name he actually smiled. I grabbed his arm. "We'll make it, Toby, I promise. Just pump. Okay."

I was at the top of the companionway step when he shouted my name. I turned, and he clenched his right fist and brought it to his heart in the Rastafarian sign of respect. He held it there until I returned the salute, then threw his weight behind the handle and began to pump, sending filthy water gushing across the deck and back to the ocean where it belonged.

The water in the passageway was now level with the floorboards. I didn't want to admit it but the motion of the boat, even in the heavy seas, was becoming sluggish.

I burst through the engine room door as Willie looked up. He was slick with sweat, smeared with oil, and dripping blood from a gash on the back of his right hand.

"The batteries are charging but that's not the problem," he roared. "There's so much crap in the bilges it's blocking the electric pumps. I clear one, and another one blocks. The pump under the galley has already burnt out. Got any good news?"

"Hardly," I yelled. "Toby's working the deck pump but I doubt he can keep it up for more than half an hour without we spell him."

The boat rolled hard to starboard. Filthy water poured out of the sump and swirled around our knees. When she rolled back, the water surged across the engine room leaving scum half-way up the hull and a coating of oil over everything.

The engine room lights dimmed. There was a sharp crack from behind an electrical panel followed by a plume of acrid smoke. "Last fucking cruise I'm taking with you, Turpin." Willie spit the bitter taste of melting wire out of his mouth and slid across the oily floor towards the panel. "The breakers are tripping; the water's getting to the connections. Fuck it, we're losing her. You're an officer, do something."

"The forefoot," I said.

"What?"

"The forefoot. We hit the bottom hard coming over the ledge. Pete thought we might have done some damage; he checked at the time but only found a few inches of water the bilge. I'm going forward to take another look."

Willie stopped what he was doing, grabbed a large flashlight from the shelf above his head and checked the batteries. He tossed the light towards me and quickly went back to the smoldering panel.

No running down the passageway this time, the oily water was over the floorboards and it was like skating on ice.

I reached the forepeak, wrenched open the door and with a whispered apology to the late Sergeant, grabbed his body and floated it out of the way.

The forepeak was a fountain of rushing water. Whatever it was the damage was here beneath the jumble of ropes and sails. I burrowed into the piles, tossing everything behind me until the sergeant's body disappeared under a mountain of gear.

My heart sank; the cabin sides were paneled with plywood, and the screws holding them were hidden beneath a thick coating of paint. I needed the fire axe from the engine room.

I struggled back along the passageway. The water was already deeper and I blundered into one of the open hatches, smashing my ankle against the combing as I fell into the bilge. Dragging myself along like a lame dog, I made it to the engine room and looked into Dante's inferno.

The thundering engine was lost amidst clouds of steam from the filthy water sloshing around it. At first I couldn't see him and then Willie appeared through the haze. He was on his belly with his head down the sump fighting the bilge pump suction pipe as though it were the boa constrictor from hell. Every time the boat rolled, he disappeared beneath a torrent of filthy water only to reappear, retching, when it rolled back.

I used the legs of the workbench to drag myself towards him. "Typical. I go forward to do the hard work while you take a sauna," I said.

The boat rolled and he went under. As he came back up, he hauled the end of the heavy pipe from the water and showed me the strum box, which was clogged with rubbish.

"This is now the only pump that's working," he gasped, "but no matter how hard I try to keep it clear, as soon as Toby starts to pump, it clogs. There must be fifty years of garbage in the bilges. You wouldn't believe some of the things I've fished out." He tried to laugh and threw up into the sump.

We lay together gripping the pipe. "We're losing her," I said.

"No we're not." The voice came from the specter at the door and for a moment I thought Sergeant Ascari was back from the dead. "We're not losing her, take the engine raw water cooling pipe off the inlet and put it in the sump."

"Do it, Willie," I yelled and rolled towards Pete as he slid down the bulkhead into the muck.

"Jesus, Pete, you scared me to death." I got my hands under his arms and began dragging him back along the flooded passageway towards his cabin. He made a weak attempt to stop me and then gave up.

"Got to watch you two lunatics all the time," he mumbled. "Can't trust you with the *Lady*, can't trust you with any lady come to that."

"Does your sudden appearance mean you're not going to die?"

We made it as far as the cabin door before he spoke again. "We're all going to die, Dick, but not today and not on my yacht."

Toby appeared at the bottom of the companionway steps.

"Pump's blocked again," he shouted. Then he saw Pete. "What the fuck—"

"Its okay, Toby, Captain Blackbeard thinks he knows how to save the ship. Give me a hand to get him back to his cabin, then go to the engine room and help Willie. He's disconnecting the engine's water cooling pipe from the seacock. We're going to run the bilge water through the engine and pump it out through the exhaust. Once you get it working, stay there and keep the end of the pipe free of rubbish. And tell Willie I need him in the forepeak with the fire axe. If we can keep her afloat for another half hour we might just save her."

Toby looked towards the forepeak where the gear was piled over his father's body, then looked down at Pete. One glance was enough, he slid his hands beneath Pete's arms, and together we carried him into the cabin and lay him on the bunk. We wedged him in, then I ran forward and Toby ran aft.

The old schooner was massively built, but the years had taken their toll and keeping her repaired was an endless cycle of make and mend. The forefoot, where the elm keel joined the oak stem, was fastened together by heavy bronze bolts. At the scarf, where the two faces of the wood come together, a series of long wooden pegs, or stop-waters as they are known, run crossways along the joint. In a yacht of the *Lady*'s vintage, the joint would be bedded on red-lead putty or tar. This was an area that had caused Pete trouble before.

I was tearing at the panel over the scarf joint when Willie arrived with the fire axe and pushed me aside. He whaled into the paneling with the spike. And when this proved too slow, reversed the axe and brought the blade crashing down. The wood disintegrated and within seconds we were able to rip it away with our hands. Once we had inflicted enough damage, I grabbed the flashlight and wiggled my head and shoulders through the hole and looked back to where the sea was rushing in.

The damage wasn't to the forefoot, but to the planking just above the keel. We might have sprung a plank or lost the caulking out of the seams. It was difficult to tell. But whatever the cause, we couldn't get near enough to the leak without destroying more paneling and a disused bunk that acted as a workbench.

I gave Willie the news and quickly stepped back. Without hesitation, he swung the axe and reduced more of the paneling to matchwood. The bunk was next to go. Ten minutes of chopping and ripping brought us to the area above the leak.

It was the seams. A gap around quarter-of-an-inch wide, spanning three frames, ran for a distance of about seven feet. The planks were still hard against the frames, so they hadn't sprung. My guess was that someone who should have known better had driven the caulking iron right through the seam and then, in desperation, packed the seam with epoxy glue. When we struck the reef some of the brittle epoxy had probably shattered and fallen out. The forward motion of the boat had done the rest and whatever caulking-cotton remained in the seam had been sucked out. It was a battle every wooden boat restorer faced: everyone with a bucket of epoxy thought they qualified as a shipwright.

Willie threw down the axe. "Jesus, Dick, what do we do now?"

"We get to play little Dutch boy," I said and dragged him into the passageway. "Go to the galley and take down a section of plywood headlining. Then get a saw out of the tool locker and cut off some eight foot strips. Make 'em about six inches wide. And while you're at it, grab a hand-full of ring-nails; Pete keeps them in a drawer above the starboard bench in the engine room. If you find any tubes of caulking compound, bring those too."

I left Willie sloshing his way aft and made my way to the saloon for a couple of foam cushions. Wooden boats have survived with worse damage to the hull, but already we had taken on tons of water and I wondered if there was another hole somewhere else. There is a formula for working out the amount of water entering a boat through a given sized hole. The formula eluded me but I remember reading somewhere that a one inch hole, three feet below the waterline, would let in more than two thousand gallons of water an hour. With what the *Lady* had already swallowed, we didn't have much time.

I waded back to the forepeak, rammed the cushions over the open seams, and used pieces of the shattered bunk to wedge them in place. The cushions helped but not much, the water was still pouring in. Each gallon would increase the pressure until finally the boat gave up the struggle and went down.

The engine was rumbling in the distance, and once I heard somebody shout.

It was taking Willie far too long. I jammed another piece of wood against the cushions and was about to go looking for him when he waded through the door. He had everything I'd asked for and more. He'd brought the strips of plywood, and a bucket of wedges he'd found somewhere. His pockets were bulging with ring-nails and he was dragging along a five gallon pale of roofing-tar.

He yanked a hammer and a tenon saw out of his belt and shoved them towards me. "Go to it, Noah," he said.

I moved back, so that we could change places, and after a lot of shuffling Willie was able to reach the cushions and hold them in place.

I lay the first strip of plywood across the frames and marked off the length with a touch of the saw. Then I cut it and lay it in place to make sure it fit. Next I hammered a line of nails around the edge of the ply, setting them about an inch apart and making sure that each point broke through the surface on the opposite side. I used the blade of the axe to pry the lid off the bucket of tar and then dug into it with my hands and slathered a thick coating onto the face of the ply.

When all was ready, I slid in beside Willie and told him to ease the cushion out of the way. The second it was clear, I jammed the plywood over the seam and drove in the nails. A couple of them bent, but by the time the last one was in, the leak between the first two frames was down to a trickle.

Halfway through the repair, Toby burst in with the news that the water in the bilge was going down but now the engine was overheating.

Willie followed him back to the engine room and reattached the cooling pipe to the seacock. With clean seawater again circulating through the engine the temperature began to drop, and after a few minutes it was back to normal.

It was late afternoon by the time we had the last piece of plywood in place and the leak reduced to a dribble. Willie went back to repairing the electric pumps and after a couple of hours the bilge was almost dry.

If I was tired before, I was exhausted now. Yet it wasn't until I climbed on deck that I realized the seas had gone down and we were no longer pitching as violently. The sky was still thick with cloud, but in places brushstrokes of sunlight bled through, painting the translucent waves an amazing shade of green.

Willie had followed me up the companionway steps. He was clutching something in his fist. "Here. Toby made this for you. Said to tell you he cut the mold off the bread." He shoved the sandwich into my outstretched hand, which was still black and reeking of tar. "Toby also caught the latest weather forecast, something about high pressure to the north causing the storm to accelerate and move away. Problem is it's taking the wind with it."

The forecast was right. As night fell the wind became fitful, at times gusting to thirty knots then dropping away into lengthening periods of calm.

By midnight the occasional star was visible overhead. Eventually the wind died altogether, leaving behind a sloppy, tormenting sea that rolled the yacht far to port and then lazily back to starboard again.

We took it in turns to steer, and found the boat rode easier with the engine on tick over and the staysail and reefed main hauled tight amidships and sheeted flat.

As the seas went down our speed crept up until we were doing three knots and at last steering a course for home.

Regular checks showed the repairs were holding. Some water was finding its way into the bilge, but the electric pumps were easily keeping ahead of the flow.

Every half-hour one of us went to sit with Pete, and once I changed the dressings on his chest and leg. He was weak, his wounds inflamed, and when I took his temperature it pushed the mercury to a hundred and four.

The horrible motion brought on by the sloppy seas made sleeping impossible and dawn found the three of us on deck.

I joined Toby at the rail to take a piss. I unzipped and looked up.

Temptress was laying a mile off, dead in the water, wallowing in the swell.

49

Toby saw the motor yacht at the same time and began to shout a warning. He shut up fast when I made a furious silencing motion with both hands.

I ran to the throttle and pulled it all the way back, then hit the red button and killed the engine. Willie heard the engine die and dashed towards the companionway steps. Then he saw my hand on the throttle. Instinct told him to look around, and within seconds he had spotted the yacht.

The *Lady* rose on the swell. A block creaked in protest.

No one spoke.

Willie fished the binoculars out of the box by the wheel and walked to the rail. "She's a ghost ship," he whispered. "The Mary-fucking-Celeste." He peered and then handed me the glasses.

The motor yacht was beam-on to the seas, gently rolling in the dying swell. I brought the glasses to my eyes, adjusted the lenses until the boat swam into focus then, beginning at the bow, slowly ran them down the length of the yacht.

Nothing seemed out of place. Even the inflatable was there, sitting in its chocks on the deck beneath the helipad. I brought the glasses forward and focused on the wheelhouse. The wing-bridge door was open and I could see the jagged hole in the combing where the Harley had gone through, but there was no sign of life.

"How many people are on board and where the hell are they, Willie?"

"Six, by my reckoning. Snake Eyes and the girl, Andropof, Van Norte and maybe a couple of crew."

"Why are they just sitting there?"

"You ask too many questions, Dick. Her engines are down or she ran out of fuel—who knows, who the fuck cares—it could be anything, she's there, and she's ours for the taking."

Toby opened his mouth to speak then shook his head and moved away from the rail.

I felt a breath of air on my cheek and watched as a cat's-paw danced across the swell, ruffled the surface of the water, and then moved on.

Willie noticed it, too. "Wind's coming back," he said. "It's now or never."

"How many weapons do we have?"

He didn't hesitate. "We lost some on the island. I still have the Uzi and there's a Glock."

"Nothing with any range, that means getting close." I swept the binoculars over the yacht and still she looked deserted.

Another cat's-paw sent ripples skipping across the water only this time it held steady from the west. It wasn't much, but it was enough.

"We're upwind and they haven't seen us," I said. "They'll hear the exhaust note if we use the engine. We can't use the main or foresail either; we'll have to get alongside using the jibs. It'll help to get a line on her, but if that doesn't work then we'll jump. Toby, you can steer the *Lady*."

Toby looked at each of us in turn then, without a word, walked to the base of the mast, undid the halyard from the pin-rail, and slowly began lowering the main.

While Toby and I worked the sails, Willie went below for the weapons.

Back on deck he handed me the Glock and three spare clips.

He cocked and locked the Uzi, slid the strap over his shoulder, and went forward to prepare a mooring line.

Toby slid behind the wheel and fixed his gaze on the motor yacht.

I secured a line to a bollard at the stern. Then took the coils of rope and walked forward, carefully passing them around the outside of the rigging until I was amidships, where I tied them off.

Temptress was directly downwind, beam-on, with her port side to the breeze. There was just enough wind to keep the jibs full. We were on the port tack, ghosting towards her at three knots, heading for a patch of water fifty feet from her stern.

The gap between us slowly narrowed.

I brought the binoculars to my eyes. Nothing, the whole yacht was deserted. Then I saw it. Someone had closed the wheelhouse door.

Willie saw me tense and brought the Uzi up to the rail.

Perhaps the door had closed with the rolling of the yacht.

A minute ticked by.

Suddenly a figure stepped out of the wheelhouse and disappeared aft.

"Should I start the engine?" Toby hissed.

I caught the fear in his voice and turned to reassure him. "Steady," I whispered. "Our luck's holding; he didn't see us." I braced myself against the bulwarks, waiting for gunfire that never came.

Time dragged on, each second seemed like an hour as slowly the motor yacht filled the horizon. Once we reached her stern we would let fly the jibs, turn hard-a-port, and rely on our momentum to carry us alongside. If they saw us, Toby had orders to start the engine and ram her.

Two hundred yards and still they hadn't seen us.

A block creaked—it sounded like the tightening of a noose.

The *Lady* lifted on the swell. I chambered a round in the Glock and picked up the stern line.

A hundred yards and Willie checked the coils of the mooring line in his left hand.

The leech of the jib fluttered and stilled.

"Jesus, I've wanted to do this all my life."

I spun around to find Pete next to Toby at wheel. He'd dragged on a pair of cutoff Levis and an old white shirt that was already soaked with blood. He was clutching an ancient cutlass in his right hand.

"Oh shit, no," I said, and dropped the mooring line. Before I could stop him he slid the cutlass into his belt and wedged himself behind the wheel.

"It's classic, Dick. Just like Nelson would have done it. We have the weather gauge. We can lie alongside and board her." He gripped the spokes and cast an eye towards *Temptress,* measuring distance and wind.

I looked down; blood was dripping from his shorts and pooling on the deck at his feet. "Pete, listen to me, you're bleeding to death, let's get you below."

"No! I'm finished, Dick, and this is how it will end." He dragged the cutlass from his belt and nudged Toby out of the way to give himself swinging room.

When I looked across the water *Temptress* was less than fifty yards off. I was going to have to force him away from the wheel, but I knew I could never do it.

"Shit. Toby, watch him, do what he tells you," I said.

Pete grinned and waved the cutlass at Willie. Willie shook his fist at the motor yacht and grinned back.

We were thirty yards from *Temptress* when the wind died.

What now? Starting the engine would have the same effect as ringing a fire alarm.

Pete glanced over the port quarter, spoke to Toby, and raised his hand. "Wait for my signal," he rasped. Toby nodded and padded towards the jib sheet.

Our speed dropped to almost nothing. We were now wallowing off *Temptress*'s stern and in danger of drifting by.

Then I felt it: a small breath of wind from abaft the port beam.

Pete twirled a finger and Toby gently eased the jib sheet. When Pete clenched his fist, Toby made the sheet fast again.

The *Lady* began to move.

Pete held the course as the boat picked up speed.

Another signal from Pete and Toby tightened the sheet a notch.

We began our slow turn to port.

Willie hefted the mooring line.

We were back up to two knots and slowly gaining speed.

Our bowsprit carved an arc close to the motor yacht's stern. Then we were inching alongside.

The breeze strengthened and Pete signaled Toby to ease the sheet, spilling the wind to slow us down.

Our bows drew level with the yacht's port quarter.

Suddenly, two crewmen, armed with coffee cups, appeared on deck. Willie dropped the nearest with a double tap from the Uzi, then switched to full automatic and hosed the yacht from stem to stern.

The *Lady*'s engine roared to life and we crashed alongside.

Willie leapt onboard and ran forward with the line.

Pete saw him go and spun the wheel.

I waited until our sterns were almost touching then climbed on the rail and threw myself across the gap. I landed on top of a polished stainless steel bollard, my leg shot from under me and I went down, dropping the Glock.

Instinct told me to roll. I did, and found myself looking down the barrel of an AK-47.

"What took you so long?" said Debbie and clicked the safety to off.

50

Looking down the barrel of a gun can spoil your day. Looking down the barrel of an AK-47 on full automatic fucks it completely.

I searched for the Glock and saw it lying in the scuppers next to Debbie's feet.

A burst of gunfire rattled the yacht and my sphincter shrunk to the size of a pinhead.

Debbie looked down her nose and let out a snorting laugh. That she knew what was going on in my shorts filled me with anger. So, to mess with her head, I thought I'd stick my finger down the end of the AK's barrel. I even raised my hand but someone came charging down the deck shouting 'Shootadesonofabeech' and unless Willie was practicing his Che Guevara accent, I knew it wasn't him.

"Why wait?" I said.

"Why indeed." My good eardrum exploded and gunshot residue ripped into my face. I heard a scream and opened my eyes to see 'desonofabeech' tango cross the deck using his entrails for a partner.

A stream of bullets splintered the teak rail above my head. Debbie spun and fired a long burst towards the upper deck. "Come on," she shouted and kicked open a door and disappeared inside the boat.

I scooped up the Glock, popped the safety, and rolled through the door after her.

The door opened onto a passageway fitted with oval windows overlooking the deck. Inboard, varnished doors gave access into cabins and the various working areas of the yacht. Forward, a panelled mahogany staircase led to the bridge. Looking aft towards the stern, a similar staircase climbed towards the upper deck and the helipad.

Debbie was crouched at the bottom of the stairs leading to the bridge. She lowered the AK and replaced the empty magazine with one from the pocket of her cargo pants. The magazine hit home and she hauled back the charging handle and chambered the first round. She took a quick look up the stairs then threw herself across the stairwell and lay with her back against the wall.

I shuffled towards her on all fours and did the looking up the steps thing.

"Would you mind telling me what the hell is going on, but speak up, you've fucked-up my good ear," I said.

That brought a chuckle from Debbie and a burst of gunfire from the top of the stairs that shattered the window in the passage behind us.

I poked the Glock around the corner and without looking fired two rounds up the stairs.

My shots were followed by the unmistakable ra-ta-tat of an Uzi somewhere towards the bow.

We pressed ourselves against the wall. "Do your guys have any Uzis?" I said with as much sarcasm as I could muster.

"They're not my guys, and no, they don't have any Uzis."

"Then it's our lucky day. Willie's still with us."

She took another quick look up the stairs and almost lost the top of her head as three shots blew out the remaining shards of glass behind us.

"Falling out amongst thieves could get you killed," I said.

"Fuck you." She let rip a long burst up the stairs, which ended in an agonizing scream. "Follow me." She threw herself round the corner and sprinted up the steps.

"You're the reason we never wanted women in the military," I yelled and took off after her, Mr. Glock leading the way.

The fingers of the guy doing the shooting were missing all the way to his elbow. He'd made it to a connecting door some twenty feet along the passageway, where he lay in a moaning heap. The walls were splattered with blood from his mangled limb, and in places it dripped from the ceiling.

Debbie stood over him. She pointed the Kalashnikov at his head and I waited for her to squeeze the trigger. But instead of killing him, she turned and handed me the weapon, then reached down and pulled the belt from his waist and fixed a tourniquet around his bloody stump.

"Should have shot him," I said. "Save getting your hands messy."

I kept one eye on the passageway and the other on Debbie the murderous nurse. Being cross-eyed was giving me a headache.

"If I can't stop your crazy Welsh friend from killing everyone on board, this guy might be my only witness." She synched the tourniquet until it was tight and rolled the guy onto his side. Then she wiped her hands on his shirt and reached for the AK.

I took a step back, putting a couple of feet between her and the end of the barrel.

"Are you going to shoot me?" she grinned.

The grin faded when I gave her the death stare.

"Why shouldn't I?"

"Pull the trigger and you will be charged with murdering a federal officer."

"Feral officers don't impress me."

The grin was back. "Do you know how to use that weapon?"

she said.

I didn't take my eyes of her. "AK-47," I said, "designed by Sergeant Mikhail Timofeyevich Kalashnikov. It has a barrel length of 415mm and weighs less than four and a half kilos with an empty magazine. This model fires six hundred 7.62mm rounds a minute, but only holds thirty in the clip so, unless you can carry twenty clips and change them at a rate of one every three seconds, you're fucked. Ninety million of them in circulation and used by scumbags and redheads everywhere."

I was too busy being clever to hear his approach. "Very funny, smart arse. Now give the gun back to the lady." The command was accompanied by a poke in the back.

"I'm not sure that's a good idea," I said.

Another poke in the back. This time with feeling.

"I said give the gun back to the lady. Do it now, stock first." His accent was bull Afrikaans and my patience was wearing thin with Mercenaries R Us.

Debbie raised her hand. "Best give me the gun, Turpin. Johan doesn't have a lot of patience."

"Do it, arsehole," he growled and to brighten his day punched me in the kidneys.

"Okay, okay. Take it," I gasped.

Debbie stood and tugged the gun out of my hands.

"You saved my life, Johan."

"Ya, well, we look after our own."

"True," she said and shot him through the head.

I took one look at Johan and made that my last.

"You're good," I said.

"So are you. That's why we chose you and your renegades. But perhaps we should keep the explanations for later. Right now we need to move.

She field-stripped Johan of his weapons and tossed me my very own AK. "Minister Van Norte and the man you call Snake Eyes are onboard somewhere. Find them and we'll find Andropof. And please, try not to kill Andropof, my government wants him."

Another burst of automatic fire rattled through the yacht.

We ran down the steps and came to the door leading to the dining room where a few days earlier this whole shit fight had begun.

"How many of your men are on board?" said Debbie.

"Just Willie and me. Pete caught a couple of rounds back on the island. If he isn't dead, he's driving the *Lady*. Young Toby's with him."

"Where's Fisher?"

"Dead."

"You kill him?"

"No, but I thought about it."

She kicked open the door and we went through. She went left, I went right.

"Fisher was working for me."

"Guess that clears him then."

"What?"

"Nothing. How many more surprises have you got?"

"A few. You think you're good, but you're sloppy. You left a candy wrapper next to the tractor on the island.

"That's what you picked up. Pete almost gutted you."

"In your dreams."

We edged our way around the long dining room table. Someone had taken the time to roll the shutters down over the artwork and strip the room ready for sea.

The yacht rolled and glasses and bottles clinked in their cabinets.

"Besides the two I saw you kill, and the three head-honchos who are on the loose, how many more scumbags are on board?"

I said.

"Two. They were working for Snake Eyes. He promised them the yacht once he got clear in the chopper, but you fucked that up nicely."

"You said were. What happened to them?"

"I killed them."

The door leading to the front of the yacht crashed open and before I could react Willie rolled into the room. Debbie dropped out of sight as a murderous blast from the Uzi raked the walls and splintered the chairs.

Willie sprang to his feet and let out a war cry. He was naked from the waist up and smeared with blood and soot. He had his trademark bandana around his head and his left ear was hanging by thread.

"Debbie, stay down." Willie swung the Uzi towards the spot where she'd dropped to the floor. "Slide the gun out. *Do it now!*" I roared.

The AK slid into view. I moved forward and picked it up. I lay the gun on the table then grabbed Debbie's hand and pulled her to her feet.

Willie tracked us with the Uzi; his eyes rapidly going from Debbie to me, looking for the trap.

"Easy, Willie, she's a federal officer."

"Then let's shoot her now, boyo, the last time I dealt with them, they lost my parcel."

"What …?" stammered Debbie.

"That was FedEx, Willie," I said.

Willie never took his eyes off Debbie. "What happened to the engines?"

"One's unusable. We hit a rock coming out of St. Peters and bent a prop. I took care of the other."

"Is she telling the truth, Dick?"

"Most of it," I said.

Willie reached for the AK and pushed it across the table.

Debbie looked at me.

I gave her the nod.

"Can the engine you disabled be repaired?" Willie asked.

Debbie reached for the gun. "It's doable but not without some serious work, and the engineer's lying up top minus an arm."

"So, unless the scumbags can whistle up another yacht, they're stuck out here with us."

"Yep ..."

"*Aw fuck!*"

We threw ourselves out of the dining room and into a hail of gunfire.

The *Lady* was powering away, Snake Eyes was at the helm and holding Toby in front of him like a shield. The fusillade was coming from the *Lady*'s foredeck; it was wild and inaccurate, but with automatics it was only a matter of time. In the military we called it pray-and-spray, meaning if the slugs didn't get you the ricochets would.

Willie and Debbie hosed the foredeck and the firing stopped. Willie immediately dropped the empty Uzi and launched himself over the rail. He crashed into the *Lady*'s rigging and slid out of sight behind the bulwarks.

I ran aft to where the gap between the two boats was at its narrowest. The guns on the foredeck were back in action, blowing chunks of teak and aluminum from around anything that moved.

I dived for cover behind a stanchion as Debbie hit the *Lady* with a long burst.

Suddenly her gun fell silent and bullets began slamming into the metalwork around me. Above the noise I heard her scream. She was shaking her rifle and pointing at the magazine.

"Shit." I jammed on the safety catch and sent my AK skidding towards her along the deck. She scooped it up and sent a withering burst of fire towards the motor yacht's foredeck.

It bought me a few seconds.

I climbed on the rail. Flung myself at the *Lady*, and dropped into the sea.

51

By the time I spluttered to the surface the *Lady* was ten feet away and disappearing fast.

Debbie was down to single shots, which meant she was running out of ammunition. There was another long burst of automatic fire then all shooting stopped.

I struck out after the boat, knowing I hadn't a cat in hell's chance of catching it. I was sobbing with frustration, gasping for breath and swallowing water. Then I saw the *Lady*'s aft mooring line slithering towards me like a snake. I lunged, first I had it—then it was gone—then I had it again. I wrapped two turns around my wrist and the line snapped tight and dragged me under. I went straight down, almost losing my arm. The propeller zinged in my ears. The rope jerked and I shot sideways, spinning through the wake like a hooked fish.

I lunged for the surface and clamped my other hand onto the rope. The yacht was doing about seven knots. It felt like seventy. Blood from my palms coated the rope as I struggled to haul myself towards the stern. If anyone looked over the side, I was dead. I might be dead anyway with the whirling prop just inches from my feet.

The thought was encouragement enough. I started to climb, hand over hand, dragging myself out of the water. Fifteen years ago I would have been up the line and amongst the bastards so fast I'd have blown myself dry. But at the rate I was going, I'd be wet for a week. I was hanging beneath the cut-away stern. The rope was cutting into my hands and my lungs were on fire. If I stopped now, I would never have the strength to get going again.

Like most traditional sailing yachts, the bulwarks on the *Lady* are set back a couple of inches, leaving a narrow strip of deck on their outboard side. If I could get my fingers over the edge of the deck then I might be in business.

Pain shot through the muscles in my arms and I felt the rope slip. Tightening my grip only made the cramps worse.

Above, I could see the line of scuppers where they were cut into the woodwork between the bulwarks and the deck. I let go the rope and lunged. My fingers slid into a scupper and locked onto the wood. I pulled myself up and swung my left foot onto the edge of the deck.

I clung on like a limpet until the cramps eased and I regained my breath. Then, with a final heave, I reached up and clamped my hands around the cap-rail. Both hands were now in full view of anyone who looked aft, but that was a chance I had to take.

The gunfire had stopped and no one was causing mayhem, which meant Willie and Pete were either prisoners or dead.

Someone shouted, and I almost let go, then I realized the voices were coming from towards the bow. I risked a quick look over the bulwark. Toby was behind the wheel and Andropof was holding Pete's cutlass to his throat. As I watched, Toby put the wheel down and brought the yacht into the wind.

This was my chance. I rolled over the rail and slithered forward until I was hidden behind the deckhouse.

After a few seconds the blocks began to creak as they hoisted the fores'l. By rights they should have hoisted the main first and I thanked God they hadn't or they would have seen me for sure.

Temptress had fallen astern and was appearing and disappearing on the swell. There was no sign of Debbie. And, unless the engines could miraculously heal themselves, there would be no help there.

I risked another look and saw Andropof say something to Toby and prod him with the cutlass.

A sudden commotion told me they were coming aft to hoist the main.

The *Lady* rolled on the swell. Empty of wind, the fores'l boom slammed across the deck. Hoping the noise would distract them, I scrambled into the deckhouse and down the companionway steps. A sudden shout had me scurrying for cover, but instead of gunfire, it was followed by the sound of the mains'l rattling off the boom and the luff sliding up the mast.

Where the hell were Pete and Willie? If Van Norte and Andropof were onboard then so was Snake Eyes. I hoped to hell there was no one else.

I had to find a weapon. Pete kept a 9mm stainless steel Smith and Wesson 908S clipped to the underside of the chart table. I prayed it was still there.

I crept along the passageway.

The chart room door was open. I was about to step inside when Pete's rasping voice, followed by the unmistakable accented English of Van Norte, stopped me in my tracks.

Van Norte was ordering Pete to plot them a course to somewhere that I couldn't quite make out. There was a crash and I took a quick look. Pete was on the floor and Van Norte was laying into him with his feet. He was shouting in Patois, and from what little I understood, Pete had told him to go fuck himself.

Pete looked as though he'd been put through a meat grinder. The wound on his chest had burst open and he was soaked in blood. He'd taken such a beating that I hardly recognized him. Van Norte was feeling brave, taking on a man half dead, normally Pete would have chewed him up and spit him out.

I stepped over the combing and slammed the door behind me. Van Norte stopped using Pete as a football and spun around. His eyes darted towards the door, but seeing no escape the cowardly bastard raised his hands and stepped back.

"Turpin, wait," he said.

But I'd had enough, I was waiting for no man, and he knew it. He lunged left and I straight-armed him across the nose. He would never be handsome again, but why care, he'd soon be dead. He let out a snot-filled sob and threw up his hands to protect his face. Perfect, I grabbed him by the balls and drove him backwards across the cabin. As we passed the chart table, I scooped up the ancient brass dividers that Pete swears came from Drake's *Revenge.* When Van Norte brought down his hands to pry mine off his puréed gonads, I drove Drake's dividers into his left eye. Drove them to the hilt and gave them a twist. He hit the deck and I kicked the dead fucker for good measure.

Pete moaned and then vomited. I went to him. "Finish it, Dick. Get them off my yacht then come back for me," he said.

"Jesus, Pete, just how much blood have you got left, you must be stealing it from somewhere." He lay in the corner where Van Norte had kicked him. I gently pulled him into the middle of the cabin and rolled him onto his side. Then I ran my hand under the table, found the butt of the pistol and wrenched it out of the clips. I dropped the magazine, checked the load and slammed it home—eight hollow-point rounds and one in the chamber.

"Pete, listen to me." I peeled off my wet shirt and wadded it up. "Press this to the wound and keep it there. I'm going to retake the ship, just like Nelson, Pete. Are you listening? Just like Nelson. Don't fall asleep, Pete. You hear me, don't fall asleep!" His breathing was ragged but he managed to draw the shirt to his chest. "I'll be back, Pete, I promise, just hang on."

A single tear ran down his cheek.

I peered around the door and checked the passageway. They were pushing the boat hard, she was healing to the breeze, and I could hear water sloshing in the bilge. My guess was that whoever was aboard would be aft by the wheel, but it wouldn't be long before someone came looking for Van Norte and the information the lubberly bastard had been trying to thrash out of Pete.

I made my way towards the bow, looking in each of the cabins in turn. The door to the saloon was open. As I looked in, a shadow fell across the skylight overhead and Willie stepped in to view. He glanced down, our eyes locked, and then he was brutally shoved forward by Snake Eyes and the barrel of a Kalashnikov.

I quickly stepped back into the shadows.

Snake Eyes stopped and looked down into the saloon. Although I could see him, I knew he couldn't see me. He began to move forward and then hesitated, as if he knew something was wrong. I thought about leaping into the cabin and trying for a head shot, but immediately canned the idea as too risky, and after a few seconds he moved on.

The passageway brought me to the forepeak where just a few hours ago we had hammered the plywood strips over the leak. The tools were still scattered around and after a quick search I found the axe and slid it down my belt.

Aft of the forepeak was a set of vertical iron steps. They were bolted to the bulkhead and led to the forehatch above. The hatch comprised of two wooden doors built into a traditional shellback storm cover. Above the doors, a small sliding hatch rolled back on bronze runners. The whole thing was made of teak, finely crafted and, apart from the varnish, virtually original.

The *Lady* was cutting through the swells, driven on by her engine and sails. She was plunging, and I could feel the seas bursting against her bows. If they pushed too hard they would blow the temporary repair and send us straight to the bottom.

Whichever way I looked at it, time was running out.

The iron ladder was no problem, but when I put my weight behind the sliding hatch, it wouldn't move. I jammed my back against the ladder and tried again. The hatch creaked and gave a fraction. Through the gap I could see that the brass hasp had fallen down over the staple. The opening was just wide enough to wiggle a finger through and, after a couple of tries, I managed to flick the hasp off the staple and slide the hatch back an inch. It wasn't enough to give me a view of the deck, so I waited and after a few seconds eased it back some more.

All was quiet except for the noise of the sea against the bow and the creaking of the blocks overhead. I eased my head through the hatch and looked back along the deck. We were on the starboard tack, heading north or northeast. Both the main and foresail were set and above me the two jibs were straining to the breeze.

Working my way along the deck towards a psychopath with a Kalashnikov wasn't a sound idea. I needed to bring the scumbag to me and then spring out of the hatch like a jack-in-a-box and do the business. I didn't have a red nose, but he was sure to see the funny side of my stainless steel gun.

The boat sailed too close to the wind and the jibs began to flog until whoever was steering gave the wheel a turn putting her back on course and quieting the sails.

The flogging sails gave me the answer.

I made sure the deck was clear and slid out of the hatch and belly-crawled to the jib sheet where it ran through the block on its way to the winch. One swing of the axe and the sail went berserk. With the severed rope still attached, it streamed out over the leeward rail, flogging the air and shaking the entire rig.

The noise was horrendous. I scrambled across the deck and down the hatch as someone came running forward to see what was going on. I was hoping it was Snake Eyes, so I could shoot him, but when I squinted through the gap above the doors, I saw Andropof staggering along the deck like a drunk.

He stopped next to the hatch and cursed. Then he lunged for the severed sheet thrashing about above his head and I thought if the idiot caught it, it would kill him for me. He might be a genius but that obviously didn't extend to boats.

A shout from aft forced me to move. I threw back the hatch and launched myself across the deck.

Debbie wanted Andropof alive but I couldn't care less. He was pirouetting around the foredeck like a demented ballet dancer. I swung the fire axe, leading with the spike, but the way he was bobbing and weaving after the flailing rope played havoc with my aim. It was like trying to swat a gnat.

I gave up dancing about behind him. "Give you a hand?" I said.

"Ya, ya," he replied. He didn't even look. Then something clicked and he spun around.

Why, I don't know, but at the last moment I twisted the shaft and instead of a spike to the brain, gave him the flat of the blade across the side of the head.

His knees buckled and he crashed to the deck.

Tossing him overboard seemed like a good idea, but there was more shouting from aft and it was coming closer. I grabbed him by the arms and dragged him backwards across the deck. His pants snagged on an eyebolt and I kicked him free, ripped open the doors, and tumbled him head first down the hatch. Then I followed him, slamming and locking everything behind me as I went.

Andropov was unconscious at the bottom of the steps. I should have tied him up, in fact I should have killed him, but I had Debbie in the back of my mind and something told me we might need a bargaining chip. However, I didn't want another killer running free, so I propped his right leg on the bottom rung and stomped on it.

Footsteps pounded across the deck above and someone hammered on the hatch. I imagined Snake Eyes driving Willie forward at the end of a gun, so I ran aft along the passageway and up the companionway steps. I pivoted towards the stern and knew I'd made a dreadful mistake. Willie was behind the wheel and Snake Eyes was holding the AK to his head.

Snake Eyes gestured towards my hand. "Turpin, so you are on board. Please drop the gun."

The automatic hit the deck at my feet.

"I should have known that was you down in the saloon. I take it Van Norte is no longer with us?"

"Take it any way you want. You can shove it up your arse for me."

Willie laughed. "Way to go, Dick. Tell him how you fucked his sister."

Snake Eyes slammed the barrel of the gun across Willie's neck, but I'd caught the gesture and while Willie took his beating, glanced along the deck.

Toby was making his way down the starboard side. He stopped opposite the bar amidships and snatched Pete's cutlass out of the scuppers.

"I need this buffoon and the Rasta kid to sail the boat, but I don't need you, Turpin." Snake Eyes stepped away from the wheel. He had to put some distance between Willie and the end of the gun to have any chance of killing me without Willie jumping him.

Willie gave the wheel an eighth of a turn and brought the wind onto the beam. Snake Eyes never noticed. His gun was pointing at Willie, but his eyes were locked on me.

"Hey, Dick, I thought his sister was good but his mother gave better head," said Willie.

"Shut up, you Welsh pig," he snarled and took another step

back.

Willie nudged the wheel and the wind moved further aft.

We couldn't keep our double act going for much longer and were fast running out of ideas.

"Hey, how about a deal?" I said.

"Yeah," said Willie, "give him five bucks, that's what it costs for a turn with his missus."

Snake Eyes ignored him and flicked his eyes towards the pistol on the deck at my feet. "I have a fortune in pink diamonds and I'm the one with the gun." he sneered. But then he couldn't help himself. "What deal?"

"I'll let you live," I said.

"Always you play the comedian, Turpin."

He took another step back. One more and he would have the distance he needed to use the Kalashnikov.

The wind was now almost dead astern. Above Willie's shoulder the leach of the main collapsed and the end of the boom began to lift.

Time, we needed time.

I stepped forward and put myself in the killer's face. Snake Eyes was a professional, he knew the moves, but he had lost his edge by allowing us to bait him and slow him down.

And suddenly I knew why.

Toby sprang forward with the cutlass and slashed at Snake Eyes' head.

But the killer was no longer there.

The wind hooked the leeward side of the mainsail and it slammed across the deck. The violent jibe rolled the boat hard to starboard; the boom scythed through the running backstays and smashed Toby to the deck.

Snake Eyes hurled the rifle at me, then scooped up the pistol and ran.

I grabbed the Kalashnikov and dropped the magazine. Empty. The son of a bitch, he'd played us at our own game.

Willie glanced at the empty magazine. "Toby, take the fucking wheel. *Do it!*" He dragged him out of the scuppers and snatched the cutlass out of his hand and began waving it around his head. "I'll have the bastard now," he roared and raced off along the deck.

I hurled myself at his legs and brought him down as two hollow points slammed into the deckhouse, showering us with chunks of teak and glass.

"Jesus, Willie, he's got Pete's Smith and Wesson."

"Now you tell me. Fucking officers, you're all alike, treat us like mushrooms ... kept in the dark and fed shit."

"He'll have checked the magazine and know he's got seven rounds left. He thinks we're unarmed, Willie, but he's got to make sure. That means taking a chance and showing himself. If he doesn't draw fire then he'll come after us."

"What do you suggest?"

"We move forward. Let him see us. Make him think we're hunting him with more than just a cutlass and this." I produced the fire axe from behind my back.

"Good plan. Who goes first?"

"You, I'm an officer not a fungus."

He grinned and took a quick look around the corner of the deckhouse.

"Nothing. Maybe he went down the forehatch."

"I locked it from the inside. He'll have a hell of a job to smash it open."

"Your turn."

"Thanks."

I took a quick look around the opposite side of the deckhouse. "Shit."

Willie tensed.

"You see him?

"No. I see the deck box with the diving gear."

"You think he's in there?"

We both laughed.

"Spear guns, Willie," I said.

"Boyo," he said.

"*Go*."

Willie ran to starboard, I ran to port, and we threw ourselves down behind the deck box.

There was no gunfire.

I took a deep breath and cracked open the lid and looked inside: Six scuba tanks, masks and snorkels, three sets of fins, four spear guns but no spears.

I gave Willie the news.

"Shit, maybe we can snorkel him to death," said Willie as a familiar voice echoed along the deck.

"Thanks for the pistol, Turpin. I've got seven rounds left and you've got shit. Who needs a deal now?"

Willie lifted the lid of the deck box, yanked out a twenty-two liter aluminum scuba tank and slammed it onto the deck between us.

A large chunk of the lid disintegrated as two hollow points did their work.

"Five rounds left, Turpin. It's enough; kiss your ugly friend goodbye."

"Don't you dare, boyo. Give me the axe and tell him I'm hit."

And suddenly I knew what he was going to do.

"Shit, it's too risky, Willie. There has to be another way."

"We're out of ideas, Dick. He's knows we're unarmed and he's coming for us. Just do it."

I took a quick look around the box. Snake Eyes was creeping

down the starboard side, holding the pistol in a two-handed grip.

"Willie's hit," I shouted. "Please, let me help him."

His reply was to the point. "Step out to where I can see you."

"Not yet," Willie hissed. "Keep him talking and draw him nearer. Give me a chance to get around the other side of the box."

"He's hit in the head and he's bleeding badly." I sobbed for effect and stole another look. Snake Eyes was creeping along, keeping his back against the bar.

"He's not close enough. Bring him closer," said Willie. Then he let out a long Hollywood moan.

"Jesus, Willie, don't overdo it."

"What was that," roared Snake Eyes.

"Oh God, I think he's dead, you've killed him," I wailed.

"Stand up where I can see you and I might let you live."

He was close now, almost opposite the front of the box.

There was a loud clang.

"Oh shit," said Willie.

"What the fuck ..." spat Snake Eyes.

"He's dead. He's dead," I blubbered and sprang out from behind the box as Willie's next swing smashed the post off the scuba tank and sent it spinning down the deck like the pinwheel from hell.

Snake Eyes fired one round at me and zinged two off the scuba tank. He'd have done better to run.

Three thousand pounds of compressed air per square inch instantly released through a one inch hole, is a sight to see. The tank slammed into the bulwarks and ricocheted onto an eyebolt in the deck. The eyebolt gave it lift and it smashed into Snake Eyes at chest height, carried on upwards, caught him under the chin, ripped off his jaw and snapped his neck like a dry twig.

With a whoop Willie leapt out from behind the box and, waving the axe, did a war dance over the dead man.

52

A few buckets of seawater got rid of the blood. And this time Toby didn't argue when we tossed Snake Eyes overboard where some poor shark would probably choke on the evil bastard's remains.

We left Toby on deck to tend ship and Willie and I went below. Pete wasn't good; he was running a high fever and slipping in and out of consciousness. In his lucid moments, we told him what had happened and what we planned to do next, which brought a ragged smile to his lips.

After a few minutes, Willie went on deck to help Toby drop the sails, while I did what I could for my friend and his wounds. Pete was drifting back into unconsciousness when Willie shouted that we were coming alongside *Temptress* and I was needed on deck.

The seas had built over the last couple of hours and the motor yacht had taken on more of a roll. Willie eased us alongside and threw the engine into reverse, bringing us to a stop about ten feet from the other boat.

"Just you?" shouted Debbie.

"Yeah, just us. It's over," I shouted back.

"Is Andropof alive?"

"Yes, but he doesn't know it yet."

"What does that mean?"

"It means he's got a serious bump on the head and a double jointed leg."

She mulled this over. "Okay. This is what I want you to do.

Head for St. Peters at full speed, someone from my agency should be there to take care of Andropof. They'll organize a helicopter to come looking for me and then send out a tug to tow this thing to the naval base in Puerto Rico. Tell them to start the search southwest of Mexican Hat, they'll figure out the rest."

"Are you coming with us?" I asked.

"No. Gotta stay with the evidence."

"Another fucking officer," said Willie and before I could stop him he was at the rail. "Listen, lady, we're not going anywhere until you look at Pete. According to Dick, you've had medical training, and he wouldn't be all shot to hell if it wasn't for you."

"You don't know who you're fucking with," Debbie fired back. "My government has been chasing these people for two years. If you don't want a lot more trouble than you've got already, then I suggest you do as I say."

Willie leaned against the bulwark and folded his arms. "Lady, we have a saying in Wales that goes like this ... Fuck you!"

The two of them stared at each other as the boats slowly drifted apart.

Finally Debbie shook her head. "Okay, bring that thing alongside," she spat. "I'll give you fifteen minutes, max."

Willie continued to stare until he was sure he'd driven the message home. Then he turned his back on her, walked to the wheel, and slammed the engine into gear.

We had drifted too far apart to make going alongside a simple maneuver, so Willie drove around in a wide circle and lined us up for a new approach.

As we edged alongside, Debbie pulled herself up onto the rail. She was carrying a large first aid kit and the minute we were in range she tossed it across to me. She waited a few seconds, until the boats almost touched, and then jumped. As she hit the deck she turned angrily towards Willie. "Take the boat a hundred yards off and keep circling," she snapped. "I don't want you going aboard *Temptress*. That vessel is now the property of the United States Government. Get it?

"Aye, aye, missy." Willie touched his forelock and spun the wheel, turning the *Lady* hard to port.

I pushed the first aid kit into her hands and directed her towards the companionway.

She drew back. "Where's that young friend of yours, Toby?"

He's there …" I pointed aft to where the body was lashed to the rail.

"Oh, sorry," she mumbled.

I sniffed and dabbed my eyes. "Thank you, you're very kind."

She stood a second in silent prayer, then spun around and I ran to catch up as she dashed for the stairs.

I showed her to Pete's cabin and followed her in.

Pete was barely holding on but the glint in his eye told me he was still in the game.

Debbie stripped away the old dressings and carefully probed and cleaned his wounds. Satisfied, she applied some antibiotic powder from the first aid kit and then covered the wounds with gauze and fresh bandages.

Fifteen minutes stretched to twenty. Every time she tried to leave, Pete whimpered and reached for her hand. Finally, she managed to trap his arm beneath the sheet and tuck him in. He made one feeble attempt to free it and then lay still.

"I've done all I can for him; now it's up to you to get him ashore as fast as possible. Even then—"

She stood and headed for the door.

"What about Andropof?" I said. "You should look at him, too."

She looked at her watch. "Where is he?" she sighed.

"This way." I grabbed her arm and propelled her along the passageway towards the next cabin. We reached the door when suddenly she stopped.

"You lousy son of a bitch." She slammed the first aid kit into my chest and barged me out of the way.

By the time I reached the deck she was screaming at Toby and trying to wrestle him away from the wheel.

Astern, Willie and *Temptress* were a smudge on the far horizon.

53

It was one of those rare Caribbean days. The trade winds were a hush and the sea glassy calm. There was no line to mar the horizon, just a blend of shimmering blue where the ocean touched the sky and the distant island of St. Peters lay suspended in air.

Willie brought the engines of the fifty-foot Hatteras down to idle and the sports fishing boat dropped off the plane and coasted to a stop. We wallowed for a moment in the remnants of our own wake and then lay still.

Astern, the spreading white of our contrail disappeared into infinity. Somewhere out there it crossed the inbound tracks carved through these same waters by *Temptress* and the *Lucky Lady* some three months ago.

Willie had managed to restart one of *Temptress*'s engines and motor her back to St. Peters, anchoring in the bay just twenty-four hours after Toby and I brought the *Lady* in.

That's when the fun started.

During a tough sail back to the island, Debbie—if that was ever her name—did her best to keep Pete alive and we were grateful for that. But she couldn't forgive us for the scam we had pulled to get her away from the motor yacht.

The minute Willie anchored our prize; Debbie stormed aboard, leading a band of 'foreign advisors' who had arrived earlier by helicopter to take possession of the yacht.

Willie threw them off, and that night, under cover of darkness,

I swam out and joined him. Debbie was incensed and threatened to send a SWAT team to get us off.

We sat tight. There was something on the yacht that Debbie and whatever agency she worked for, wanted, but to get it they would have to play the game.

Perhaps it was the anonymous phone call that brought the international press sniffing around, or maybe they were just worried we might discover the yacht's secret, but one morning Debbie showed up requesting a talk. She said her boss would listen to our salvage claim on condition we immediately left the yacht and took nothing with us.

Willie gave her a torrent of Welsh and told her to come back with a lawyer, put it in writing, and bring a case of beer.

It took them a week to sort it out. Then, less than hour after signing a bullet-proof salvage agreement, *Temptress* disappeared over the horizon behind a U.S. navy tug.

For a while, things ashore were as wobbly as the broken bridge. But Toby's return with the stolen government funds, along with stories of our daring-do, was enough to keep us out of jail and, after a couple of weeks, the long list of charges against us were quietly dropped.

I thought that would be the end of it, but I was wrong. Debbie returned to the island a couple of times to—as she put it: 'tie up loose ends.' When I asked what loose ends, she just threw back her head and laughed.

By her last visit we had fallen into an uneasy truce. As long as I never asked about the fate of Andropof, she agreed not to ask about the injured engineer that she had left behind on *Temptress*, who, like Wies, had mysteriously disappeared.

"You made some important friends, captured a dangerous criminal, brought about a better government and helped put away some serious drug lords. Why don't you just leave it at that?" It was her parting shot.

I never saw her again.

Willie hit the stop buttons and the noise of the diesels faded away. He made his way down the ladder to the cockpit.

All was quiet but for the gentle lapping of the water on the hull and the occasional tap of a wire trace against the outriggers.

I opened the teak box and let Susie's ashes mingle with the tide; they sparkled in the sunlight and then were gone.

A hint of a breeze ruffled the glassy sea.

Pete pushed himself up out of the fighting-chair and limped to the side of the boat. He scattered a handful of flowers from a flamboyant tree onto the water. The flame-red petals reflected like blood against the white hull until they, too, were carried away by the tide.

Behind me, I heard Willie climbing the ladder to the flying-bridge. At the top he turned and took a small velvet bag out of his pocket. He looked down at each of us in turn, then dropped the bag of diamonds and booted it like a rugby ball into the blue.

"Let's go fishing," he said, and turned the key.

The End

Photograph by Janet Brown/OceanMedia

Gary Brown is a journalist and the author of numerous articles about boats and the sea. After leaving school he traveled extensively, picking up work along the way. With family connections that go back to the last great days of sail, it was inevitable that his travels would eventually lead him to the sea. Life as a fisherman, boat builder and sea gypsy led him to the quill and a career in broadcast journalism. He lives on the island of St. Martin with his wife, Jan.
Visit his website at www.garyebrown.net

Made in the USA
Charleston, SC
25 May 2010